Power of the Gods:

Sabrina LaMore

Scott M. Stockton

This is a work of fiction. Names, characters, businesses, places, events, and incidents are either the product of the author's imagination or used in a fictitious manner. Any resemblance to actual persons, living or dead, is purely coincidental.

Copyright 2017 by Scott M. Stockton
All Rights Reserved

This book, and the entirety of my Power of the Gods story, is dedicated to my mother.   She always believed in me and my dreams, even when everyone else in my life hadn't.   Although I've me others along my journey who have given me love and support, she will always be the first to believe. To believe that anything I dream in my mind, can be possible if I want it to be.

Hello there.

I'm pleased to see you've come to join me on this journey.

Welcome to my mind, dear reader...and may the path ahead you lead deep into a world of unknown. A world much like your own.

In fact, it's nearly identical.

Maybe you've opened this book for an escape...

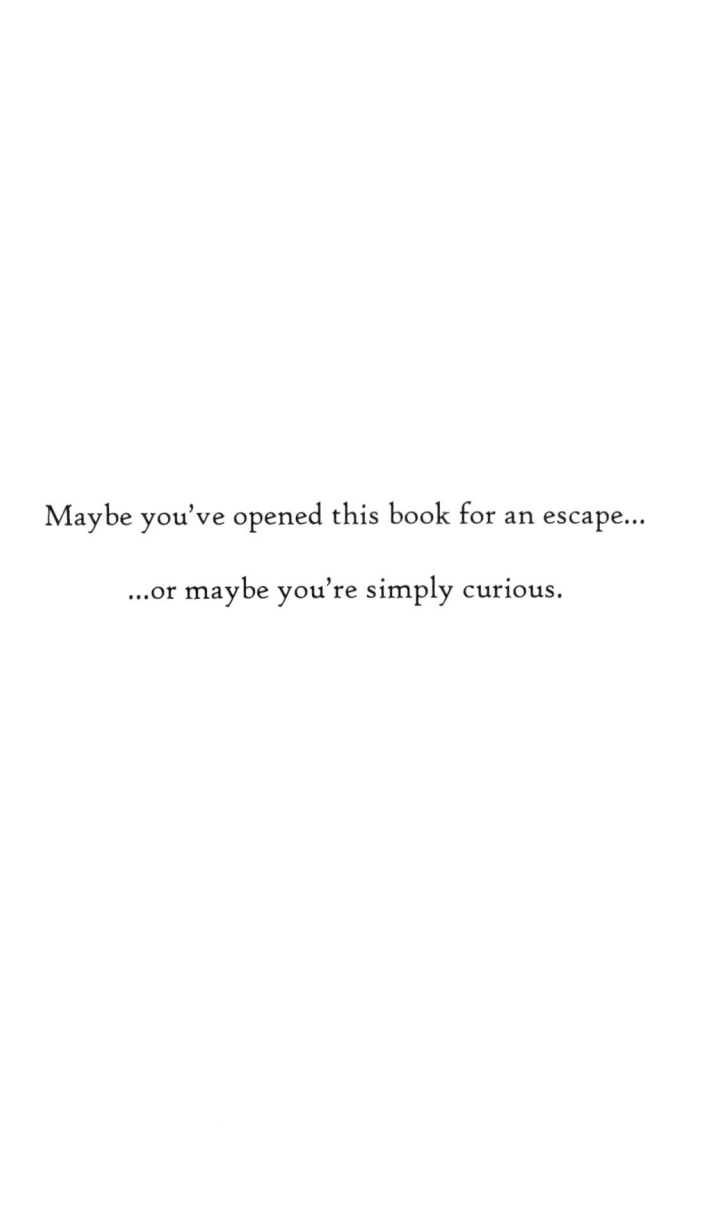

...or maybe you're simply curious.

Either way, I greet you now...for we won't meet again until the very end of this story.

Remember this...for it is sure to be a long one.

Book One

"One should not fear what they have no control over."

- Sabrina C. LaMore

Part One

The Beginning

Chapter One

Shall We Begin?

She was born in the winter solstice during a time when the world was still new. Meaning, it wasn't ready to understand. At the hour of midnight on the third of January, an angry snowstorm had announced the arrival of the girl that gave Warren County a piece of dark history. Sabrina Celestine LaMore…was a rare seed. The small city of Warren, Pennsylvania, doesn't talk about her much…for fear of "what she'd do". Scientists say, we humans only use small percentages of our brain. Although, Sabrina LaMore tends to "bend the rules". Don't worry, what most people didn't know…won't kill them.

Victor LaMore was the type of man that always proved to be decent.   He was good with children, and he quite often used his fortune for kind purposes.   Being born into millions of dollars is rare, and many people in the city of Warren were grateful he'd shared his money when others truly needed it.   Victor proposed to, and married his wife Erika during springtime, and the wedding had been held at LaMore Manor in the rose gardens.   Erika had come to Warren to visit her grandmother, whom is now deceased, and she had met young Victor while shopping.   The two seemed to hit-it-off right from the very start. Sometimes, love works that way.   It wasn't his wealth that captured her eyes, but his charm and handsome stature.   Victor took pride in his physical appearance, and without boasting an ego – just as some men do when found to be attractive. His sporting moustache gave him an old-fashioned, yet dignified look that told Erika he was respectable.   Complete with jet black hair and wavy bangs above his green eyes, he was quite unique.   He always spoke in professional manner, and he could settle an argument without raising his tone.   Something most people can't do, even while trying.

     However, even the most steadfast of men have a flaw or two.   What many people, during that time didn't know, was that Victor had a secret.   Something so "different", he hadn't told Erika until she was pregnant with their *first* and *only* child.   Victor…was telekinetic.   He was able to move any object with his mind.   Sometimes just thinking about it, or simply directing himself to move something *without* touching it.   Erika had heard of it before, but not as the same term it's now known to be today.   In truth, hearing about paranormal ability of the mind was thought to be madness fueled with fantastical lies.   She didn't believe in such "stupidity".   She thought a force like that could only belong to the gods themselves.   However, she quickly changed her mind when her husband "showed it" to her.   Obviously startled at first that Victor could do such things, she made a vow to stay away from the man she so dearly loved.   Victor pleaded for her to stay, and promised he'd never hurt her with his rare gift, but Erika was just too surprised to listen.   So...he let her go.

Erika stayed with her mother for short while.   During this time, she did some reading up on telekinesis.   After realizing that it was in fact very real, and people studied it in various places, she went back to her husband.   She knew, deep down, that he loved her, and she couldn't keep his unborn daughter away from him.

Victor welcomed her back with loving arms, except, there was only one problem.   During the time Erika was gone, Victor had an affair.   Erika was appalled by this and immediately demanded to know who it was.   Victor said the woman's name was Marsha Nelson, and was just another woman who lived at the other end of town.   She meant nothing to him.   Heartbroken and distraught, Erika didn't speak to Victor for the rest of her pregnancy.   Then, on January 3rd, Victor met up with Erika at the hospital...and their daughter was born.

Erika chose the name, Sabrina.   Her daughter was born with jet black hair and cat-green eyes, just like her father.   After looking at their precious baby, Victor and Erika forgot about the affair and decided to stay together, and raise Sabrina.   Erika had only hoped that everything would be "okay" with her daughter.   When she had studied telekinesis, she found out it was a genetic trait.   Victor could have easily passed it on...just as he had inherited his own.   She confessed her worry to her husband, and he in return...said it was only a matter of time...before it would take effect.

Chapter Two

Awakening

Sabrina LaMore sat quietly in the large library of LaMore Manor.   Unlike other thirteen year olds, Sabrina loved to study.   Just the thought of learning more about the topics she loved, fascinated her.   Sabrina had always liked mainly science, but learning about certain history sparked her interest too.   Sabrina was very intelligent for her age…and very serious.   At school, while the other kids played at recess, Sabrina chose this time to stay by herself.   She would either read, or sit and watch the others. Many adults were puzzled by this.   Especially the teachers.   Victor and Erika were often questioned about Sabrina's anti-social personality.   However, her parents had no answers.   It didn't even bother Sabrina that nobody spoke to her...that was how she liked it.

    Sabrina also showed a rare appearance. Her beautiful black hair was much longer than most girls her age.   She had only had it cut once when she was younger...and she hated it that way. Her hair was sacred to her, and she loved it long and shiny.   To her, it felt very unnatural to alter something that was meant to grow.   Sabrina's clothing was mostly dark colors, since she had a fondness for black.   Although, she fancied red too. Not just any red...scarlet, crimson, and blood red were her favorites.   Light colors were too "common" to her, and she only accepted them in art and paintings.

    As Sabrina sat at one of the round tables in her second favorite room of the mansion; her bedroom was her first; she was suddenly interrupted as the doors of the room opened.   A short, middle aged woman wearing a maid's outfit, stepped inside and caught Sabrina's attention with a wave of her hand.

"Sorry for the intrusion, Miss LaMore, but lunch is now served" the woman said with a heavy Spanish accent.   Sabrina closed her book on Japanese Culture, and spoke softly without a change of expression.

"Thank you, Rosario.   What is it today?"

"Smoked salmon, one of your favorites" Rosario answered.   Sabrina nodded and placed her book back on one of the many bookshelves that aligned the walls of the room.   Rosario closed the double doors as she left, and Sabrina walked slowly over toward the large vast windows of the library.   Outside, the cherry blossom trees were in full bloom.   Sabrina's favorite season was winter, but she liked it when the flowering trees around LaMore Manor bloomed in the spring. The library was on the second floor of the mansion, and Sabrina was looking at the tops of the trees.   Considering her family's wealth, Sabrina had traveled overseas before.   She'd seen London and Paris, but where she *truly* wanted to go…was Japan.   She promised herself to go there one day, no matter what the cost.

Sabrina walked slowly into the large dining room where her parents were already seated.   Since she had been in her library most of the morning, Sabrina hadn't seen her parents yet until now.
"Hello, dear" Erika said, as she saw her daughter walk in.   Sabrina didn't reply.   She simply walked over to the dining table with a straight face and sat down.   Victor and Erika had noticed this behavior in Sabrina for quite some time.   Their daughter was *changing,* since she approached puberty.

A man wearing a black suit, soon came through the door with a dinner cart that held their food.   His name was Dmitri Vallenway, and he'd been the butler of the mansion ever since Victor was nineteen.   He was from Cheshire, England, where he was born to a English father and a Russian mother.   He was greatly trusted by Victor personally, having spent all of his life living with him thus far.   In truth, the two men weren't very far apart in age.   Dmitri had been only twenty years of age when first hired by Victor's parents.   He was trusted by them personally as well, having met in England on holiday.   Dmitri was the first person Victor ever confided in about his telekinetic ability, and to his surprise, the butler hadn't rejected him.   In fact, Dmitri was Victor's only true friend for a long time before he was comfortable enough to share his secret with a select few others in his world around him.

      Rosario Guten, had been hired as a maid back when Sabrina was born.   She too, was from overseas being born in Madrid, Spain.   She migrated to America with her family in her twenties, but now spent her life working for the LaMore family line in her early forties.   She was hired by Erika personally when felt she needed extra help taking care of the mansion after Sabrina's birth.   The home was simply too large for only three people to take care of prior to her joining the family.

Sabrina waited with little patience, as Dmitri handed over her plate. She had been a bit on edge ever since she'd woke that morning. She had a slight headache, and she could feel something *new* inside herself. She couldn't tell what it was, and little did she know, it was something that would change her life...forever.

"Is something wrong, Miss LaMore?" Dmitri asked. Sabrina looked down at her salmon and spoke.

"No" she said with a short, dull tone. Victor wasn't convinced, and motioned to Dmitri for his attention.

"Would you please bring my daughter some medicine, Dmitri? I think she has a headache" Victor asked.

"Right away, sir" Dmitri answered. Sabrina shot a look over toward her father.

"I'm fine" she said blandly. Victor continued eating and Erika spoke up.

"No, you're not. You have sweat running down your face" she said. Sabrina then gave a glare out of annoyance. Her mother was right, since Sabrina had been sweating ever since she had entered the room.   Something inside her was waking up.   She could feel it in her veins, and in the objects of the room.   Some type of energy force was surrounding everything.   Sabrina began to breathe heavily as she stared down at the table.   What was happening to her?   She felt as if her head was going to split apart.

"Sabrina?   What's wrong, dear?" Erika asked cautiously.   Victor looked over at his daughter, and dropped his fork.   Sabrina looked up at her parents.

"I...don't know" she said uneasily.   Victor then stood up and went over beside her.

"Stay away from me" Sabrina warned.   Victor ignored the request and he came closer.   Erika noticed as the dining objects on the table, slowly began to vibrate.   Sabrina glared darkly at her father for not listening to her.

"What's going on, Victor?" Erika asked.

"Sabrina...calm down.   You're just feeling sick...that's all" Victor said carefully.   Sabrina felt her headache increase and her eyes dilated.   The feeling inside her wanted out.   It screamed for her to set it free, and Sabrina finally gave in to it when Victor took her by the hand.

"Let go!" she demanded roughly.   At this point, Victor fell backwards by some unknown force, and there was a loud *crack* as a thick and ugly line, swerved it's way through the top of the dining table abruptly.   Erika's drinking glass shattered and she gave a short scream as she stood up quickly.   Sabrina's eyes rolled back as she suddenly fainted to the floor beneath her.

Victor looked at his daughter in surprise, and he stood up slowly.   Erika put her hands up to her face in alarm.

"What the hell just happened?!" she exclaimed.   Both Dmitri and Rosario came running into the room from the sound of the commotion.   Victor knelt down beside his motionless daughter and he put a shaky hand on her forehead.   Her headache was now gone, and he then looked back at the line in the table.   The wood was completely split in two, and he could slightly see the floor below it.   Looking over at his wife, he spoke with a whisper.

"It's time" he said.

Chapter Three

The Fairgrounds Incident

Sabrina opened her green eyes timidly, as she laid in her white canopy bed of her bedroom. She noticed a figure seated beside her as she turned her head. Widening her eyes, she realized it was her father.

"Daddy?" she asked quietly. Victor turned his head when he heard his daughter's voice.

"Sabrina…you're finally awake" he said. Sabrina sat up slowly and looked at her father, curiously.

"Who's Sabrina?" she asked. Victor now was confused, and he looked at his daughter carefully.

"What do you mean? You're Sabrina" he said. Sabrina then began to shift away from her father.

"No...I'm not" she said cautiously. Victor stood up and tried to figure out why his daughter was acting this way. Sabrina never played tricks on people, for the very thought of it was *immature* to her. He knew something wasn't right.

"You're name is Sabrina...it always has been" he said. Sabrina shook her head in alarm.

"No! My name is Clementine!" she spoke aloud. Victor's eyes suddenly widened at the mention of that name. He remembered, when Sabrina was a little younger, she had had an imaginary friend...named Clementine.

The bedroom doors suddenly opened, and Erika stepped inside. She saw her daughter, and was delighted she was finally awake after being unconscious for five hours.

"Oh, Sabrina...I'm so glad you're okay" she said. Sabrina gave a nervous look of tension, as Erika walked toward her.

"I'm *not* Sabrina! My name is *Clementine!*" she shouted.

Erika froze in her tracks with a look of shock. She glanced over at her husband, who was just as surprised.
"What happened?" she asked.
"I don't know. She's been acting this way since she woke up" Victor said. Erika turned back toward her daughter, and began to advance near her.
"Sabrina...what's wrong? Do you feel okay?" she asked warily. Sabrina moved around near the edge of her bed, and stared at her mother with a baffled look.
"My name is Clementine...and I feel fine" she said. Erika moved closer and Sabrina suddenly fell over the edge of her bed. As Erika tried to catch her, Sabrina crashed to the floor and banged her head. This time, she was conscious, and she looked at her mother with a sudden change of expression. Her green eyes gave a glare of hatred as she stood up slowly.
"What are you doing in *my* room?!" she

asked coarsely.   Victor and Erika exchanged looks of confusion and worry, after their daughter spoke.   Sabrina seemed to have an instant change of tone and thought after hitting the floor.

"Sabrina?" Victor asked.   Sabrina's eyes darted toward her father quickly.

"What?!" she asked rudely.   He realized now, his daughter recognized her own name.   He just couldn't figure out what exactly had happened with her state of mind.   Sabrina glared scornfully at her parents.

"Get out" she said shortly.   Without saying another word, Victor and Erika left Sabrina's room with concerned looks.

Sabrina walked over to her bedroom doors and locked them securely.   She then went over to her window and gazed at the back yard.   She gradually remembered what had happened earlier during lunch.   She remembered how different she felt, and how strange everything was during that time.   *"What is this...feeling?   What's happening to me?"* she asked herself, rubbing her head gently.

After closing her claret colored curtains, Sabrina walked over to her classic, electronic gramophone.   She quietly placed an old recording disc of Beethoven's 5th Symphony on it, and started the turntable.   She closed her eyes as she let the chords of music flow through her ears, and around the room.   Sabrina loved older music.   She liked music from the 40s to the early 60s, but classical helped her relax.   As this was happening, Victor had previously decided to go back and talk with his daughter.   As he walked through one of the darkened halls of LaMore Manor, he could hear Sabina's music drifting with the air serenely.   It was the only noise in the north wing.   The mansion was so large, one wouldn't even know Sabrina was there, since there were so many walls and rooms throughout the entire façade.   Victor had never counted the rooms, but he was told there was close to 110 in his magnificent, gothic mansion.

    Victor finally approached Sabrina's bedroom doors, and he knocked on them lightly.   Sabrina opened her eyes, and was quite miffed at the fact that someone interrupted her.   She stopped the record and walked over to her doors, opening them forcefully.   Victor, a little surprised, backed away slightly.   Sabrina stood in her doorway with a plain expression, and her piercing green eyes fixed upon her father.

"What do you want?" she asked with a faint whisper.   Victor looked at his daughter with keen interest and somewhat fear.   She had definitely changed, and this bothered him.

"I was wondering…if you'd like to go to the fair…with your mother and I?" he asked.   Sabrina was silent for a moment, and she didn't move her eyes.   Victor didn't know if he should speak any further, so he in return, was silent.   Sabrina turned her gaze upon her grandfather clock in her room.   It was just after four o'clock.

"I'll be down in twenty minutes" she said, as she shut her doors before her father could reply. Victor turned away and went to go find his wife.

Sabrina was the type of person who didn't like to go out much.   Mostly due to the fact that she was a quiet person who kept to herself.

Although, today she felt she needed to get some air and focus on her thoughts.   She usually went to LaMore Manor's garden to do this, and walk the large floral hedge maze.   Or even go out on her balcony, from her bedroom.   She had surprised herself, by accepting Victor's invitation to go to the Betts Park Fair.   "At least I'll get some ice cream" she told herself.   Sabrina had a weakness for foods that were sweet.   She liked many types of cakes, pies, and ice cream, but her favorite…was sugar cookies.   There was just something about them she adored and couldn't resist, especially the warm soft kind.

      Dmitri drove the LaMore family to the fair in a blue and gray 1987 Lincoln Continental Givenchy.   Victor originally wanted to go in his white Mercedes-Benz limousine, but Erika said it wasn't necessary.   They were only going to a fair, not a mayor's ball.

      Sabrina stepped out of the luxury sedan, and looked at the amusement rides busy in motion, across the parking lot.   Victor offered for

Dmitri to join and spend time with them in the fair grounds, but the butler humbly told him he'd stay in the car, since he needed a nap.

Victor bought his daughter some strawberry ice cream, as Erika was busy looking over several choices of snacks at a concession stand.   Sabrina was pleased at the fact her headache was now gone, and as she sat at a small picnic table with her parents.   Her attention was drawn to one of the amusement rides nearby. The ride was known as the "Balloon Race", and it made Sabrina curious.   She watched as the hot air balloon shaped seats carried their passengers around in a circle formation, with a light slant.   It was a ride that Sabrina had never been on before, and she now wanted to.

Sabrina casually walked over to the ride with her ice cream cone, as Victor and Erika observed with watchful eyes.   She entered the waiting line, and soon it was time for her to get into one of the seats.   With her ice cream in hand, Sabrina began to walk into the riding area, but was soon stopped by a man who had been watching her. He was the ride's operator, and he quickly put his hand on Sabrina's upper chest to stop her.

"Hold on there, girl, you can't go on with your ice cream, you'll have to wait" he said. Sabrina fixed her eyes angrily on the man.

"Take your hand off me!" she said, as she slapped it away. "I'll go on if I *want* to!" The man was suddenly surprised, and he became quite angry.

"You're not going on at all!" he said, and pushed Sabrina out of the line.

Sabrina was outraged. She dropped her ice cream cone to the ground with a slush-like splash, and began to walk back toward her parents to see if they could do anything about the man. She could feel her rage building up inside again, and as before, she had the *feeling* again. Sabrina got halfway toward her parents and then stopped walking. She *knew* she didn't have to let her parents deal with this situation. Sabrina turned around and brought her glare upon the ride. She could feel the energy again...it was around everything.   Every object, big and small…and even the people too.   She no longer had a headache, since the feeling wasn't *brand new* anymore.   Sabrina began to like this feeling.   It made her feel good…and powerful.   Something that was hers…and hers alone.   She saw how the ride worked and moved, and as if she had a lasso, Sabrina grabbed a hold of the ride's energy and very existence.   She wanted to teach these people a lesson.   If she couldn't ride it…then no one would ever ride it again.

      As the Balloon Race spun in its constant circle, the passengers could suddenly feel themselves going faster.   The power of the ride had increased, and the ride operator was confused by this.   He knew he hadn't used the controls to change the ride's speed, and yet…it happened by itself.   The passengers were scared now, as the ride became ever faster.   The hanging seats began to vibrate from increased tension, and the motor let out a grinding sound.   The operator was worried and he tried the emergency break, which didn't work.   Sabrina's gaze never moved from the ride.   She knew she had control, and she wasn't giving it up.   She wanted it to go faster, and she could taste the metal from the ride's façade in her mouth.   It was a part of her now, and Sabrina spread her fingers stiffly apart as the energy transferred from her, to the ride, and back again.

The metal bars and rivets of the ride bent with a moaning sound, as the bolts and connectors yanked apart.   The ride simply wasn't designed to go over eighty miles an hour, and it finally gave into to Sabrina's wrathful control.   What happened next…many witnesses talked about for several weeks.   The hanging seats of the Balloon Race tore off from the extending iron arms, and most of the passengers soon found themselves either flying into nearby objects, or crashing to the ground with extreme force.   As for the ride operator, he met his fate when one of the large metal rods was thrown through his stomach and out his back.   Screams were coming from everywhere, and Sabrina's parents watched in horror of what their daughter had done.   Sabrina, herself…wasn't done yet.   Her new power demanded more, and she was simply having too much fun.   She turned her gaze upon a large oak tree beside her.   Which only stood for half a second, before being twisted forcefully, and then severed in half.   The innocent tree fell to the ground, landing atop a random woman, with a few heavy branches puncturing her chest.   A few people had noticed Sabrina standing there the entire time, and they now were running away in terror from what she was doing.   They looked at her as if she were an alien from another planet…not even realizing or caring that she was indeed a human being.   Victor grabbed his daughter from behind, breaking her concentration. He turned her around and began to shake her with angry force.

    "Stop this now, Sabrina!   No more!" he demanded.   Sabrina stopped, even though she didn't want to, and softened her expression.

    "Why, dad?   They *needed* that" she said.

    "No, Sabrina, they didn't!" Victor retorted. Sabrina then made her usual bland expression.

    "You don't understand, dad…I'm fine.   I

feel *much* better now" she said daintily.   Victor looked into his daughter's eyes.   She was different now.   There was no mercy…no soul. She was so relaxed by what she had done…that she was maddened.   He slowly began to back away from her with widened eyes.

"Something's wrong with you…you're not…natural" he whispered.   Sabrina stared at her father without blinking and made a small smile.

"Don't worry, dad, I'm as natural as they come" she said.   With that said, Sabrina turned away and began to walk back toward the parking lot.

Chapter Four

Meredith

    Erika and Victor laid next to each other in their large bed, with only the bedside lamps lit. Erika was doing her usual nightly reading of a random novel, and Victor worked on his studies. Every Monday, Wednesday, and Friday, Victor worked at a private college.   He was a teacher of World Culture, and he also did much research. This was one reason he liked to travel overseas. It was just after midnight now, and Victor found himself unable to concentrate as he thought about the events that had happened the other day at the fairgrounds.   Erika felt the same way, and she tried to focus on the lives of the characters in her book instead.   LaMore Manor was very quiet too.   Dmitri and Rosario had gone to bed a few hours ago, but Victor wasn't sure about Sabrina.   If she wanted to, Sabrina could stay up all night.   Sometimes, on the weekends when she didn't have school, Sabrina would wander around the mansion.   This had caught her parent's attention before.   They had seen her one night, walking slowly down a darkened hall with a small candelabra in hand.   She looked as if she were sleepwalking with the candle's light hauntingly reflecting off her eyes.   Needless to say, her parents didn't bother her.

   Victor set down his thick book, and turned his attention on his wife.   Erika moved her soft brown eyes and looked at Victor curiously.
   "What?" she asked in a low tone.   Victor almost didn't want to speak what was on his mind, but he knew he needed to talk about it.
   "There's something about Sabrina...*something strange*" he said.   Erika set down her book on the nightstand beside her.
   "Well, that is *obvious*" she responded.

"Our daughter can move *objects* with her *mind*." Victor gave a short glare out of annoyance.

"That's *not* what I meant" he said.

"What then?" Erika asked.   Victor sighed, and then spoke.

"When I was her age, and when I hit puberty, I discovered *my* power too, but..."

"But what?" Erika urged.

"It was never as strong, or out-of-control as *hers* is.   She's displaying power that I've never seen before, and...she's even stronger than *me* now" Victor said.   Erika sat up from her pillow, and looked at Victor in alarm.

"What are you saying, Victor?   Is Sabrina going to be okay?" she asked.

"I don't know...I think she is, but...the power is *different* with her.   As if she's increasing it somehow, whenever she gets angry.   I saw the look in her eyes that day, when she killed those people.   There was nothing there." Victor explained.   Erika could tell this was serious, and she didn't know what to do.   She remembered reading, that telekinesis was linked to emotions, and could be brought forth with intense urges, desires, and stress.

"My God, Victor, what if Sabrina realizes how strong she is…and…decides to *practice* her power?" Erika asked with worry.   Victor, whom had been thinking the same thing, shook his head solemnly.

"I think she already has" he whispered.

Erika sat there in worried thought.   Her mind asked her questions and played a few random scenarios of what might happen if people found out about Sabrina's *gift*.   Scenarios about the police, or social workers trying to take her away for murder.   However, Erika also realized that one could hardly *prove* it was Sabrina who'd killed all those people, since she never really touched them, and her *weapon* can't be physically seen.   What happened at the fair had been ruled out as a freak accident and malfunction with the Balloon Race ride, and the fair owners were now facing several suing charges over the deaths of twenty-five people.   However, no one could explain the severed tree nearby.

"What do we tell Meredith?" Erika asked.

"What do you mean?" Victor asked in confusion.

"Well, we said Meredith could live with us now, so…what do we say if she finds out about Sabrina's power?" Erika asked again.

"We'll just have to tell the truth, and hope she takes it well" Victor said.   Erika made a sarcastic frown, since she felt Victor's idea wasn't going to work.

"Are you sure?   You *know* how she can *be*" she said.

"Yes, I'm sure.   And if she doesn't like it, than she doesn't have to stay here" Victor said.

Meredith Ishtar was Erika's younger sister. Just recently, Meredith's home had caught fire by a tragic accident.   Meredith wasn't home at the time, but she had lost most of her belongings. Victor and Erika felt bad about her loss, and invited her to come live at LaMore Manor for as long as she wanted.   Meredith agreed, and she was due to arrive the next day.   Meredith was known as the "fireball" of the family.   She had no problem speaking her mind, or taking drastic measures to get what she wanted.   She was also quite quarrelsome to many people, but just not right away.   And if she didn't like something, or didn't like what you had said or done, she'd let you know in her usual sarcastic way.   Deep down, however, Meredith *did* have feelings of sensitivity, just like everyone else.   She just rarely had shown them right off the bat.

The next morning, Sunday, Meredith arrived in her car by ten o'clock.   Sabrina watched from the Sunroom, as her aunt drove up in sporting blue Porsche and greeted Victor and Erika.   The Sunroom was on the second floor, above the main entrance to LaMore Manor, and it had it's own balcony.   Sabrina wasn't too fond of Meredith's rudeness, and therefore, she rarely spoke to her.   She narrowed her eyes, and walked away from the windows.

　　　Dmitri carried in Meredith's suitcases to the main front hall.   Meredith walked in as well, with Victor and Erika following.   Rosario gave a formal bow to Meredith when she entered.

"Welcome back, Miss Ishtar" she said. Meredith took off her decorative thin peach colored scarf, and placed her purse in Rosario's hands.

"Hey, Rosie, would you be a dear and take the rest of my things up to my room" she said, without even making eye contact. She then walked past the maid, not caring to hear a response. Rosario gave a look of irritation, and then followed Dmitri up to the third floor.

Meredith stood in the middle of the front hall, looked up at the chandelier on the ceiling, and around at the surrounding walls. She had a fixed expression, and she seemed annoyed as she raised one eyebrow and spoke.

"This place gets bigger every time I see it…I hope I don't get lost again" she said with mild sarcasm. "They should've made *this* the White House instead." Victor wasn't too pleased with his sister-in-law already, and he quickly countered her remark.

"Meredith, you know very well that

wouldn't have worked, my home is made of gray stone" he said. Meredith made a smile out of annoyance with Victor, and walked into the living room.

"Yes...thank you, *Vic"* she said. Erika looked at her husband.

"I can tell this will be a jolly day" she spoke sarcastically.

Victor and Erika entered the living room, and found Meredith seated on the loveseat, already situated and holding a Vogue magazine. Her long dark blonde hair lightly dangled over the back of the loveseat.

"So how is mom doing, I haven't heard from her" Erika spoke up.

"Getting old, other than that she's fine" said Meredith, as she turned a page of the magazine. "She loves to garden now, and she sucks at doing it. She can't grow a damn thing if her life depended on it. What time's lunch?"

"Around one thirty, Rosario said she had something planned for your arrival" Erika said. She sat down beside her sister, and grabbed one of the other magazines off the coffee table.

"I hope it's nothing fattening, I gotta keep my figure, sis.   But that's nice of her" Meredith explained.   Erika nodded in silence.

Victor walked over to the fireplace, and picked up a dark blue ring box, and handed it to Meredith.

"You left this here, when you stayed with us last Christmas" he said.   Meredith looked up and smiled.

"Thanks, Vic, I forgot about my sapphire" she said.   Victor actually made a small smile as Meredith took her ring back.   He then walked over to the sofa and sat down.

"So, sis, where's the munchkin, I haven't see her yet?" Meredith asked.   Erika looked up and realized her sister was talking about Sabrina.

"Oh...she's around.   Probably practicing her music" Erika said quietly.   Meredith set the magazine on the coffee table and stood up.

"Well, let's go see her then" she said. Erika stood up as well, and looked at Victor with caution as Meredith made her way to the south wing staircase room across the hall.   Victor knew his wife was worried about Meredith discovering Sabrina's ability.   So he took her by the hand and they followed Meredith up to the second floor.

     Each room in LaMore Manor was named, and its name was printed on the doors that allowed you to enter them.   It was easier for one to navigate around the mansion to help not be lost. Although, due to the home's size, it was still difficult, and you would have to live there for a while in order to remember where everything was.   Meredith actually knew where the Music Room was, and she had no trouble finding it.   She came up to the room's double sliding doors, and she could hear the sound of a piano.   Meredith opened the doors slowly and entered.

     The Music Room, was one of the larger rooms of LaMore Manor.   It had a high ceiling and a row of vast windows, which let in lots of light while the drapes were open.   Victor had been told, that it had been chosen as a room for music so the sounds would flow around nicely.   It was large enough to host a small party or get-together, even though the Ballroom was located elsewhere.

Walking slowly, Meredith found her niece seated at the antique, ivory grand piano of the Music Room, facing away from her.   Sabrina's long black hair dangled freely down her back, as she played Beethoven's Moonlight Sonata elegantly.   The slow melody that the piano strings produced, drowned out Meredith's footsteps, as she walked toward her niece.   Meredith had only come up a few feet behind her, when Sabrina spoke with a genial, yet bland tone.
"Good morning…Aunt Meredith…"

Meredith suddenly stopped moving, as her niece stopped playing the song. Sabrina turned herself around, and looked at her aunt with an expressionless face.   Meredith made a small smile, and spoke.
"My, how you've grown" she said.   "I haven't seen you for a while."   Sabrina   stood up from the bench, and closed the piano's lid.
"You stayed here with us for Christmas last year, Aunt Meredith, and you arrived on December

23rd. It is now April 27th, of this year. I don't believe my growth has changed much in 115 days" Sabrina said precisely. "But yes, I have grown a bit since then."

Meredith, both impressed, and yet annoyed, acknowledged Sabrina's factual information. Erika spoke up, and confronted her daughter.
"Now, Sabrina, there is no need to be rude to your aunt. Like it or not, she is going to be living with us now" she said. Sabrina turned to her mother, and then looked back at her aunt.
"I apologize, Aunt Meredith, I was only making a statement" she said. Meredith gave a short laugh.
"Heh…don't worry about it" she said. Sabrina then nodded.

Looking out the large windows of the Music Room, Sabrina noticed the sky becoming dark. A storm had been on its way recently, and it seemed to have arrived now as thunder made itself known with a few low rumbles. Bothered by the presence of her aunt's arrival, Sabrina decided to go out to the back lawn of LaMore Manor, to the gardens, and floral hedge maze.   She carried her dark green umbrella along with her, and even though her mother had told her to wear a coat, since the temperature had dropped, and the air was moist, Sabrina refused to do so.   The rain came down steadily, as she walked the corridors of the maze.   Every few moments there would be a lightning flash, followed by the thunder, but this didn't bother Sabrina.   She was alone now, and having her quiet thinking time.   It wasn't that she hated Meredith, it was just the feelings and vibes she got from her.   Thoughts as well.   Meredith was always so down inside, angry, and annoyed by everything, and Sabrina couldn't handle it. Sabrina realized that ever since she was born, she could get that from people.   Their feelings, thoughts, and vibes.   They never came easily either, and were quite distorted sometimes. Almost like weird scenarios playing in her mind. It felt better to her, knowing she could get away from it for a break.

    Sabrina also knew of her father's ability of

telekinesis, and this....absolutely fascinated her. She'd read about it once, in the library, and continued to do so from then on. Parapsychology, the study of the paranormal and unknown, was an interesting topic.   One that could be explored and have so many different results every time.   Sabrina knew, what had been happening to her, was no coincidence.   She wasn't sure if what she had was telekinesis, however, it certainly seemed like it to her, and for some reason she couldn't always just "do" it.   She figured, that if she truly had telekinesis, it was something she must practice to master, just like learning the piano, or solving a math problem or a chess game.   And if it was a part of her, she was going to except it, for she knew, there was no reason to fear something she could not control. She was born with it, and it was hers now....she was going to work with it.

     Sabrina coughed a few times, and wiped her nose as she walked the maze.   Her body was cold from the wet air, and she felt sickly.   She had been walking around for an hour, taking a few breaks now and then to rest, but she figured she must go back inside, before she caught a cold. She stood in the center of the maze, coughing, and looking at the silver colored metal statue of a unicorn on a tall marble pedestal. The rain was pouring hard, and the lighting had gotten worse. She felt so sickly, as she turned around, and decided to go back, a lightning bolt abruptly hit the unicorn statue with a quick flash. Startled by the event, Sabrina screamed and fell to the soggy ground below the statue. She stared at the sky, with the swirling black clouds, and the unicorn wobbling in the heavy wind. The lightning had knocked the statue off balance, and she knew it was going to fall... Her fear wouldn't let her move, as she watched the heavy statue fall toward her, and land across her legs. Sabrina screamed and felt the pain from her legs go throughout her body. Frantically trying to move the statue off of her, her hands moving wildly, she suddenly felt her strength increase, and the statue literally flew off of her with a twist and hit the ground with a thud beside her. Crying, and also terrified, Sabrina eventually passed out from the pain as the rain down poured onto her body.

Chapter Five

A Growing Power

Victor slowly paced the hallway in front of Sabrina's bedroom, while Erika and a doctor stayed inside looking after Sabrina's heath. He previously went out to look for his daughter during the storm, and had heard her screams from the hedge maze. It just about drove him crazy when he found her laying on the ground unconscious and the unicorn statue laying beside her. He hadn't known what happened exactly, he only assumed it had fallen on her, and was terrified of her condition. Losing patience, he opened the doors of the room and asked if his daughter was okay. Erika sat on a chair beside the bed, with Meredith as well, and the doctor stood up from Sabrina's bed.

"She has a broken leg, Mr. LaMore, and a terrible migraine. Her body temperature is 104 degrees. Being out in the cold weather for so long has given your daughter a terrible sinus cold, and she will have to be medicated" the doctor said with a serious tone. "Her other leg is bruised, but both of them will be fine in time. I recommend constant rest, and for you to notify me directly if her condition worsens."

Victor stood there with a bland look, and then turned away while putting his hand up to his face
"That damn statue....damn it all to hell!" he said aloud. The doctor gave Erika his phone number, and told her to call him if anything worse happened or when Sabrina showed signs of healing, and then walked out the door with Meredith showing him the way out. Victor slowly approached Sabrina's white laced canopy bed, and sat down beside her. Sabrina, whom had been sedated with medication, was sleeping soundly

now, although her fever was still present.   He leaned forward and kissed his daughter's forehead lightly, and then got up and hugged his wife.   Erika held tight to her husband as she looked past his shoulder at her sleeping daughter.

"I really hope she'll be ok, Vic" she said softly, and tears welling up.

"She'll be fine, Erika.   All children fall ill at least once or twice, and let's just be thankful she wasn't extremely hurt and only broke a leg" Victor replied.

Later on that evening, Victor, Erika, and Meredith sat down in the living room, relaxing after a long day.   Sabrina had been sleeping for hours due to the fact that she now had pneumonia, and Victor and Meredith each took turns checking up on Sabrina's condition frequently while Erika lay napping on the couch.   The rainstorm outside had continued, but calmed a bit since the morning, and the mansion was quiet, while Victor and Meredith engaged in small conversation.

"There is something I noticed" Meredith said, as she turned her head to Victor.   Victor drew his attention to his sister-in-law.

"What?" he asked.

"Sabrina got sick very quickly.   She only had a bad cold earlier, and now its pneumonia. I've never seen a sickness come so fast" Meredith answered.   Victor nodded in agreement, and glanced at the mantle clock above the fireplace, which chimed an elderly chime for 9:30pm.

"It's time for her medicine again, and the tea should be ready" Victor said.   Meredith stood up and grabbed Sabrina's medicine.

"I'll take it up to her.   It's my turn anyway, and I made the tea.   You can stay here with Erika if you want" she said.   Victor nodded again, and Meredith went off to the kitchen.

After placing Sabrina's medicine and tea on a silver serving tray, Meredith walked up to the second floor where Sabrina's room was at the end of the long hall, which turned to the right, in order to reach the end.   As Meredith casually approached Sabrina's bedroom, she could slightly hear a creaking sound, coming from wood.   The hall light was on, but slightly dimmed and

Meredith could see the light from Sabrina's room, beneath the doors. The doors themselves were slightly bowing outward, which she realized was the source of the creaking sound. With the tray in one hand, balanced against her side, Meredith turned the knob of one of the doors, and they opened rather quickly, with a slam against the wall behind them in the hallway. Startled at first, Meredith stepped back, and almost dropped the tray. There was a wavy feeling coming from the room out into the hall, sort of like air, except it wasn't. Rather it was a force. Meredith walked in and gasped at the sight of the room, finally dropping the tray with a crash. Sabrina's bed floated above the floor lightly as if it were on a cloud, while Sabrina tossed and turned from her raging fever. Her eyes were closed and she didn't notice her aunt in the room, or what she was even doing. Her black grand piano slid slowly and sluggishly across the floor by itself, leaving marks in the carpet. The grandfather clock's glass door opened completely, almost breaking the hinges. Sabrina's bookcase floated as well, while the books slid off the shelves almost one by one, but in no particular order, and never hit the floor. They started drifting in the room's air like feathers, with their pages flapping while they dangled. The wardrobe had opened as well, and the hangers inside were bending themselves out of shape. Meredith slowly started to back out of the room, but the force around her seemed uncertain, and non-directional as it moved around. She couldn't see it, but could feel it pressing against her, and Meredith started to breathe heavily. It felt as though it was going to crush her.

      The bolts which held up the small chandeliers in the room unscrewed themselves a bit, and the chandeliers, dangled aimlessly with little sways back and forth as they flickered. The silver tray that Meredith had brought with her, started to bend and warp with a crunching sound. Meredith could see Sabrina moving her head back and forth on her bed, as though she was being tortured. The pain from her migraine had worsened, and the bed posts snapped in half as the wood splintered. Meredith had no clue what was happening. All she knew was, it seemed to be coming from her niece; since every time Sabrina moved, more objects and force moved in unison. Even the bedroom windows start to crack, showing lines in the glass.

"Victor!..." Meredith managed to call out, while lying on the floor. "Victor! Erika! Help me!"
By this time, Victor and Erika had been on there way down the hall when they heard Meredith's voice. They ran to the room, and suddenly felt the "unknown force" and saw the floating objects and distortions of the room. Erika knelt down beside her sister, while Victor ran over to Sabrina's bed. He lightly shook his daughter to wake her. Sabrina opened her eyes wide, and let out a short scream, and that's when everything was let loose. The windows shattered, the grandfather clock's display door flew off its hinges, and the bed slammed against the wall. Victor carried his daughter out of the room, while Meredith and Erika left as well. As soon as Sabrina's presence was gone from the room, everything had stopped moving. Even the books that were floating, simply fell to the floor.

Victor drove his daughter to the hospital, where she now laid in bed, sleeping once more. Her doctor and a few other nurses watched over her, talking in hushed tones amongst themselves, while Victor, Erika, and Meredith stood out in the hallway. Erika hugged her husband, wiping some of her tears from her face. Meredith stood off to the side of them, slightly trembling. She, of course, was breathing normal now, but had been constantly thinking of what she'd seen back at the mansion. She stood there with her arms folded and held against her, as though on a constant alert.

"What...what was that?..." she started to say, in a tense tone. "What was happening back at the house? That...wasn't normal...it couldn't have been."

Erika raised her head up from Victor's chest, and looked at her sister. She saw Meredith's serious and frightened face, and tears starting to trail down her cheeks. "What have you been hiding from me?" she asked. Erika came over to her sister, and then hugged her gently.

"I'm sorry, Meredith. We should have told

you" Erika said softly.   Meredith hugged her sister back, and spoke in uncertainty of what to say.
    "Told me what?   I don't…even know what the hell that was…or what was happening.   It scared me, Erika"   Meredith said through softened tears.

    Sabrina's doctor came out of the room, and approached Victor, while the nurses stayed inside.
    "Mr. LaMore, I'm glad you brought your daughter to me.   Her pneumonia is at a heightened state, and she will need to be looked after.   I'm keeping her for a few weeks or longer, maybe a month.   We have the medication she needs, here on demand, and I will be in everyday, even if I need to on Sundays.   She is currently getting her rest, and I'm leaving for the night.   Angela and Greta are the nurses whom will be watching over her tonight, and if I need to, I can come in" said the doctor.   "She will be alright, I have treated this before many times."
    "Thank you, doctor" said Victor quietly.   Sabrina's doctor nodded to Victor and Erika, and

then left, walking down the hall.   One of the nurses, Greta, opened the door, and looked at Sabrina's family.
    "You can come in now" the elderly woman said.   Victor walked in, with Erika and Meredith behind him, and they all sat down near Sabrina's bed.   Angela, the young nurse, had given Sabrina an IV and wrote down notes on her clipboard.
    "Greta and I will come back in a half hour, to check up on her.   You're allowed to stay here with her if you like" she said.   "For now she needs her rest, so I recommend hushed tones as you talk amongst yourselves.   You're very lucky.   I don't intend to scare you, but if she would have stayed at home any longer, she may have died."

    Erika placed her face in her hands, while sitting next to her daughter with Victor.   Meredith observed from her chair, slightly at a distance from Sabrina.   What she had seen before, still lingered in her mind.   After the nurses left, she then asked Victor and Erika, again, what exactly had happened.   As Victor had said before, there would be no secrets from Meredith, now that she was staying with them, and so, he told her. He told her about how Sabrina had inherited his telekinetic ability, and how it was progressively becoming stronger, seemingly every day. Meredith could hardly believe what she was hearing, and almost didn't, but after what she'd seen, she decided it was probably the truth. Victor and Erika really had no reason to lie to her.

"When you mentioned about your power in the past, Victor, I admit I always thought you were making it up. I'd never seen it. And now...I just don't know what to think... Is this even natural?" she asked.

"Yes, it is" Victor said simply. "It truly is natural. It just seems so different with her, and it's stronger than mine."

"You don't have to stay with us, Meredith, if it makes you uncomfortable. We haven't really told anyone else" Erika said. Meredith stared down at the floor, and thought to herself. She really had nowhere else to go, and Sabrina was indeed part of her family. Victor and Erika had been kind enough to let her live with them, for as long as she wanted. After about five minutes of

silence, Meredith raised her head and spoke.
 "I'll stay" she said dimly. "But I must say, I wish you would have told me sooner."
 Victor and Erika both nodded.
 "I know, and I'm sorry for that" Victor said. "We just didn't know how you'd react."
 "Well...it's pretty surprising, Vic. My niece is able to move things without touching them, and I still feel like I'm honestly in some sort of dream" Meredith responded. "Have you given any thought about what the rest of the family will think? What about Gabriella? Or your parents? Or even *my* parents?"
 Victor frowned at thought of his sister, Gabriella, knowing about Sabrina. Gabriella LaMore was the type of person to believe Sabrina was diseased, if Victor had mentioned her ability. Or even possibly controlled by the devil, or a demon of some sort. Gabriella knew of Victor's own ability, and she never mentioned it, for the very thought of it, bothered and frightened her.
 "I'll deal with that situation when it comes" he finally said. Erika sighed at the thought of this leading into a secretive problem.

"Well, alright, Vic, if that's how you see it. You know how Gabriella can be, and if she doesn't like it, she'll try and do something about it, and tell the whole family" said Meredith.

"I know" Victor said somberly.

Chapter Six

Clementine

In the 6th century B.C., it was believed the spirits of the dead would speak through the stomach region of the living.

From the Latin words 'Venter' meaning "belly" and 'Loqui' meaning "to speak".

Hence the word: Ventriloquist

Sabrina slowly opened her eyes, while lying on her hospital bed. The room was quiet, and the light from the window shown through, as she stared up at the ceiling. She could faintly remember being brought to the hospital by her parents, and she felt as though she had been sleeping for years. During her two week stay at Warren General Hospital, Sabrina had finally and successfully fought off pneumonia. Her body felt much stronger now, and her breathing was normal again. No longer did she have such a terrible migraine either. She looked around the room with slight caution, and realized no one was there. She sat up, and saw a vase of white carnations sitting on a little table next to her. There were also a few "get well" cards as well. There had been a few times in the past two weeks, when she'd woke while being ill, but she didn't remember much. Sometimes a vision of someone giving her liquid meals by mouth, but not for very long before passing out again. Most of the time, she had been sleeping. This caused the nurses to give Sabrina an IV needle in her wrist for feeding nourishment as well as one for her medication.

Sabrina stared at the needles in mild disgust, for she never liked anything foreign, puncturing her skin. She pressed the "call help" button to summon the nurse, and she sat on the bed, with her legs draped over the side.

Within a few minutes, Angela, Greta and the doctor as well came in and saw Sabrina sitting up silently on her bed.

"Oh, Miss LaMore...you're awake" Greta said in surprise. Sabrina stared at them with a blank look across her face.

"Where's my parents?" she asked blandly. Sabrina's doctor came over to her, and began to check her temperature, and the monitors.

"They aren't here as of yet, Sabrina. It's 10:15am, and they usually stop by and see you after noon" Angela said.

"How long have I been here?" Sabrina asked with the same tone. "What happened to me?"

"You have been here for two weeks; you had pneumonia, and you're quite lucky. You've recovered well" said the doctor.

Sabrina looked down to the floor, and

thought to herself.　She remembered the day of the storm, and being in the hedge maze too.　The lightning bolt, and the falling statue.　She slightly shivered at the thought of the pain again.　The doctor told Greta to call Sabrina's parents to let them know their daughter was fully conscious, while Angela helped Sabrina to stand and walk around for a bit.

　　"You have to start using those legs of yours again" she said with a small smile.　Sabrina almost fell at first, while her knees bowed, but soon she was standing up straight, and walking around again just as before.

　　After a few hours passed, and Sabrina had a nice breakfast, she was discharged from the hospital, and ready to go back home.　Victor and Erika both had come for her, while Meredith stayed back at the manor to wait for them.　They began to walk out of the hospital's lobby, when suddenly Sabrina's eyes widened and she clung to her mother's side like glue, staring out the front windows.

　　"No!　I'm not going out there!" she spoke

out with a raised voice.   Erika and Victor, both surprised and confused by their daughter's reaction, looked out the windows.   Outside, a rainstorm was in progress, with slight thunder. Sabrina began to quiver, and she turned her head away.

"Not in the rain…" she whimpered into her mother's side, burying her face.   Erika held Sabrina tightly, and then sat down on one of the benches, while Victor knelt down to face his daughter.

"What's wrong, Sabrina?   Is it the rain?" he asked quietly.   "Does it bother you?"

Sabrina said nothing, but simply nodded her head in silence.   Victor and Erika soon realized that Sabrina had now developed a fear of the rain, from her experience, and the trauma of being knocked unconscious during the storm.

"I don't want to be sick again" she whispered again.   Victor nodded, and helped Sabrina stand up again.

"Alright, we'll wait until the rain stops, and then we'll go home, ok?" he said.   Sabrina nodded again, and turned away from the windows.

"Okay."

Sabrina arrived home finally after about a half hour, and she immediately went upstairs to her room.   After being away for a little while, she felt the need to clean it.   Unknowingly to her, many of the broken objects where now repaired, since she didn't remember breaking them with her mind.   She did, however, notice them out of place and it made her wonder who'd been in her room while she was away.   She felt the presence of her father's aura in the room, and decided to lay the matter to rest.   She trusted Victor more so than her other family members, and this was mostly due to the fact they had one thing in common. Although, having telekinesis in common didn't change Sabrina's mind.   She still felt very defensive and territorial over her belongings.   An act of kindness from her father was alright for now, as Sabrina would settle back in with the thought of being home again.

Erika and Victor sat down in the living room with Meredith.

"I was wondering what took you guys so long to get back.   Is she doing ok?" Meredith asked.

"Yeah, she's fine now, except…" Erika started to say.   Meredith gave a look of confusion.

"Except what?" she asked again.   Erika shook her head.

"Sabrina seems to be…afraid of the rain" Victor said with a serious tone.   At first, Meredith gave a short little laugh, thinking Victor was only joking.

"What do you mean, Vic?" she asked, as she then began to straighten her face.

"Not just the rain, but also storms.   She's afraid she'll get sick again" Erika added.
Meredith stared at them in shock.

"Oh my god, Erika…is she going to be ok?" she asked again.

"I don't know" Erika said sadly; and she got up from the couch and walked over to the window, looking out at the side lawn.

"I think she's only afraid of it temporarily. After all, she experienced a trauma, but I don't think it will last very long" said Victor.

"Well, let's hope not" Meredith said.

Victor got up from his seat, and began to walk out of the room.
"Where are you going?" Erika asked quietly.
"I'm going to take Sabrina out for a little bit. Maybe buy her a present to help her feel better" he returned.   Erika nodded, and went back over toward the couch, where she had left her coffee on the coffee table.
"Be home in time for dinner, ok?" she said.
"We will" Victor said.   He then left the room, to go find his daughter.

Dressed all in black and red, her favorite colors, Sabrina entered her father's beige Mercedes Benz coupe.   Victor had at least five Mercedes Benz cars in his collection, which were stored in the LaMore Manor garage.   His coupe classic happened to be his favorite, and had been the first one he ever bought; back when he was seventeen years old.
"Where are we going, dad?" Sabrina asked gently.   Victor started the engine, and slowly

drove out of the long driveway, passing the tall black iron gate that surrounded LaMore Manor and the lawns.

"I just thought we'd go out for a bit. Maybe stop at a few stores" he said casually. "We haven't done much lately; the two of us."

Sabrina looked out her window without speaking. She watched the trees and homes go by in a soft blur with the speed of the car. It wasn't fast, it was more as though drifting along down the road, and the sun peeked through the clouds of the previous rain storm which had finally passed over.

Victor drove into downtown Warren, and parked the car on central Liberty Street. He walked with Sabrina down the sidewalk, and asked her if there was anywhere she'd like to go. Sabrina replied with a simple "no" and Victor gave a sigh. He suddenly looked across the street, and saw a little store, which seemed to be crammed in between other stores in the little building. The sign above it was named "Little Dreams". Most of the buildings in Warren hardly went above 5 floors high, except for the old clock tower bank, and the county courthouse; since it was mostly a historical old fashioned town.

"Come on" he said, as he began to cross the street.   Sabrina followed without a word, but made a frown out of annoyance.   They both entered the little store, which was dark, and lit only by two rows of lights on the ceiling, and the single display window.   It had at least four rows of high shelves, which held many items old and new.   Some collecting dust over years of rejection.

An elderly man standing behind the counter, fixed his eyes on his only customers, and pushed his glasses back up to his face, since they had been falling slightly.

"Hello" he said with a genial tone, and made a small smile.   Victor replied and began to look around while Sabrina simply stood at the beginning of the aisles.   The man came out from behind his counter, and walked over to her.

"Can I help you find anything, Miss?" he asked.   Sabrina looked up at him after staring at the floor.

"No bother; I don't see anything here I like" she said quietly. The man raised an eyebrow, and looked at the girl's father.

"Oh, I'm sure there is something" he said. "Just take a look. You'll never know until you do." Sabrina then sighed lightly, and walked down the aisle in front of her.

Every object she saw, all looked as though they had been neglected and thrown into the trash by several people, and then scavenged to be brought to these shelves. However, she was somewhat curious of them. As though she was meant to come to this little shop, to see what the world had forgotten, and cast aside. The old man behind Sabrina stood there in confidence with his hands behind his back; as though he knew she'd find something, no matter what. Meanwhile, Victor had chosen a few items for Erika, Meredith, and himself. Sabrina was alone on her side of the store, and when she came to the end of the aisle...that's when she saw her. Sitting low on the floor, tucked away in the corner, was a doll. It had long black hair, and was wearing a solid white frilled dress, with a large white hat to match.   The hat had a pink ribbon tied around it, and covered the dolls eyes, somewhat eerily.   It was rather large in size for just a normal doll, and this intrigued Sabrina.   She knelt down and picked the doll up slowly; and for a minute, everything seemed to stop.   There was no sound.   No movement.   Just her and the doll, which seemed to have an instant bond.   Something Sabrina felt she had been missing, and finally found.   She looked under the hat at the dolls eyes…and discovered there was only one.   It was a glass eye of a brilliant green color, much like Sabrina's own eyes, while the other side had nothing but a hole of emptiness.   Sabrina wasn't sure why, but the look of the doll almost made her cry, and she held it tight to her body.

"This doll is a ventriloquist's doll, and my oldest find" the elderly man said.   "I found her years ago, while traveling in Europe."   Sabrina looked up at the man with slight tears in her eyes.

"How did she lose her eye?" she asked.

"I don't really know.   I found her that way." said the man, as he shook his head in disappointment.   "I was told she survived a terrible fire, which is why her dress is slightly singed on the back.   Other than missing her eye…I think she's a real beauty.   Probably over a hundred years old now, I'd say."

"I promise to take good care of her" she said.   The man smiled, and led Sabrina to the front counter, with Victor following behind.

"I know you will" he returned.

After Victor and Sabrina came back home, Erika noticed how her daughter went directly to the staircase and up to her room.   She asked Victor what he had bought for her, and he explained how they found the shop called "Little Dreams" and how Sabrina found the old ventriloquist doll with one eye.   Erika was upset at first at the fact her husband bought Sabrina something she didn't know how to use, and was broken to begin with.   However, after Victor explained again, how happy Sabrina was with her gift, Erika decided to leave the matter to rest.

Sabrina sat on her canopy bed in her room,

quietly looking down at her doll, which she held in front of her, facing her chest.   Staring at it with both curiosity, and also delight.   She felt something about the doll...something that wasn't natural.   It felt as though it may have had a living presence.   This slightly confused Sabrina, for she knew, that could not be possible.   She placed her hand inside the back of the doll, holding onto the movement gears comfortably.

"Hi" she said softly.   "My name is Sabrina. What's yours?"

The doll sat in silence for a few minutes, yet Sabrina never took her eyes off it.   She stared directly into the doll's face intently, as if it were an actual person.   The doll moved it's mouth open sluggishly as Sabrina moved her hands, but not her own mouth.

"Clementine" the doll said in a light, childlike tone.   Sabrina made a small smile and spoke again.

"Where are you from?" she asked. Responding sooner this time, the doll opened its mouth again with the same child's voice.

"Your world."

Erika climbed the steps to the second floor, and began to walk down the hall to Sabrina's room.   She hadn't seen much of her daughter, and she wanted to talk with her more.   And about the doll as well.   When she reached Sabrina's bedroom doors, she could hear her daughter and another voice speaking.   She stopped and carefully put her ear up to the door.

"I like you Sabrina…can we be friends?" Clementine asked daintily.
"Of course we can" Sabrina replied.
"But…what will the other's say?" the doll asked.
"It doesn't matter what others think.   I protect you now, Clementine" Sabrina said seriously.

Erika leaned back and looked at the door in bafflement at the sound of her daughter.   She then opened the door slowly, and came into the room, seeing Sabrina's back turned to her, while on the bed.

"Thank you, Sabrina…we'll be friends forever" Clementine said.   Sabrina smiled again, while still being her usual serious self.
"Yes, we will."

"She knows about us, Sabrina" Clementine said.   "Can she play with us too?"   Sabrina looked at her doll in confusion, wondering what she meant.
"Who?" she asked.
"Your mother…"

Sabrina turned her green eyes, and quickly moved her body around, facing Erika straight on.   Erika jumped slightly in alarm, and said hello to her daughter.
"Sounds like your practicing is getting good, Sabrina" she said with a weak smile.   "It's time for bed now."
"I'm not tired yet" Sabrina said with a short dull tone.   Erika's smile faded, and she then became stern.
"I won't tell you again, Sabrina.   It's time

for bed now" she said.

"Sabrina will go to bed after she's done playing, Erika" said Clementine happily.   Erika now was angry, and quickly walked up to Sabrina, snatching the doll from her grasp, and surprising her.

"I've had enough of this" Erika said, as she walked back to the door.   "The thing is broken to begin with, and you don't need it."

"Sabrina!" Clementine called out.   "Sabrina help me!"

Erika froze when she heard the doll speak without its controller, and dropped it to the floor. Sabrina glared at her mother in the slight darkness of the room.

"How did you...do that?" Erika asked cautiously.   Sabrina stood up from her bed, and came over, picking up her doll, and shielding it in her arms.

"You are not to touch her ever again" she said darkly.   Erika gave a sudden look of shock.

"Now wait just a minute, young lady!   You don't speak to me that way!" her voice rose.

Clementine's head, then started to turn slowly with a grinding sound, until it finally faced Erika in the opposite direction of its body, with its single glass eye seeming to slightly gleam.   Erika couldn't speak, while she looked into the doll's face.

"I think it's time to leave now Erika…Sabrina seems angry with you…and that upsets me too" she said.

Erika backed away, and opened the doors behind her.

"Okay…" she said mildly, and then shut the doors, leaving Sabrina and Clementine alone.

Sabrina looked down at her doll in her arms, and Clementine's head swung back around in its normal position quickly.

"She's not very nice.   I change my mind.   I don't want her to play with us, okay?" Clementine said cheerfully.   Sabrina nodded in silence, and walked over to her bed, where she pulled the covers back, and laid her doll down beside her.

"She just doesn't understand, Clementine. And from now on, you speak whenever you want

to" Sabrina said.   The dolls head faced Sabrina, and spoke just once.
    "Okay."

Chapter Seven

A Splitting Mind

For the next few days, Sabrina practiced her ventriloquism with Clementine. Being someone who naturally learned quickly to begin with, she found she had the knack for it, and was able to make Clementine "come to life" easily. Erika had confessed to Victor and Meredith that she didn't like the doll. Ever since Erika was young, she had a small fear of dolls, mostly china dolls, and Clementine made her feel uncomfortable. Victor and Meredith shared the same feeling on the matter as Erika, considering every time Sabrina made contact, it was through the doll only.   Sabrina had always been quiet before, but now she almost seemed to be a mute.   During meal times, Clementine sat in Sabrina's lap.   Victor thought of taking the doll away a few times, but Erika told him what happened the night she tried to do that exact same thing.   So, instead of upsetting his daughter by taking away the gift he'd bought for her, he simply would only try to get her to speak.   However, when Sabrina actually spoke, her responses were either bland and dull, or spiteful and harrowing.   Most of the time she seemed to be without emotion or expression.   A zombie-like effect of a trance which followed her every action.

    Meredith, being her usual self, would sometimes make comments on her niece's demeanor, only to miff Sabrina, and react with more speaking from Clementine and silence.   In Meredith's thoughts, she came to the simple conclusion that Sabrina was mental, and decided to ask Erika and Victor if they'd take their daughter to see a psychologist or therapist.   Erika actually agreed with Meredith, even though Victor said no.   He felt Sabrina was only trying to express her true self in her own way, and would eventually grow out of it.   Although, everyday Sabrina seemed more and more distant, and Erika made the call for a psychologist appointment.   Victor told his wife, that if there wasn't any improvement, then Sabrina would no longer see a doctor for her "troubles".   He refused to believe her actions were caused by anything, other than her own way of being herself.

      Sabrina had also begun to practice her telekinetic ability.   It no longer bothered her, and she liked how she felt when she used it.   Knowing that the world would never accept her for who she truly was, Sabrina decided that if anyone ever gave her a problem, or took advantage of her in some way…she would give them a reason to be afraid.   Since from what Sabrina had learned…it has never been mankind's desire to get along.   Too many people base so much on the differences in life, so they fear and reject them…while not even realizing, that differences are what keep the balance in life going. Things like stereotypes and sexual preference, or race and identity, never bothered Sabrina. She was willing to accept anyone for who they were...as long as they accepted her too.

Sabrina sat in the middle of the floor, holding Clementine, and thinking to herself. She was in, yet another room of the mansion that seemed to relax her while in thought. It was the Clock Room, and the inside was filled with many antique clocks that had been passed down and collected through the LaMore family line. The mansion itself, had many clocks of its own, but the rarest and eldest of the clocks, were kept in this room for protection. On the right side of the room, was a long line of grandfather clocks against the wall. From the start of the room at the door, to the end by the windows. Each were different and unique on their own, and with their own chimes as well. The left side of the room consisted of shelves for the mantle and bracket clocks, as well as wall space for the regulators and cuckoos. Victor would often come to the room and wind the clocks with Dmitri and sometimes Rosario as well; although they were never set to the appropriate time schedule, since Victor liked to hear the chimes at separate times, instead of all at once.   While in the room, Sabrina heard nothing but the sounds of every clock ticking at different rates.   The room was on the third floor, and just after the Ballroom; which was rarely used these days.

On the floor in front of her, sat a little wooden stand, which held a row of spoons and forks, which Sabrina had propped up as though they were standing by themselves.   She had read in books in the library, that many people used silverware in testing telekinetic movement in brain wave patterns.   How they would bend them as proof of the results, without touching them physically.   She knew her ability was getting much stronger within her, and at an increasingly rapid rate, but she wanted to be sure she could control it.

Holding her doll with one hand, Sabrina

reached out her arm slowly until her hand hovered over the silverware stand.

"Alright, Clementine...it's time for a test" she said quietly.   Staring down at the forks and spoons, she began to focus her thought and energy upon them.   The room started to feel wavy to her. She felt the energy surrounding the silverware easily, as they started to wobble in the stand.   In her mind, she wanted them to bend, and could see a mental picture of them doing so in her thoughts. One by one, each fork and spoon quickly bent directly in half as she let her energy flow out of her.   The silverware severed into pieces, and the wooden stand shattered completely into several small jagged fragments as they scattered across the floor.   A few of the forks and spoons had even flung with tremendous speed and embedded themselves into the wall.

Pleased with her results, but not changing her concentration, Sabrina closed her eyes and focused on all the energy of the room.   She could feel the movements of the clocks as her energy built up inside her and let loose.   The clocks themselves all started to slow down rapidly, with the sounds of the ticks and chimes coming to a dull and slurred reverberation and resonance. The pendulums swung back and forth increasingly slow, until finally coming to a stop. The walls of the room creaked and moaned slightly, while the grandfather clocks started to slide across the wooden bare floor with a grating sound. They all moved in aimless direction; a few bumping into each other, and the floor boards cracked in a circle around the spot Sabrina was sitting in.

Suddenly, as the door of the room opened, and Victor walked in with a look of shock on his face, Sabrina stopped her focus quickly, and the grandfather clocks stopped moving across the floor. She stood up slowly, and turned herself around, facing her father and holding her companion. The pendulums all continued to sway as they had before, while every clock ticked once again. Victor stood in the doorway; his hand on the doorknob and staring at his daughter with widened eyes.

"Sabrina…" he whispered.

His daughter simply raised an eyebrow with her scowling look and spoke in a casual, yet sarcastic manner.

"*Yes*, father?"

Victor didn't know how to respond to this. He didn't even want to move from his spot, much less speak. Sabrina stood in the middle of the crowded forest of grandfather clocks that surrounded her, not moving an inch.

"*Well?* You *do* have something to *say...don't you?*" she asked. Victor finally found the courage to talk.

"Its...time to go now" he said.

Sabrina walked slowly toward her father, with the grandfather clocks moving away, and clearing her a path, while tearing up the floor boards a bit from their dragging weight.

"Where are we going?" she asked.

"Your...mother and I...have someone for you to meet" he responded. Continuing to walk closer, Sabrina spoke again in the same tone.

"I don't want to meet anyone. I'm just fine" she said. Victor was soon face to face with his daughter as she stopped and stood in front of him, staring at his face.   He took in a deep breath, and looked back at her, and focused himself.

"It's time to go now, Sabrina.   Get yourself ready" he said with a slight stern tone.

Standing there in silence, Sabrina lifted her scowl and replied calmly.

"Alright" she said.   And then walked past her father, heading toward the staircase.

Dmitri drove the LaMore's to the doctor's office downtown in the limousine.   He waited in the car, while Victor, Erika, and Meredith lead Sabrina inside.   They sat in the waiting room, with Sabrina staring down at the floor, not speaking a word.   She knew why she was there, and she certainly wasn't very pleased about it. She got the vibe from her parents that they thought she was crazy, but not so much from her father.   It was mostly from Erika, and Meredith as well.

A woman suddenly came from the next room, and smiled gently.   She was in her mid thirties, with semi long light brown hair, and was dressed in a dark blue business suit.

"Hello there" she greeted Victor and Erika cordially. "I'm Dr. Roberta Stein; it's nice to meet you."

"Hi, Dr. Stein; I'm Erika. We spoke on the phone" Erika replied with a handshake. Victor and Meredith introduced themselves as well.

"This must be Sabrina" the doctor said, as she looked at the silent girl. "I'd like to talk with her first for a bit, so you can all just relax in the waiting area. It won't be long."

Sabrina looked at the psychologist without speaking, but narrowed her eyes. Dr. Stein walked back toward her office room, and gestured for Sabrina to follow her. After closing the door, Dr. Stein sat in her desk chair, and asked Sabrina to sit in the guest chair in front of her. Behind her, hung Roberta Stein's degrees in Psychology, Social Services, and also Parapsychology; in black frames.

"So, Sabrina, how are you feeling today?" she asked casually. Sabrina sat quietly in the chair with her usual poker face, and clutched Clementine tightly.

"I'm fine" she said.

"Have you done anything exciting lately? Gone to the mall maybe?" the doctor asked.

"No."

"I guess you don't get out much, huh?" the doctor asked.   Sabrina made a scowl, and looked at Dr. Stein in annoyance.

"*No*...Dr. Stein."

"Oh, you can call me Roberta" said the doctor.   Sabrina then sighed from frustration, without opening her mouth.

"You shouldn't ask so many questions, Roberta...its impolite" Clementine said lightly. Roberta Stein raised her eyebrows slightly.

"Oh...oh really now?" she spoke, with a nod of her head.   "Sabrina, do you know why you mother asked me to talk with you?"

Sabrina made an angry expression and the pictures on the wall behind her cracked with a sudden breaking of the glass in each one.   At this moment, Roberta's welcome smile, faded quickly and she stood up from her chair, while looking at the dark girl in front of her.   The small knickknacks adorning her desk began to slide toward her and hit the floor with a few thud-like noises.

"T-tele..kinesis..." she managed to say, out of amazement.

"Erika doesn't mind her own business, Roberta.   She doesn't let Sabrina play and be herself" Clementine explained.   Roberta stood motionless for a minute, while the objects in the room eventually stopped moving.

"You may leave now...Sabrina" she said uneasily.   Sabrina stood up, and then walked out of the room, closing the door behind her.

Roberta Stein came into the waiting room again, and Victor and Erika noticed her change of mood right away.

"I'd like to speak with you two and Meredith now, please" she said.   Victor, Erika, and Meredith noticed the broken pictures and the objects on the floor when they came in the office.

"Mr. LaMore, I'm concerned about Sabrina's emotionless demeanor.   And I'm not sure if you're aware of this, but your daughter has an extremely powerful gift" Roberta said. Victor gave a short laugh.

"We know" he said. "She was born with it." Dr. Stein then shifted her eyes between each of her guests.

"Yes, well...I'm also diagnosing her with Dissociative Identity Disorder. Your daughter has two personalities, Mr. LaMore, and she will most likely need to be medicated. I would like to see her again, if it's alright with you" she said. Victor nodded and looked at his wife and sister-in-law for their approval as well. They both nodded in silence, and Erika turned away, putting a hand up to her eyes. Victor was also slightly surprised at how quickly Roberta Stein had noticed all of this in Sabrina's personality. Being a professional, he supposed she knew what she was talking about.

"I'm hoping medication is a last resort. I think with progress, she can learn to talk by herself; without the doll" Roberta said.

"Thank you for your time, Dr. Stein. I realize this may be shocking to you" Victor said.

"I'm here to help, Mr. LaMore. I'll do what

I can" Roberta said. "I know her ability is strong within her, and I believe it will increase in strength over time. She is clearly comfortable displaying her ability without consequence. This leads me to believe she is most likely developing it."

"Yeah…I had a feeling she was doing that" Victor admitted. After what he witnessed in the Clock Room prior to visiting the doctor, he knew Sabrina wasn't going to hide her ability. He wanted his daughter to express to herself…and now she was doing it.

Part Two

Enter Eleanor: Fire Sorceress

Chapter Eight

Not A God

Fire is the only known non-living phenomenon, needing oxygen to survive. It is also the only destructive force, able to bring rebirth from its ashes.

    Sitting at her desk, Sabrina held her doll close to her, while working on a math quiz. She was now age seventeen, and in high school. Over the years, since she was thirteen, she had practiced her ability of telekinesis; mastering it well.   Just as she'd been in her early teen years, Sabrina was much of a loner, and barely spoke to anyone in school.   The other students mostly did the same around her.   Some were baffled by her, while others were slightly afraid.   Many thought it was strange she carried Clementine with her all day.   Some would even make rude remarks to her.   Although, after giving her usual glare with her deep green eyes upon them, the other students would quickly quiet themselves.   Sabrina would walk down the halls to her other classes; her long onyx hair swaying behind her with the light bouncing along the strains evenly.   With her blank expression across her face, the students knew who she was; they knew she was very wealthy, and they knew there was something about her…that wasn't average.

    The classroom teacher, Mrs. Norma Baker, stood at the chalkboard at the front of the room, writing math problems.   Her class sat in silence as they worked on their quiz.   They were in silence, for this was how Mrs. Baker always wanted it.   A stern old woman in her age; she seemed to rule the classroom with an iron fist. In all the years of her teaching, her former students would surely tell, that any misbehavior or laziness of attention, would give you a trip out of the class and to see Mr. David Castle; the head principal. Baker and Castle seemed to have an "alliance" as the students would say. It seemed as though Castle would let Baker treat her students any way she wanted; no matter how strict. Some of the students accused the two of "secretly fucking" and this made them chuckle at the thought of old Mrs. Baker cheating on her husband just to make the status of "Teacher of the Year" *every* school semester. This never bothered Sabrina. In fact, she knew Mrs. Baker was more curious about her "quietest student" rather than annoyed.

Mrs. Baker set the chalk back in the tray, looked at the clock on the wall, and then faced her class.

"Alright, class, pencils down" she spoke allowed, clapping her hands and waking some of her students from the quiet. "Bring your papers to my desk; finished or not." Each teenager left their work in a pile on the desk and sat back down. Two of Sabrina's classmates; Lois Platte and Tammi McVay, whom always seemed to be together where ever they went, giggled to each other while gossiping about a few of the boys in the room, and swayed their hips as they walked passed them. Sabrina noticed this, and had been slightly annoyed; for she thought their very existence was utterly incompetent of being mature. It was these two girls, whom often made many remarks of Sabrina as well. As though, they couldn't focus their energy on anything else when they saw her.

       Sabrina was the last of the students to bring her paper to Mrs. Baker; approaching her slowly, and holding Clementine close. The eyes of Baker and Sabrina met for a moment, and no words were spoken. Sabrina walked back to her seat with the entire classrooms eyes upon her body. Mrs. Baker looked at Sabrina's paper, and was surprised to find every answer she viewed was correct, while a majority of the other students had made mistakes.   She looked at Sabrina, and then called her to the front of the room, along with Tammi, Lois, and another student named Bryson Blackwell.

"I would like you four to solve the problems on the board, and when you're finished, you may sit down again" she said.

Tammi and Lois complained slightly, until they saw Baker's stern look, and went up to the blackboard.   Sabrina stood at the end, beside Bryson, and finished her math problem in about five seconds.   To everyone's surprise, she soon was walking back to her seat without a word. Mrs. Baker stood up, and directed Sabrina to go back to chalkboard and finish the problem. Sabrina turned around, and spoke quietly.

"I'm sure you'll find it to be finished already, Mrs. Baker" she said.   And then finally sat down again.   Norma Baker went up to board and viewed the math problem; only to find Sabrina had been correct all along.   She took off her glasses, and thought to herself, while looking at her student.   Never, in all of her years at the school, had she seen this from any of her students. Sabrina seemed to be able to do any math problem, and always find the solution, quicker than the others.

"It's obviously wrong..." Lois spoke up sarcastically. "She was done too quick." Mrs. Baker then looked at Lois and put her glasses back on.
"Pay attention to your own, Lois, since you've got it wrong, yet again" she said. Some of the other students laughed a bit, until Baker made her "look" again. The bell that signaled to switch classes suddenly rang, and the teacher motioned for them to leave.
Sabrina was the last to leave the room, and Norma Baker spoke to her as she was leaving.
"You've been doing well, Miss LaMore, but if you want to continue in my class, I suggest you leave your doll at home. This is a place of learning, not for play" she said with a solid tone. Sabrina stopped, and turned toward the old woman with a glare.
"Clementine is more than a doll...and you

should appreciate that" she said with the same tone of voice.   Mrs. Baker stood in silence, and then watched Sabrina leave the room.   That, was the first and only time, any student had ever talked back at her, in the same manner.   She walked quickly out the door, and found Sabrina was now gone; lost in the crowd of students scurrying around the halls to their classes before the bell rang again.   She then went back to her desk, gathered her books and planner, and made her way down to David Castle's office.

    She knocked loudly on the glass windowed door, and soon heard him say "come in".   The gray bearded, African American man looked up from his work, and saw her standing there.
    "Hello Norma, what brings you here today?" he asked.   Norma Baker sat down in the chair in front of Mr. Castle and set her books on his desk.
    "I'd like to talk with you about a student of mine" she said.   David reached for his coffee.
    "Another one giving you a hard time again, I presume" he said.
    "No actually.   I'm intrigued by Miss

Sabrina LaMore" Norma replied.   David looked up and set his coffee down again.

"What about her?"

"Well, aside from the fact she never speaks in class, especially to the other students, her math skills are extraordinary.   She is well above her grade level, and displays a learning capability unlike any student I've ever taught" Norma said. Mr. Castle looked back down at his paper again, and began writing his thoughts.

"You're not the first teacher to come and tell me this, Norma.   I've had all her other teaches in my office saying the same thing about her learning ability the last few days.   Are you suggesting she doesn't need to be in your class?" he asked.

"Actually, with your permission, I'd like to schedule a possible meeting and discuss this with her parents, and have you and some of the other teachers present if they want" Norma said. "Bumping her to a more advanced class may not be a bad idea either.   I believe she needs a challenge in her learning."

Mr. Castle looked at Norma intently, and

then set his pen aside.

"Well Norma, you're one of my long time teachers of this school, and if you don't mind me saying so, I consider you a friend of mine. We've known each other for a while, and if you feel Sabrina LaMore may need this, then I trust your judgment. I will call her parents at the end of the school day, and see if they can come in" he said. Mrs. Baker made a small smile, and then stood up.

"Thank you for your time, David. I have to be going now, since this is my planning period" she said. Mr. Castle motioned for her to leave, as he sipped his coffee.

"Have a good day" he returned.

As Sabrina rode in the LaMore limousine on her way home, Dmitri chose this time to start up a conversation with the girl, and tell her some unexpected news.

"How was your day at school, Miss LaMore?" he questioned. Sabrina looked over from the window and spoke mildly.

"Productive" she said, and Dmitri nodded.

"I remember my school days of your age

too.   Seems so long ago now" he said.   Sabrina made a small sigh.

"Dmitri, what is the news you wish to tell me?" she spoke blandly, since she'd already known this was the reason why Dmitri started talking to her.   Dmitri made small smile at the inquisitive teen.

"Get straight to the point, yes?" he said with a slight chuckle, and Sabrina nodded.   "Well, it seems your aunt Gabriella and her daughter are coming to live with us for a while, just as Meredith is currently" he said.   Sabrina then fixed her look upon the butler quickly.

"Explain" she said with a sharpened tone.

"Well, Miss LaMore, it seems your aunt's husband, Mr. Lee Mang, has been causing some trouble, though I'm not aware of the whole situation, so you may have to ask your father. Gabriella *is* his sister after all" Dmitri said.

Sabrina walked through the front doors, and began to look for her parents.   She walked with Clementine through the front hall, and could faintly hear voices coming from one of the rooms nearby.   She eventually found Victor, Erika, and Meredith seated in the Lounge, with another woman standing off to the side.   She was tall, like Victor, but slightly shorter, and had short dark hair that dangled just above her shoulders.   She held tightly to a small handkerchief, which she had been using to dry her frequent tears.   Her eyes, reddened and swelled, and her breaths were frequent.   As if trying to calm herself.

    Sabrina stood in the doorway, and Victor noticed her there.
    "Welcome home, Sabrina.   There is someone I'd like you to meet.   This is your aunt Gabriella, my sister" he said.   Gabriella LaMore turned toward her niece and spoke softly with a shuddered voice from crying before.
    "Hello dear" she said.   "I know you've never met me before, but that's because I used to live quite a ways from here" she said as she dried her eyes once again.
    "Where are you from?" Clementine asked her pleasantly.   Gabriella froze for a second, when Sabrina made her doll talk.   She stared at

the doll as if it were an insect, but finally found the courage to speak.

"Florida. I lived in St. Augustine" Gabriella responded, and then hung her head a bit. "With my ex-husband."

Sabrina continued to stand there in silence, as she felt her aunt's aura. Victor got up from the loveseat and spoke up.

"We're going out for a little bit, Sabrina. Gabriella will be living here for a while, and we're going to show her around town" he said. Gabriella looked up at her brother and slightly widened her eyes, speaking with a small whisper.

"Are you sure we should leave my daughter here alone?" she asked. Victor walked over to his sister.

"Eleanor will be fine, wherever she is. And besides, it's just for a few hours. Let her get used to the house. I know it's quite a change from where you used to live" he said. Gabriella nodded in silence, but still kept a worried expression. Sabrina stared among her family members, and then walked slowly away from the room.

Victor, Erika, and Meredith then left with Gabriella, and since Rosario went out grocery shopping, and Dmitri drove; Sabrina was alone in the mansion…except for one other…

It was late spring now, and warm zephyrs surrounded the manor as they blew through the trees.   It was relaxing to Sabrina as she walked around the spacious back lawn, going past the floral hedge maze.   She walked toward the willow tree gardens, near the very back of the property, where not even the neighboring homes could see her.   The sun shown down nicely and it wasn't even hot upon her face.   It was just right, and the smell of the flowers floating through the air softly like music helped Sabrina's soul escape the world.

As she walked casually with Clementine in her arms among nature, she began to sense another human presence somewhere close by.   It was new, yet it had the same aura slightly as her family did.   Every person's aura was different, but Sabrina came to realize she could tell her family had a similar presence in their bodies, that she could sense. Not only was this presence slightly familiar, but also intriguing. There was something about it...something powerful...like her own. Both warm and dark. A type of presence that felt uncanny, but she wanted to know what it was. It felt distorted.

As she walked through the flowerbeds in the large willow garden, she finally saw a figure standing. It was a girl, as she could tell from her clothing, and she was about her age, maybe a year younger. She stood, facing away from Sabrina amongst the daffodils, her long platinum blonde hair drifting in the wind as it slightly curled around the ends. She wore a solid black dress, of an older Gothic design from the 1940's and a large black hat to match. The yellow ribbon on the hat was tied to a bow, and dangled quite long in the wind, along with her dress blowing gently as well. Her ankle strap style heeled shoes, stood on a few of the daffodils without mercy, matching black in color. Sabrina walked up to the girl and stood beside her, but not very near. The world around them was quiet and serene, except for the sound of the wind gliding around their bodies.   They stood there for a few minutes; neither of them speaking, and the girl held tight to a gold bell-shaped locket that hung from her neck.

"You must be Eleanor" Sabrina said quietly. The girl opened her eyes, and breathed in heavily before speaking.

"Well…I'm certainly not anyone else" she blandly replied.   "And you're Sabrina, I presume. Mother told me about you."

There was another pause between the two, and both still hadn't faced each other.

"Your mother is afraid of you" Sabrina said suddenly, yet casually.   Eleanor made a small gasp and turned her head, fixing her brilliant blue eyes on her cousin.   Sabrina then turned her head in return, as they finally looked into each other faces for the first time.   "She's quite foolish…is she not?" Sabrina spoke again.   Eleanor looked to the ground, and turned away again.

"She doesn't understand…and neither will you…so don't bother me…" she voiced.

Sabrina looked at her cousin with interest, and could sense the depression weighing heavily upon her, and the angry aura raging inside like a forest fire.   Although, she realized Eleanor's anger was not with her, but it wasn't something she could easily suppress either.   It had moments of exploding, and Sabrina felt she could relate to some of her feelings.

"There is something very diverse about you" Sabrina said.   Eleanor then made a small laugh, but she didn't think anything was funny; only annoying.

"Of course there is…" she said quietly, and she raised her right hand up slightly.   With a wicked smirk to herself, she snapped her fingers gently, and hot flames formed easily in her hand, as if she were holding them by some unknown means.

Sabrina noticed this, and turned her green eyes quickly at the blonde girl near her; yet still stood without moving.

"Quite impressive" she said to her.

Eleanor turned herself toward Sabrina, but didn't move.

"There is something about you, too.   You

give off an enormous amount of energy; more so than any other human I've met" she said. "I feel it floating around you, drawing in other energies nearby."

"Tell me something, Eleanor. Do you honestly consider yourself godly?" Sabrina asked in sarcasm. Eleanor then narrowed her eyes with slight anger.

"I should be..." she voiced in a grisly tone. Sabrina made a sigh, and turned toward the blonde girl completely.

"You are sadly mistaken, cousin...no god stands here" she said.

"Then test me..." Eleanor retorted.

"No thank you" Sabrina said dully; clearly bored with the situation. Eleanor made another small laugh.

"Don't tell me you're afraid..." she said, as the flames in her hand grew larger. Sabrina stood in silence, without a change of expression.

"Fire is the natural third element of nature. You're only scared of it, because it's hot; and burns; and blackens...I find it beautiful all the same." Eleanor said quietly.

Sabrina raised an eyebrow with her serious glare upon her poker face.

"Sabrina has no fear of fire" Clementine said in delight.   Eleanor then became annoyed at the fact Sabrina would no longer answer in person, but rather a doll instead.

"Then show me what you can do…" she said provokingly.   Eleanor's fire raged high above the two, and then raced itself toward Sabrina abruptly with a powerful speed.   Sabrina simply stood there, and quickly countered by bending the flames around her body, as the fire scorched the flowers and most of the willows to a blackened crisp.   The branches of the willows fell behind Sabrina and the flowers partially turned into a blackish powder.   Eleanor gasped quickly with eyes of surprise, and soon found herself flipping into the air and landing on her back to the solid ground.   She sat up quickly, coughing as she caught her breath, and the remaining flames surrounded both her and Sabrina.

"What…the…fuck…" she exclaimed. Sabrina approached her cousin, and stood above her, peering down with her darkened glare, and

her black hair blowing around her.
"You are powerful, yes, but not a goddess of this world...and nor am I.   We are simply developed among our species" she said to her.

Eleanor stood up slowly, holding her black hat, and staring at her cousin darkly.
"Don't do that again..." she warned. Sabrina then made a small smile, which hardly anyone in her entire life so far, had ever seen before.
"I'm not going to fight you...I'm rather intrigued by you" she said.   Eleanor dusted herself off, and straightened her dress; her hair; and put her hat back on, worn slightly to a tilt, just as before.
"Well...I must say...I've never met anyone like you before, Sabrina" she said, returning a smile.
"Welcome to LaMore Manor, cousin" Sabrina said, holding out her hand.   Eleanor slowly took it in return, and they greeted each other.   A bond between the two had begun. They felt comfortable with each other, unlike

anyone else in their life.   They knew they could trust each other.   And their bond…would never be broken…

Chapter Nine

To Feel the Air

By early evening, Victor, Erika, Meredith, and Gabriella all arrived back to the home. Gabriella and Eleanor were each given their own rooms in the mansion, just as Meredith had been; and on separate floors. This somewhat relieved Gabriella, and Eleanor's room was located just down the hall a bit further from Sabrina's room. Also by that evening, Sabrina began to feel a bit lightheaded again, although no migraine this time. However, she felt slightly different. And so did her surroundings. She somehow felt extra-sensitive to the temperatures around her. Especially outside, when the wind blew and moisture in the air flocculated.   The smell of the water in the air was enhanced now, but only for her it seemed.   Sabrina noticed this new feeling within her whenever the weather changed; which was quite often.   Realizing her energy was developing again, she decided to experiment with it later on after dinner, when a small storm made itself known with a low roll of thunder.

  Eleanor walked out onto the back terrace of LaMore Manor, and soon found Sabrina standing on the back lawn, looking up into the dark and clouded sky.   She came up to her cousin, and stood beside her in the night wind.
  "Something wrong, Sabrina?" she asked lightly.   Sabrina looked at her cousin, and new found friend.
  "There's something happening with me again" she said.
  "What do you mean?" Eleanor questioned.
  "I can feel everything out here right now. The wind; the moisture in the air; and I know this

is going to sound illogical, but I think I can feel the clouds..." Sabrina said, looking back up into the sky.

Eleanor looked at Sabrina in bafflement, but she knew she was telling the truth. Ever since the time they met earlier that day, she and Sabrina had spent the whole day together. They talked about their interests, and fears, and when they each discovered their "power" within them. They realized how much they had in common as well as their differences. Eleanor now felt she could tell Sabrina anything, and knew it would be safe.

"Sabrina...are you saying you can feel the weather?" Eleanor asked in a slight whisper. Sabrina looked at her cousin again, with her green eyes gleaming in the dark of the night, and nodded lightly. They both noticed how every time the lightning in the clouds flickered above them, Sabrina seemed to flinch a bit, since she was sensitive to the electrons as well. Although, this didn't bring Sabrina any physical pain either. Eleanor then snapped her fingers again on her right hand, and lit a flame.   She and Sabrina both watched, as the flame moved slightly toward Sabrina, and then away from her quickly; as though the wind was projecting from her body. With the light from the flame in the darkness, Eleanor could actually see the wind patterns flowing gracefully around Sabrina, encircling her body like a miniature tornado.   They moved evenly, as if it was natural, and Eleanor's eyes widened slightly.

"Are you...doing that to the wind?" she asked.   Sabrina nodded again.

"Yes, I am" she answered.   "I just realized I could."

Eleanor was amused by this, and she made a small smile at the new ability.   Sabrina...could now control the weather.   Her abilities were increasing at a rapid rate, and even though she now had atmokinesis; the ability to control the weather with the mind; Sabrina's strongest energy within her was still her telekinetic trait.   Eleanor had been born with pyrokinesis; the ability to create fire and manipulate it, however her ability only grew in strength as she aged naturally.

Sabrina's ability, seemed to grow abnormally, and branch out.   While this happened, her telekinesis became stronger as well; becoming the most powerful force within her soul.   She was indeed unique, as was Eleanor.   To most people, these abilities would seem god-like, and unnatural; leading them to not believe in them.   However, it truly was natural for the two girls standing on the mansion's lawn…and it was only the rarity, and fear of the difference, that made most not believe in it.   Sabrina and Eleanor knew there were other people in the world like them.   Some with extreme abilities of the mind, that they probably felt they should hide, or just hadn't discovered or understood yet.   Eleanor shared Sabrina's thoughts on how society would never accept them, unless they were similar to them.   Sabrina felt, that in order to understand someone as complex as herself, it would take a lot of effort and time, and most people in the world just wouldn't do that.   For a while now, Eleanor had been the only person she could open up to, and actually speak without Clementine's voice.   Although, with her Dissociative Identity Disorder; of her mind being split mentally and directly in half of two personalities; Sabrina still used Clementine while in conversation with her cousin. Eleanor didn't mind this. She actually liked Sabrina's uniqueness, and had long waited to find someone who could understand her in return.

Soon enough, rain drops began to fall upon the two girls and eventually started raining. Eleanor frowned and made a comment as she wiped some of the drops from her face.
"I hate rain…I hate being wet" she said allowed. She soon realized Sabrina was no longer standing beside her. She turned around, looking for her cousin and found her standing on the back porch, in shelter from the wet weather. Sabrina had a look of worry on her face, which had been rare due to the fact she was mostly emotionless.
"Sabrina…what's wrong?" Eleanor asked, walking over to her cousin. She gave a concerned expression and stood beside her.
"Sabrina doesn't like the rain" Clementine said softly.

"Why not?"   Eleanor asked again. Sabrina looked into Eleanor's eyes and Clementine spoke again with her genial child's voice.

"Because when Sabrina was little, she got hurt in a storm, and the rain made her very sick" the doll explained.   Eleanor spoke no further for she understood what Sabrina was trying to say. The two girls knew each other well in such a short time.   It seemed they were destined to understand each other's actions and thoughts. Eleanor slowly approached Sabrina, and gave her a gentle hug, even though Sabrina seemed to not know how to react to it.   She stood there in silence as Eleanor comforted her, and stared up at the sky as the night storm started to progress.

The next day, while sitting in the high school cafeteria, Eleanor told Sabrina how she felt about being in a new school and town.   They both always sat alone together at a small round lunch table near one of the walls of the room. Sometimes students would stare across the room at them, and even often wonder who the blonde girl was sitting with Sabrina LaMore. The other students knew Sabrina was very anti-social, and it puzzled them seeing the new girl getting along with her so well. Lois Platte and Tammi McVay sat just a few short tables distance away from them, and as always, couldn't keep their business to themselves.

"Who's the blonde with the black hat sitting with her?" Tammi asked her friend. Lois spoke up as she opened her milk carton.

"That's Eleanor LaMore. Apparently Sabrina's cousin" she explained. Tammi looked back over at the two girls and narrowed her eyes slightly.

"They're both weird. Sabrina always carries that hideous doll with her, and the blonde girl always wears nothing but black. You'd think she'd be too hot wearing that all the damn time" Tammi scornfully commented. Lois laughed a bit at her friend's comment and nodded.

"Yeah, including the large hat too. The teachers keep asking her to take it off, and she throws a fit about it every time. Saying its "part of her outfit" Lois said.

Eleanor sat casually with her cousin as she slowly removed the peas from her lunch plate and put them into a small pile on a napkin.   Sabrina watched as she did this, and silently got the sense from Eleanor, that peas disgusted her.   Sabrina's senses had gotten much stronger now.   She knew some of Eleanor's thoughts just by sitting next to her without speaking.   This also was getting annoying to Sabrina at times during school hours, when she was busy trying to study.   Other students' thoughts and fears would drift into her head and often distract her.   At first, it was very bothersome, but she soon learned to tune them out and concentrate on her own thoughts.   It seemed to almost work like an on and off switch, but still randomly.

Eleanor looked over at her cousin and noticed she had been staring at her, and she stopped moving.

"What?"   she asked quietly, setting her fork down.

"Sabrina knows your thoughts" Clementine said lightly.   Eleanor's eyes went wide and she stumbled her words.

"W-What do you...mean?" she asked quickly. Sabrina's eyes turned back to the book she'd been reading while sitting at the table and holding her doll at the same time.

"Sabrina knows your thoughts, Eleanor...*and your fears*" Clementine said in a general eerie, yet happy tone. Eleanor made a small laugh and looked down at her open milk carton sitting on the table below in front of her.

"I don't have fears" she said simply. Sabrina's eyes slowly looked over at her cousin as she gently raised one of her brows.

"Dear, Eleanor...everyone has fears" Clementine said innocently.

"Well not many" Eleanor retorted, starting to get angry now. She glared down at her milk as the carton began to vibrate lightly and steam rose out through the top. "I'm only afraid of spiders."

Clementine fell silent as Eleanor now focused her attention on the carton in front of her.

"You have a more prominent fear than spiders, and you're afraid to face it" Sabrina said with a direct tone. Eleanor narrowed her eyes in

annoyance and the milk boiled hot over the sides of the carton from the increased heat.   The curdled liquid rolled off the table and down to the floor with no sense of direction.   Sabrina glanced at the carton as it then suddenly flew briskly off the table, and colliding with the wall beside Eleanor, making a splash that caught some attention.   Eleanor looked up, blinking her eyes as though she'd been in a trance.   She saw her cousin give a stern look, and Eleanor felt her anger turn to guilt for causing a scene.
    "Sorry, Sabrina…" she said quietly.

    Not far away, Tammi and Lois sat at their table in shock by what they had just witnessed.
    "Did I see what I *thought* I saw?   Did that milk *fly* into the wall?"   Tammi asked in surprise.
    "Yeah…I think it did" Lois replied.
    "But that's impossible" Tammi said with a chuckle.   Lois calmed her expression and took a bite of her hamburger, while rolling the meat around in her mouth as she thought to herself. She'd seen the way Eleanor had been glaring at the milk, and how Sabrina seemed to have made it go

airborne as though she were some kind of talented magician of levitation.   However, it wasn't the same as that, and she knew this.   She knew there was something different about Sabrina and Eleanor…and she wasn't going to forget it anytime soon.
    "Yeah, I guess you're right" she said.

Chapter Ten

Eleanor and Dr. Stein

Over the years, since the first meeting of Dr. Roberta Stein, Sabrina had been having frequent visits with her every two to three weeks.   During each session, the doctor would attempt to get Sabrina to "open up", and generally every attempt failed.   Roberta Stein had become quite tired of the fact that Sabrina was very uncooperative with her.   Nevertheless, Sabrina's parents were paying her a hefty sum to try and get their daughter to speak fluently without the use of Clementine. Roberta Stein also studied Sabrina's overall demeanor and her abilities.   She would sometimes ask for demonstrations of Sabrina's "power" as though to get a thrill from the paranormal experience.   Roberta was very fascinated with Sabrina's mind.   It was one-of-a-kind to her, and she was the first person Roberta had ever met with such a complex ability from birth.   Although, despite being intrigued by Sabrina's powerful mind, she also feared it.   She feared the fact it kept growing in strength with no signs of decreasing.   Little did she know...Sabrina had already known this.

      By this time, Gabriella had finally told the family about Eleanor's gift.   Being born with pyrokinesis and it growing into quite a hot dilemma when Eleanor became a teenager.   She explained the reason she'd left their old home, was mostly due to the fact that Eleanor loved to play around with her gift.   She had used it in public often with no regrets and caused many to fear and question her and Gabriella.   The problem with

Gabriella's ex lover, Lee Mang, was another reason they had left St. Augustine and moved into LaMore Manor.   Nearly 2, 000 miles north of Florida to Pennsylvania.   Gabriella was afraid of her daughter's ability, and asked if Victor and Erika could help her cope with the anxiety.   Victor then mentioned to Gabriella about Sabrina's abilities, and how she had been seeing Dr. Stein for nearly five years now.   He offered to take Eleanor there as well, and feeling she had no other choice, Gabriella agreed to it, hoping there would be a positive change.   Gabriella reacted rather upsettingly to the fact there was yet another family member with the "Devil's power" and she felt very uncomfortable even speaking to Sabrina from then on.   Especially when Victor described how her trait seemed to be increasing very rapidly in an unusual way.

"I hope you're right about this Dr. Stein, Victor" Gabriella said as she rode in the car with her brother.   Eleanor sat quietly in the backseat, unwilling to speak after knowing where she was going; miffed at the fact her mother didn't trust her, and wanted her to see a "doctor" about her "problems". Eleanor knew very well about her ability and how to control it, and in her own eyes, she certainly didn't have "problems" that needed to be dealt with.

After waiting in the lounge room of the small office building, Dr. Roberta Stein finally opened her door with a smile, saying hello, and motioning for Eleanor to enter her office room. Eleanor gave a crossed look, as she didn't like the woman already, and slowly got up from her seat; walking silently into the room.

"Take a seat, Eleanor" Roberta said pleasantly, as she then sat down in her own desk chair. Eleanor looked around the room, noticing the pictures on the walls, and the knickknacks on the desk, which were now adorned with candles accenting the room's personality. Before Eleanor left the mansion, Sabrina had told her about what Roberta Stein was like, and how she too, didn't like her.

"So, Eleanor, how are you feeling today?" Roberta said with her welcoming smile. Eleanor narrowed her eyes and spoke with a rude tone.

"Look, if you're going be this cheery and pleasant the whole time, then I might as well leave right now.   Just get to the point ok?   I already don't like being in here as it is" she said directly.   Roberta's smile faded and she narrowed her eyes as well.

"Well, your mother was certainly right about you having an attitude issue and problems with authority" she said in mild sarcasm, attempting to defend herself.   Eleanor's rage soon started to build within her as the temperature of the room began to rise.   Roberta noticed her candles starting to melt and deform as the wicks quickly ignited themselves while the wax poured over the desk, and onto the floor.   She could feel her body heat rising with the room, and her sweat rolling down her face in droplets while Eleanor glared at her.   She watched as the blonde girl leaned slightly forward in her chair, with her radiant blue eyes gleaming from behind her black hat's shadow.   Roberta's hair started to dry out and frizz quickly in the heated room and she felt very uncomfortable and dehydrated.   Eleanor made a smirk and spoke with a dark tone from her

lips.
"The last person who told me I had an "issue"...had the joy of having their face burned and melt from their skull slowly...in the middle of a playground...with over twenty kids watching" she voiced.   Roberta swallowed hard with her dry throat and began to cough.   Eleanor stood up and walked slowly toward Roberta's desk, still fixing her concentration on her.
"S-Stop it..."   Roberta said uneasily. Eleanor smiled gently as the wax from the candles now began to burn, creating smoke throughout the room.
"As you wish.   I was actually having fun...weren't you?"   she snidely teased.   Roberta coughed even more, and Eleanor soon doused the flames in the room quickly by taking in the heat as though it was a part of her soul.   She turned away, leaving the room and walking out to the parking lot.   Victor and Gabriella rushed into Roberta's office and were astounded by what Eleanor had done to the room.   Roberta opened her window, allowing the rest of the smoke to clear, and looked over at Victor.

"I can't do this anymore, Mr. LaMore. I'm sorry...I just can't" she said as a few tears rolled down her cheeks. "Those girls are too powerful...and if word gets out about what they can do...this whole town could go crazy on them." Victor nodded in disappointment, but understood the entire situation, and knew it was probably best not to get anyone else involved. Gabriella, being in awe about the situation, couldn't find anything to say. She looked at her brother and soon embraced him into a hug without words.

"Thank you for your time, Dr. Stein. Give us a call if you should change your mind" he proposed.

Later that evening, Eleanor found herself roaming the halls of LaMore Manor, both lost in her own thoughts, and also curious about the large mansion she now lived in. A few times, she'd gotten lost, but figured it would be a good way to learn her way around the house. She found many rooms, some of which she could hardly imagine ever existed. The mansion seemed to conceal many secrets and wonders.   A maze of entrances leading into other places with stories of their own. The Grand Ballroom had glorious chandeliers so large, she swore they were heavier than a typical compact car.   The mansion seemed sad, and lonely.   As though people had forgotten it after so many years of use.   Now it just sat quietly upon its large foundation edged within the cold earth below it for the remainder of its days.

After finding her way toward the back end of the house, she discovered another completely separate wing of the mansion.   She opened its large glass doors and was immediately in sheer awe at what she found on the other side.   Eleanor had entered the Grand Conservatory of the mansion, and the view before her was simply stunning in beauty.   A complete change from the rest of the dark, and silent mansion behind her within those hallways she'd roamed.   The greenhouse was so large, it was literally just taller than two stories of the house, possibly more, and it needed its own wing.   Inside were so many trees and plants gracing the grounds among the stoned path walkway which lead her into a rainforest-like effect of wonder and beauty in a sea of earthly beings.   It was silent inside, almost like being with nature itself, and the vibrant colored flowers of many species caught Eleanor's eyes from every turn.   Around the walkways, there were little marble statues of the Greek gods and goddesses. The largest statue being, Aphrodite; the goddess of love and beauty, whom to the Romans was identified as Venus.   She was carved completely out of white and pink marble with gold trimmings around the base pedestal, and she seemed just perfect standing around all the plants and flowers growing healthy and strong.   The trees themselves, were among many varieties too, and some grew very tall toward the high cathedral-like glass ceiling of the room.   The room itself was made entirely of glass, as the walls let in the auburn light of the setting sun, as it graced across the earthly paradise through a large dome above. Eleanor literally felt she had stepped into another world and began to smile to herself, removing her hat to get better views above her.

In the distance, she could faintly hear the sound of water, and decided to follow it and find the source. The stone path lead her deep into the greenhouse, arriving in the middle of the room, where a large marble fountain sat in a circle shape. The general design was that of large water fountains displayed in parks and cities for the public to view. It had a large base, as it grew taller in smaller pedestal layers that formed something of a tower, where the water was flowing out of rapidly from all sides. To Eleanor's surprise, sitting down on the base was her cousin, Sabrina, looking at her in silence. She held her doll against her lap with one hand, and she quietly raised her other hand up, motioning for Eleanor to join her. Grabbing a few flowers along the way, Eleanor smiled and sat down beside her cousin on the fountain's base, listening to the water cascade into the base's pool. She set her flowers down beside her.

"It's so beautiful in here…I can't believe I've never seen this place before" Eleanor said softly, looking at the fountain behind her.

"I like it here. Its quiet...and serene" Sabrina spoke allowed.

"How did your father afford all of this? It's truly amazing" Eleanor asked. Sabrina didn't answer, but simply stared down at the stone floor below them. She seemed deep in thought, and she held Clementine close to her body. Eleanor looked at Sabrina in curiosity.

"What's wrong, Sabrina?" she asked lightly. Silent for a few minutes, Sabrina then gently leaned toward her cousin and whispered while looking into her eyes.

"I can make you see what I want..." she said unnervingly. Eleanor's face turned serious and then became cautious.

"Don't worry, Eleanor. Sabrina would never hurt you. You're her friend" Clementine said happily. Eleanor then smiled and picked up one of the flowers that were sitting beside her. She watched, as the radiant orange and black tiger lily slowly folded its petals upward all together, and then folded them out; moving them in motion like wings as the flower became a monarch butterfly. Eleanor gasped and was speechless at the beauty of the butterfly as it then folded its wings back up, soon to fold out again as the tiger lily it was once before.

"Oh my god..." Eleanor spoke softly. "...how did you do that?"

Sabrina leaned back again, and explained to Eleanor about her newly developed ability known as "psycho illusions". She could literally enter someone's mind now, and make them see whatever she wanted. Even creating alternate realities and fabricate people's most desired wants, or their worst fears come to life. However, this took much of Sabrina's energy and it made her body and mind very extremely tired after doing so. The illusions were also short lived, as a result of the amount of energy it took for her to create them.

Eleanor was completely blown away by this. She stared at Sabrina with widened eyes and spoke quietly.

"You're really strong, Sabrina...it's almost kinda scary" she said seriously. Sabrina kept her serious expression, and stood up from the base of the fountain.

"It's who I am. There is no point in trying to change that fact" she said dully.

"Easy for *you* to say" Eleanor replied. She then stared at the vibrant orange flower in her hand and watched as smoke started to rise from it while it began to wither, followed by hot embers and flames engulfing its entire existence. She burned the flower in her hand, watching the ashes fall to the floor below her. "Sometimes I wish to be normal…all I do is destroy…" she whispered. She felt her eyes well up with tears, as they streamed silently down her pale face as she looked at the black charred ashes in her hand where she once held the tiger lily. Sabrina, still facing away from Eleanor, closed her eyes and held tight to her doll.

"One should not fear what they have no control over" she said. Eleanor then hung her head down, staring at the floor while her tears dripped onto the flower's ashes, making them wet.

Sabrina suddenly opened her eyes as she heard footsteps in front of her on the stone path.

Eleanor raised her head up, and to her surprise, Gabriella was standing on the path looking at both of them. She held an angry look upon her face, staring directly at her daughter, and Eleanor felt upset again. Although, she didn't allow herself to cry any longer.

"I told you..." Gabriella spoke up. "...I told you to *never* use that power ever again... It's the Devil's power!" she said angrily. Knowing now, that her mother had seen her burn the flower, Eleanor stood up directly and shouted back at her mother.

"You have no fucking clue what it is! It's part of me and a part of who I am, and you can't accept it! If Lee wouldn't have hit me, then I wouldn't have burned his fucking face off!" she declared. Gabriella gasped and Eleanor's remark, and got ready to strike her daughter out of anger. Sabrina then stood directly in front of her aunt, and held a solid expression while gazing into her eyes. Eleanor was surprised and she watched Sabrina's eyes gleam into a reddish-like glow. Gabriella froze and soon became horrified as the glass walls and ceiling of the greenhouse shattered violently, sending flying jagged pieces of glass toward Gabriella's body.   She screamed in fear, and fell backwards to the floor as the glass passed through her body evenly without making any injuries, and then disappearing behind her body into the air.   Gabriella looked up and noticed she was completely fine.   The glass wasn't broken at all, and Sabrina stood directly above her, glaring down with a look of hatred.

"Next time it will be real..." she voiced with a baleful tone.   Her eyes then returned to their normal green color, and Sabrina walked passed her aunt who now lay shivering on the stone floor. Eleanor stood up in silence, and walked away with her cousin, and Gabriella starting crying lightly to herself, not even bothering to stand up.

Later on that night, after Gabriella explained to everyone what had happened in the conservatory, Victor decided they were all going to have to do something to stop them from acting so violently against the family.   Although, it seemed rather hard to do much of anything at all, considering the two girls were inseparable and could wield "weapons" beyond what most physical science could explain properly.

"We have to do something, Victor. What if they use those powers of theirs at school? What then?" Meredith asked.

"She's right, Vic. We'll have people questioning us, including police, and if they hurt anyone...how are we going to explain it?" Erika added. She walked up to her husband, staring at him with a serious expression. "Something is wrong with Sabrina...and I want to know what it is" she said stern tone. Victor sighed deeply, and looked at his wife, not knowing how to react or what to do. He knew Sabrina's ability had grown strong, and was still continuing to dominate her mind, and with Eleanor being her only trusted outlet, her reactions to anyone else would be harrowing.

"I'll think of something. I promise. But right now...I don't really know what to do" he said. The objects in the room shook slightly as the man covered his face, and his hands were shaking from anxiety. The women in the room stood back slightly, and realized they were stressing him with their questions.   Victor rarely, if ever, displayed his ability.   His telekinetic gene wasn't very strong or developed, but he could move smaller objects with just enough force to cause disruption, and this mostly happened when he was under tremendous stress.   After so many years of living with him, Erika knew to back down when this situation occurred.   Even though Victor vowed to never use his ability again, she knew he couldn't hold it in completely when upset.   She gently put her arms around his waist and laid her head against his chest to calm him.

"I'm sorry, my love..." she whispered to him.   Victor took in a breath, and let it out with relief as he closed his eyes and returned the embrace.

"Try not to worry" he said, and both Meredith and Gabriella quieted themselves.

Chapter Eleven

The Fortune

    For the next few days, members of the LaMore family kept cautious distance from Sabrina and Eleanor.   Meal times were quiet, and everyone was avoidant of conversation about recent events.   In his own thoughts, Victor was annoyed by this.   He didn't like his family being so silent amongst themselves in their own home and decided he needed to do something to help bring them together in some way.
    Sitting at the dining table, the LaMore

family ate their food casually without words. Sabrina and Eleanor always sat together at the far end of the table, while Erika, Gabriella and Meredith sat on the other end with Victor.   The grandfather clock in the room sounded its chimes for seven o'clock pm, and Victor suddenly spoke up after looking around at his reticent family.

"Doesn't anyone have anything to say?" he asked in mild impatience.   "I'm rather tired of this constant silence among us."

Erika and Gabriella said nothing and looked down at their meals, as did Sabrina and Eleanor. Meredith set down her fork and decided to speak.

"Well...what exactly would you like us to say, Vic?"   she answered with her own, sarcastic question.   She lightly pushed her food plate ahead of herself, indicating to Dmitri that she was finished eating.   The butler then came over and took the plate away quietly.   Victor glanced over at his sister-in-law with a scowl.

"Anything.   This house has been quieter than usual for three days now, and I know you all have the same thing on your minds" he said, as he looked around at everyone individually.

"Then what do you propose we do about it?" Erika spoke up; keeping her eyes down. Victor took a drink of his ice water and decided this was a good time to announce a plan he had been making for the past few days.

"Well, I *propose* we all go out this weekend. The whole family. We can go do whatever we want on Saturday, starting first thing in the morning. By early evening, I have something planned" he said. Everyone looked up from their silence from hearing Victor's words.

"What do you have planned?" Gabriella asked.

"It's a surprise actually" Victor replied. Sabrina looked directly at her father and didn't speak. Eleanor did as well, but wanted to know more about the situation.

"What would we do until evening?" she asked curiously.

"As I said…anything we want. We could go to the mall or something, and then out for dinner afterwards" he said. This now caught Meredith's attention, since she was known as the "shopper" of the family. Considering the family's wealth, Meredith loved to go out and spoil herself by buying anything that caught her eyes, and not worrying about the price.

"I'll agree to that" she said quickly with a smirk.   Victor nodded.

"Everyone else okay with this?"   he asked. Erika, Gabriella, and Meredith all nodded in agreement, and Victor looked over at his daughter and niece.

"Sabrina?   Eleanor?   What about you two?"

"Yeah...alright then" Eleanor responded. Sabrina replied to her father with a slow nod of her head in silence.

"Alright then, everyone be ready Saturday morning.   After breakfast we'll be leaving" Victor announced.

On Saturday, the first destination for the LaMore's was the mall just north of Warren. Meredith made good use of her "plastics" as she called them, letting her credit cards add to her wardrobe and jewelry box at the various fashion stores.   Sabrina and Eleanor walked together, talking quietly among themselves and avoiding most contact of other people.   Sabrina actually wanted to go home and felt uncomfortable with so many people around.   Eleanor got the sense she was thankful that she was there to keep her company.   While Meredith shopped, and had Dmitri carry her new purchases along with her, Victor decided to tell Erika and Gabriella his plan for the evening after dinner.

"The circus is in town tonight.   I pulled some strings, and got some last minute tickets for all of us.   After dinner, we'll all go home and change into something nice" he said.   Erika and Gabriella both smiled at the idea of going to the circus, but Gabriella still had something on her mind.

"What if Sabrina and Eleanor don't like it?" she asked.

"Well, it will do them good to smile for once.   If they don't like it, then at least us adults will still enjoy it" Victor replied.

For several years, the Laramie Circus had

made frequent visits to the residents of Warren County.   Their Big Top attractions have fascinated the minds of many, and had always been known to put on a good show, and have a different grand finale every time.   Victor personally knew someone who worked for the circus's company itself, and was able to get some tickets for his family even after being sold out.

After leaving the mall, Victor decided his family would dine out for Chinese cuisine before getting ready for the evening.   This, Sabrina liked very much and so did Eleanor.   Meals of the orient were among her favorite, whether it be Chinese, Japanese, or Thai.   By this time, Victor had told Meredith about going to the circus later on, which added to her excitement, since it would be her first time going to one.   During the time at the mall, Sabrina had only requested to buy one thing, and that was a solid cat statue, made of black tinted glass.   It reminded her of one of her twelve cats she had as pets back home in the mansion, and that particular cat was named Selene.   It was the oldest of her twelve cats, receiving her as a gift from her father when she was ten years old.   Selene was a kitten at the time, and Sabrina's first pet.   The statue was at least fifteen inches tall, and Sabrina would display it in her room on top of her black grand piano.

"Well, I hope you're all having a good time today" Victor said, as the waitress brought over a tray of fortune cookies to end the meal.   Sabrina stared at the tray as each of her family members grabbed one of the cookies to read their fortunes. One cookie remained, waiting for its owner to open it.   As Sabrina looked at it in deep thought, Eleanor soon snatched the cookie and handed it to Sabrina.

"Here, this one's yours" she said with a light smile.   Sabrina took the cookie from her cousin, and opened it, slowly pulling out the strip of paper that held her fortune.   While the rest of the family was busy talking, Eleanor read hers first and then showed it to Sabrina.

You must choose wisely in future choices of stable mind.   The lotus will not grow in one night's time.

Eleanor shrugged her shoulders after reading her fortune and Sabrina handed it back to her.

"I guess it means I have to watch what I think" she said. Sabrina quietly read her fortune to herself and was completely silent at its words.

Love is nature's beauty, and is found in many forms. A new lesson awaits you.

Eleanor raised her eyebrows in surprise at the sight of Sabrina's fortune in her hand. Sabrina, herself, spoke not a word and simply folded up the fortune paper and placed it into Clementine's small pocket on her white frilled dress. Her emerald eyes gleamed at Eleanor, and she soon got up from the table, and walked out to the parking lot to wait for the family to take her home. Eleanor was puzzled by her cousin's calm reaction, and placed her own fortune in her pocket as well. Victor asked where Sabrina had gone, and Eleanor stood up, saying she was out in the car, waiting for everyone to finish up.   She left the large dining room as well, and joined Sabrina in the quiet backseat of the LaMore's classic Lincoln Continental.

"What's wrong?"   she asked her gently.   Sabrina held Clementine close to her chest, staring straight ahead out through the windshield of the car where she sat.

"Sabrina thinks her fortune is wrong" Clementine said in her light voice.

"Why does she think that?"   Eleanor asked the doll.   Sabrina's eyes turned to her cousin carefully.

"Because Sabrina has no love" Clementine replied.   Eleanor slowly leaned back against the seat, staring at her cousin, and asked no further questions.   She turned her head and looked out the window, thinking to herself and Sabrina spoke above a whisper.

"It doesn't exist" she said faintly.   Eleanor made a deep sigh in response to her cousin's words, and together the two girls waited for their family members to enter the car and go back home again.

Chapter Twelve

The Fall of the Laramie Circus

Fear not the laughing clown, for he is only there to tease. You may turn your heads away from glee, and despise him if you please.

As cars started to fill up the large parking lot, Dmitri drove the LaMore's white limousine carefully through the crowd of walking people. In the distance, large purple and white "big top" tents stood at least five stories tall housing all of the main events.   Lights in matching color of the tents shone brightly on a large entry arch, which read in large letters gracing the top "The Grande Laramie Circus".   After dinner, earlier that evening, the LaMore's had gone home to change into nice clothes for their night out.   As they slowly walked together toward the entry booths, many people would glance their way, knowing exactly who they were.   It was no secret to the residents of Warren, that the LaMore's had the most money, and weren't afraid to express it. The small city of Warren had originally built itself up around "old wealth" and the LaMore family line were among the first to settle there years ago, after arriving from France in 1880.   LaMore Manor was built shortly after, in the year 1890. Which took ten years to complete the entire structure. It now remains one of the oldest homes in the town still in living use.

Meredith and Gabriella both smiled brightly while talking with each other about how excited they were. The loud music from within the circus itself echoed around the entire area for attention, as if to tell the world that this was its last night on earth. Sabrina walked gradually in her long white gown, as though she were a lazy swan poising the river flow. Her black hair had been pulled up into fancy bun, but left her long bangs down on both sides since her hair was so long. A silver colored choker graced her neck, supported by matching dangled earrings. She held Clementine tightly in front of her and spoke not a word while her family walked ahead of her. Normally, Sabrina wore her lengthy hair down and flowing free, so this was a rare sight. Eleanor walked beside her in the same fashion, wearing a shorter black dress, with her matching large hat. Her platinum blonde hair had been left down, except to one side as her hat was tilted. After giving the tickets to a man in one of the booths at the entrance, the LaMore's found their seats under the main big top arena.   The noise inside was everywhere, as people filled the seats and got ready for the show.   Victor had gotten seats right in the front row, for the best experience.   They all sat together, with Victor and Erika on one end, and Meredith and Gabriella on the other end.   Sabrina and Eleanor sat in between them all, side by side.

As the lights in the large room, slowly dimmed, voices from the audience created a flow of whispers drifting throughout the air.   A spotlight came on in the center ring, where the ringmaster appeared from the darkness, holding a microphone.   He took off his large top hat, and made a low formal bow before breaking into an introduction.
"Ladies and gentleman, and boys and girls of all ages!   Welcome to the Grande Laramie Circus!   My name is Rubin, and I will be your host for this evening.   Now sit back and relax, and let your *minds...be...amazed*!"

Victor and Erika soon made wide smiles as

the music began an uproar for the start of the first show, as did Meredith and Gabriella.   Sabrina turned and looked at her cousin while the show started up in the foreground.   She spoke in her low tone, but Eleanor could hear her clearly enough to know what she was saying to her.

"Keep yourself calm tonight" she said to her.   Eleanor looked at Sabrina in return, and formed a small smile.

"Don't worry, Sabrina, I feel fine" Eleanor replied.   She then turned her attention back to the center ring, and Sabrina still stared at her cousin in silence.   She knew Eleanor still suppressed a major fear.   A phobia of which she hadn't been able to get over, and probably wouldn't for a long time.   She watched as her cousin smiled while the circus entertainers brought in the elephants that wore bright colored décor around their necks, and carried their riders around the area.   Deep down, Eleanor was the only other person that Sabrina could relate with, and cared about the most.   She didn't want to see her lose control.   She soon turned her eyes toward the entertainment, leaving her thoughts back in her mind as she tried to find something amusing.   Her parents sat next to her, and were already busy watching the show.   The loud noise of the room was hitting Sabrina's ears with full force, and so many colors, people, and objects were moving all at once.   Sabrina could slightly find herself having a hard time focusing on anything.   Instead, she looked up above at the ceiling of the arena, which was held up by several large support beams.   Each made entirely of metal, and all latched together on the ground, and also the center top of the tent.   Instead of watching the show, Sabrina found it more interesting to view the room itself.   The parts that everyone was missing.

      Throughout the room, there were many "oooo's" and "awes" as the show progressed, bringing out more animals such as the lions and their tamers.   Even with no change of expression, Sabrina found the lions to be quite impressive as she now began to watch the tamers crack their whips at them.   Eleanor was suddenly distracted from the show, as her smile slowly faded into a more serious, anxious expression.   Within the arena's main ring now, many clowns and harlequins were running around, acting bizarre and making people laugh at the same time. Eleanor, however, was no longer in a laughing mood.   She became nervous as the clowns made their way toward her area and she clutched tightly to Sabrina's arm.   Sabrina looked at her cousin quickly, and repeated what she'd told her earlier, about keeping herself calm.   Eleanor was deafened from all other sound as the clowns finally noticed her.   They came directly toward her, acting in their ridiculous manner and getting into Eleanor's face.   The young girl raised her voice quickly, and Gabriella now noticed what was happening.

"Get away from me!   Stop it!"   Eleanor demanded.   The clowns ignored her request, and continued to tease and laugh in her face. Eleanor's fear grew inside her as she tried to look away, and she felt her rage building up inside herself.   Gabriella reached over and grabbed her daughter's arm to pull her away.   Eleanor couldn't hold it in any longer.   Her eyebrows narrowed and her eyes gleamed as she acted out of fear with a reflex. Gabriella quickly let go of her daughter's arm, as her hand was burned from unknown immense heat waves, through the fabric of Eleanor's black dress.

The once laughing clowns soon found themselves screaming in severe pain as flames engulfed their bodies rapidly. They flew backwards in the air, away from Eleanor, hitting the floor behind them. Eleanor stood there as her body heat rose, and her muscles tensed. Her fingers spread apart as she let the energy flow through her, while it demanded to be set free. Several cries and screams from the audience filled the air, as people began to burn in several different ways; some from the inside out as the flames came up out of their throats, melting away their faces into deformed masks of liquid flesh. They scrambled over each other as they rushed to leave the arena in peril. The flames were everywhere...eating everything in their path. The heat of the room was so unbearable, that many found themselves collapsing from exhaustion in a matter of minutes.   Eleanor held the large flames in her hands as everything around her began to burn and char.   The tent of the big top arena ignited at a quickened pace, beginning to trap the remaining audience members inside a blazing inferno.   A crowd of people, who managed to escape the flames, soon met their crushing fate as the several elephants, lions, and other animals made a stampede over them toward the exit.   They were scared from the fire, and made no attempt to avoid anything in their path to safety outside of the large tent.   Victor, Erika, Meredith and Gabriella were trying their hardest to get Eleanor to stop.   Although, every time something came even within a few feet of the girl's body, it was instantly fried to a crisp by the enormous amount of energy and heat she gave off.   Instead they finally made their way toward the exit, as the large beams of the arena started to fall from increased high pressure tension.   Rubin the ringmaster was instantly crushed by the center beam as it came crashing down upon his body, severing his head with a fountain of blood.   Sabrina stood behind her cousin, watching her in silence as the remaining flames encircled around them.   Eleanor had indeed lost control…and there was no turning back now.

   As the Warren County Fire Department rushed their fire engines toward the scene, the once glamorous Laramie Circus began to fade away into ashes and debris.   It did, however, hold true to its promise that the audience would forever be amazed.   The people that *did* survive, had either collapsed from intense heat and smoke, or were driven into complete shock of terror. Sirens could be heard for miles, as the neighboring towns sent their ambulances and fire trucks for assistance.   Victor watched in horror at what his niece had done in what seemed to be in a matter of minutes while the smoke clouds rose high into the atmosphere.   The air smelled horribly of burnt objects and death.   Erika held tight to Gabriella whom had been crying with flowing tears to no end.   Meredith felt her entire body shake and she fell to the ground below her, losing her ability to walk.

Back in the center ring, Sabrina slowly walked toward her cousin, as she gently bent the flames around her body with telekinesis. She calmly let down her long black hair from its bun, and stood beside Eleanor, who was just now beginning to catch her breath again.

"You didn't listen" Sabrina said in a darkened tone. She stared straight ahead into the flames, gazing into the incandescent orange glow of their surroundings. Eleanor let her arms rest to her sides, and turned her head as the wind from the night air blew her hair lightly. Her bright blue eyes were filled with tears as she spoke, stammering her words.

"I c-couldn't stop it…and I didn't w-want to" she said lightly. Her tears streamed down her face as Sabrina looked at her silently. "Do y-you know what that's l-like? To not want to stop? To want to k-kill everything around you, because all you do is hurt?!" Eleanor asked, raising her voice from anger. She wanted to say more, but her words were soon drowned by her tears as she cried from repressed feelings of hatred. Sabrina calmly pulled her cousin into an embrace and spoke in a whisper, while she cried into her shoulder.

"Yes...I do."

Chapter Thirteen

Suspicious Minds

They rode home in utter silence that evening. Each of them still seeing the blazing flames freshly within their memories of the dreadful night. It was like riding home after a tearful funeral of shattered emotions over someone's death. Only this time, the death count was over a hundred. Gabriella couldn't speak. Her thoughts in her mind raced and her hands shook quietly as the nerves felt tensed. She wouldn't even dare look at her daughter, and clutched her rosary that hung around her neck with a tight fist.   She closed her eyes and let a few wet tears align her cheeks.   Meredith stared blankly out her window of the limo at the passing trees and houses.   She too, spoke no words and fiddled with the buttons on her dress coat.   Erika held tight to her husband's hands while Sabrina and Eleanor sat nearby, side by side.   Sabrina's expression hadn't changed.   She sat there as though nothing had happened, and nothing phased her.   Eleanor kept her eyes facing downward to the car's floor, recurring the events of the evening in her mind like a silent movie.   The circus going up in flames...the people falling to the ground, burning to death.   It overwhelmed her.   Her hands slowly made two fists as she tried to repress her emotions once again.   Her tear drops fell upon her skin, and Sabrina quietly placed a hand on her cousin's arm to comfort her.   Her face still stared straight ahead and she paid no attention to anything else.   Victor noticed this, and it only answered his question he'd been asking himself for a little while now, that Sabrina could still show signs of compassion even though her mind was split.   Who she showed that compassion to…was a different story.   From what Victor had seen, his daughter only seemed to care about her cousin and her doll, rather than anyone else.

       That doll…if only he'd not bought it for her that day.   He was now beginning to see the effect it had on Sabrina, only seeming to split her conscious mind even more so than what it was to begin with.   It became Sabrina's "transitional object".   Something she needed in order to communicate with others.   She acted as though it were another person, which in fact, it truly was. The other side of her personality held deep within, struggling to be set free.   Sabrina would only let her emerge through the doll's façade, while her mentally unstable mind slowly became torn. Clementine, the social and caring one; wanting to make friends with everyone she met…and Sabrina, the vacant, emotionless shell of a body only revealing an uncanny darkness toward the world. Caring for almost no one but herself, and destroying anything that upset or disturbed her. The soul that was gradually sinking into a bottomless pit, with no desire of letting anyone in. Victor wondered and asked himself why something so horrible would have to happen to his daughter.   Why did it have to be her?   Why did she have to inherit the telekinetic gene? Why was it so unstable?   He often wondered what was truly going on in that girl's mind, and whether or not she'd ever be able to recover.   Wondering if her ability would eventually consume her mind, only to shred it completely and kill her.   Although this seemed a likely scenario for his daughter's future life, Sabrina didn't show any signs of physical weakness.   The migraines had long passed since her early teenage years, and now it only grew stronger.   Her paranormal ability acting like a parasite; using her mind as a host, even though Sabrina was fully in control.   He wanted to know more.   He wanted to know what was truly happening to her.

    When the LaMore's finally arrived home, Victor decided to do a little research in the library. He looked through every book he had on Parapsychology, and learned something extraordinary.   Sabrina's ability had only started out as an "undeveloped telekinetic gene" when she reached puberty.   For several years, the trait of telekinesis had been passed down through the LaMore family line.   However, after Sabrina was born, the gene became unstable as it grew.   The trait was more advanced in her.   Sometimes, when genetics are passed on, they take on a new stage of change.   It was growing into a rare development on its own, and was becoming potentially limitless.   With her newer abilities of psycho illusions, and atmokinesis, her trait was branching out.   Since telekinesis was linked directly to emotions, and Sabrina was already mentally unstable, a combination between the two could be disastrous.   With Eleanor having a powerful force of her own, an alliance with Sabrina would be deadly for anyone who got in their way.   Victor dropped the book he'd been holding to the floor.   He felt responsible for Eleanor's incident at the circus.   He felt he would have to try his best not to upset his daughter, or his niece, for fear they would unleash wrath upon others again.   Victor held his hands up to his head while his thoughts picked at his brain.   Some of the books in the room flew off the table by themselves onto the floor, as he let his ability flow out.   Even though he was born with the same trait as Sabrina, hers was more developed, and she was just becoming a young adult.   Who knew what it would be like when Sabrina matured into complete adulthood…and how strong she would become.

    Victor's silent thoughts were suddenly disrupted by the sound of the door opening in the library.   He turned quickly and found his wife standing in the doorway, wondering what he'd been doing.   He looked at her with his worrisome expression over the situation, and she began to walk toward him slowly.

    "Victor…what's wrong?"   Erika asked with a mild whisper.   She gently moved her long brown hair away from her eyes, and looked up at her husband, whom was slightly taller than her. Her eyes were tired and reddened from the crying she'd be doing, and her make up was smeared. She looked as though she hadn't slept soundly for days.   Victor   pulled her into an embrace, and spoke calmly to her.

"I just want you to know how much I love you, Erika. I always will. And no matter what happens...I will protect you. All of you" he said to her. Erika hugged him back in silence, for she knew why he was worried. She had the same thoughts going through her mind about Sabrina and Eleanor after what she had seen and experienced that night. She hoped to herself, that the public wouldn't find out about the two girls, since it would probably send the entire town into chaos against their whole family. After what Eleanor had done...that scenario was now highly probable.

As the two girls stood together in the long hallway that lead to their bedrooms, Sabrina opened her large doors and walked inside her room. Eleanor stood outside the door without speaking and watched her cousin turn around to look at her.

"Goodnight Eleanor" Clementine said happily. "Sweet dreams." Eleanor made a straight face as a few tears started to well up in her eyes.

"S-Sabrina...could I stay with you tonight?" she asked nervously.   Sabrina was frozen for a moment, staring back at her cousin with interest until finally speaking with her own insipid voice.

"What is it, Eleanor?"   she answered with her own question.   Eleanor forced a small smile, and stepped inside the room slowly.

"I just...don't wanna be by myself tonight" she said to her.   Sabrina turned away from her cousin and shut the doors behind her with a light wave of her hand.

"Very well then"   she said calmly.   She then got ready for bed, and Eleanor felt a little better knowing she didn't have to sleep alone that night.   Her emotions were already wracked, and she needed the company of someone she trusted. Soon, as the two girls lay together on the large white canopy bed, Eleanor spoke up again, and asked her cousin a question in the darkness.

"Sabrina...am I normal?"   she asked her. Without moving, or opening her eyes, Sabrina's reply came soft and quiet.   Eleanor gave a smile after hearing Sabrina's words.

"Yes, you are.   Goodnight Eleanor"
"Goodnight Sabrina…and thank you"

    The next morning, just before noon, Victor was suddenly woken from his sleep by the sound of the mansion's doorbell.   He quietly got out of bed, and put on his robe as he walked down the spiral staircase, and toward the front hall of his home.   Dmitri had already been awake, and as the job of being the butler, he answered the door right away.   In the doorway, Victor could clearly see what appeared to be two police officers waiting to be invited in.
    "Can I help you gentleman with something?"   he asked them.   One of the officers stepped forward and greeted Victor by shaking hands.
    "Good morning, Mr. LaMore.   We're sorry to disturb you like this…especially on a Sunday. I'm Inspector Karl Jenkins, and this is my partner Martin Landers"   he said, pointing to the other officer beside him.   Martin gave a silent nod to Victor as Karl went on talking.   "We were

wondering if we could come in for a bit. We have some questions we need to ask you about the fire outbreak last night."

Victor felt his stomach tighten into a small knot as he heard these words.

"Well…what kind of questions?" he asked in return. Karl's face became serious and he looked at Victor's eyes directly.

"Mr. LaMore…I think you know what kind of questions we need to ask you. Now, if it's not too much trouble, can we please come in?" he asked again. Victor lightly backed up, and stood to the side, allowing the officers to enter his home.

"Sure. The living room is off to the left of you" he said.

Erika, Meredith, and Gabriella soon joined Victor and the officers in the large living room of LaMore Manor. For the first few minutes, the tension in the room could be felt between everyone, and Erika spoke up out of the silence.

"What is this all about?" she asked them. The second officer, Martin, now spoke as well with a slightly raspy voice in his throat.

"I'm sure you're all aware of the fire that consumed the Laramie Circus around 9:30 pm last night" he said to them. The LaMore's each nodded and exchanged nervous expressions between themselves, although trying to hide them.

"We were there last night" Gabriella said. "We had tickets to go."

Martin quickly spoke again, raising his voice some and he straightened his face, looking at Gabriella.

"The cause of the fire is still unknown after several hours of investigation. Some of the survivors from last night are saying they had seen some "bizarre things" going on during the time of the flames" the man voiced.

"Well, what are you implying?" Meredith added. Karl gave a deep sigh and looked at Gabriella individually.

"Ms. LaMore, is your daughter's name Eleanor Mang?" he asked her calmly.

"Yes...well, no, not anymore. Her last name is LaMore now. I had it changed back to my maiden name. Her father is...deceased" Gabriella lightly answered.

"What does this have to do with my niece?"

Victor interrupted. Karl and Martin both focused their attention on Victor now, with Martin giving a slight glare.

"Mr. LaMore...some of the survivors are saying that Eleanor is the cause of the fire. They're saying she started it, by some unknown means after she got angry" Karl said. Victor gave a look of annoyance.

"*Unknown means?* What the hell is *that* supposed to mean?" he asked impatiently. Karl took a deep breath and Martin folded his arms as a show of dominance in his authority.

"Look, Victor, many people here say there is something going on with your daughter, and now also your niece, Eleanor. You all were at the circus last night, and several eye witnesses say the girl started the flames. Now...is this true, yes or no?" Karl asked, now getting impatient as well.

"Surely you understand the seriousness of the situation, Mr. LaMore" Martin added. Erika spoke up, raising her voice.

"Now wait just a minute, you can't hold us responsible for a fire which over a hundred other people could have easily started instead of us!"

she declared.

"Mrs. LaMore, I'm going to have to ask you to calm down" Martin said. Erika silenced herself, and turned to look at her husband for defense with a stern expression.

"Yes, Inspector, I am aware of how serious the situation is. I was there last night when all of those people were burning alive, but you can't just accuse my niece for the cause of it all" Victor firmly said.

"We're not trying to accuse Eleanor of this, Victor, we're only looking into the situation further" Karl added.

"The *situation*? And what might *that* be then?" Victor asked. "You're telling me that several people, who could've easily been confused while frightened in a deadly situation, thought my niece was the cause. A complete misunderstanding."

"That may be so, Mr. LaMore, but it seems unusual to me that Eleanor and Sabrina were both the last two people to leave the scene of the destruction, and without a scratch on either of them" Martin challenged. Karl then put his hand up, in gesture for his partner to stop speaking.

"We're only trying to get the facts, Victor. Honest to God, no one is accusing Eleanor LaMore of arson.   Now, those people could've made a mistake out of fear, just like you said.   And I'm willing to believe that.   There is no physical evidence that suggests that your niece caused the destruction, but we have to take into consideration of what those survivors told us"   he calmly said. Victor then nodded at the man.

"That's all well and fine then, just please don't accuse her of arson.   Eleanor was the last to leave the site, because she was terrified.   My daughter stayed with her to be sure she was alright"   he explained.   Karl stared down at the floor, taking in Victor's words and nodded his head lightly.

"Alright, Mr. LaMore, we thank you for your time.   We will call you, if we find out anything else.   You all have a good day"   he said after standing up again.   Dmitri showed the officers back to the front door, and let them leave.   Victor turned to his family and spoke to them in a serious, quiet tone of voice.

"We have to do something about this. No matter what, just try not to upset them. A lot of people lost their lives last night, and the police obviously aren't fools" he said

"Yeah, Vic, but they got nothing on us. There's no evidence that Eleanor did it, just like he said" Meredith added.

"Well, let's hope it stays that way then" Gabriella spoke up. "My daughter has done something like this before. When she was fifteen. If those officers find out about it, we may not be able to hide this." Victor looked over at his sister.

"They won't find out about that, Gabby. We just have to stay low for a while until the investigation is done" he said to her. Gabriella gave a soft smile back at her brother.

"You haven't called me Gabby since we were kids" she said lightly.

Off to the side of the room, Sabrina and Eleanor stood quietly by the doorway after hearing the entire conversation. Eleanor looked at her cousin with a quaint smile as Sabrina nodded to her silently.

Chapter Fourteen

The Christmas of Changes

For the next several months, the small city of Warren and its vicinity mourned the losses of those who perished so brutally in the fire of the Laramie Circus. There had been news broadcasts on television and radio as far off as Pittsburgh, Cleveland, Philadelphia, and New York. The residents of Warren weren't going to let their loved ones go that quickly…and nor were some of them going to forget the cause of the disaster either. Wherever the LaMore's went in town, there would be people staring at them. Some of them would move away, keeping their distance. In the affluent neighborhood of Unicorn Acres, at least six of the LaMore's neighbors moved away, out of town.   The few that did remain on their block, didn't speak with them much.   Sometimes only a simple "hello and goodbye".   In small towns, news travels fast, and before you know it, your business has become everyone else's business.   An incident such as a fire that claimed 122 lives wasn't something people were going to forget the next day…especially the cause.   In school, several of the students would often stare at Sabrina and Eleanor from afar, and none spoke to them. Even less than they did before.   This didn't bother Sabrina at all, but Eleanor was annoyed by it.   Her instant reaction to everyone would be a glare, and soon they'd stop staring.   She felt as though the entire high school thought she was an alien or mass murderer set out to kill them.   Even her teachers were slightly cautious around her, and a few times she felt like burning the whole building down, just to give them a reason to be afraid.   She figured it'd be amusing, but also make things worse for her and Sabrina.   Instead, she would later take her anger out on other things after school hours by burning them to ashes until the wind blew it away.   Deep down, Eleanor didn't like how all she seemed to do was destroy things.   She wanted to do something better, but continued to doubt she would even have the chance.   In her mind, the world would always hate her, and there was nothing she could do to change it.

Victor and Erika's nerves were finally able to calm as the winter months approached them, and soon it was the holiday seasons.   Gabriella and Meredith were soon doing things again too, including going out.   For a while, the LaMore's had just stayed at the mansion, to avoid any further questioning or accusations from other people about the previous fire destruction.   It was nice to be able to go out and do things again, especially during the holidays.   Halloween and Thanksgiving went by smoothly, and it seemed that the LaMore's problems were finally starting to dwindle.   Sabrina and Eleanor of course, had spent a lot of time together, and hiding out in the mansion hadn't bothered them at all really. It gave them time to explore the house more, and Sabrina had shown Eleanor some of the rarer rooms, like the solid glass, circular room, with a complete skylight ceiling. This room was known as the Chess Room due to the fact it had Sabrina's chess game table in it, sitting in the middle of the room. The glass ceiling gave an excellent view of the sky, and all weather formations. The walls of the room were made of mirrors entirely, and the floor had a reflective surface. When originally built, the room was known as the Glass Room, and nothing else sat inside of it. Not even Victor truly knew of its original purpose, but he believed it was meant to be a star gazing room of sorts. He thought of placing a telescope inside, but he never got around to doing it. It became empty over several years, forgotten in the back of the mansion on the 6th floor, including the even larger room that was hidden behind it. The Glass Chess Room had a secret door, and only Sabrina had known about it. Behind the door was the forgotten large room, which no one but Sabrina had been in ever since the mansion was first built back in the

1800's. The room was about the same size as the Music Room, with the same type of large scale windows that rose high up to the cathedral style ceiling. Currently, the only access to this secret room was through the Glass Chess Room, but there had been other previous entrances in the past. Those were now either closed off, or forgotten and neglected. What was inside this room, was the reason Sabrina would make her yearly visits, especially during the quiet winter months.

  Inside this room, sat the old fashioned, large grand pipe organ. It was the largest object to even be set inside LaMore Manor itself, and the original owner had been Percival LaMore; whom designed and built the mansion for him and his wife, Patricia. They were literally the first of the LaMore family line to settle there, after moving to America from La Havre, France in Europe. Hence the French origin of the LaMore family name. Percival had met Patricia in London while traveling for business. Although living in France most of his life, his family was half English and they would have frequent visits to Great Britain often.

Over the years, after Percival had passed on, the pipe organ was left there in the secret back room, and never played again until after Sabrina was born. It was during those silent winters, that Sabrina would go up to the 6th floor's back wing, and play the grand pipe organ beautifully while the moonlight shown through the large windows of the darkened interior, reflecting the shadows of the snowflakes falling from the sky across the floor.

It was late December now, as the snow had already covered the grounds of the mansion with a hearty seven inches. Eleanor woke from her sleep, and quietly looked over at her alarm clock; showing the hands pointing at 3:20am. The sound which had awoken her was distant, and soft, yet enough to jog her mind from slumber. She already knew it was music, but she couldn't tell where it was coming from, or what kind. It had a slow tempo, and almost had a creeping effect while she listened to it. Eleanor got out of bed, put on her black robe to cover her night clothes, and left her room on a mission to find the source.

She didn't bother waking anyone, as she carried her small candelabra through the darkened halls of the old stone home.   She felt nervous, but intrigued at the same time.   She wasn't really afraid, for she knew she could easily use her pyro ability to defend herself, if need be.

The sound was getting louder now as Eleanor climbed the stairs to every floor above her.   There were a total of six floors in the mansion, and her bedroom had been on the second floor.   She wondered if the other residents of the home were woken by this sound too, or if it'd only been her.   Surely, for a melody to wake her from four floors above her, it must've caught someone else's attention as well.   They were either heavily asleep, or probably thought they were dreaming.

By the time she reached the top floor, she could easily hear the music clearly enough to know what song it was.   The question was…who was playing it?   And where was there ever a pipe organ in LaMore Manor?   Throughout those many years, no one but Sabrina ever knew the large instrument existed.

Eleanor found the door which lead into the large forgotten room, and her jaw dropped as she rounded the corner to find the large pipe organ sitting at the far right end of the room.   The chandeliers of the room no longer lit up, so the organist hadn't bothered turning them on. Eleanor slowly walked toward the pipe organ, which was so large, the top pipes almost touched the ceiling.   Eleanor was amazed by it, and she could see Sabrina sitting at the organ's keyboard, playing "Greensleeves" as the chords softly echoed in the room.   The well known song, that was played on many keyboard instruments including pianos, had a serene melody that gave the large old room a more relaxed feeling.   Outside, the snow came down in heavy flakes, and Eleanor quietly sat down on a nearby bench that resembled a church pew.

    She waited until Sabrina finished playing her song, and slowly her cousin stood up from the bench and spoke before turning around.

    "Merry Christmas, Eleanor.   Welcome to LaMore Manor Cathedral"   Sabrina said almost silently.   Her quiet and dull tone of voice made a gentle echo in the room, as Eleanor stood up again too.

"That was beautiful, Sabrina. I loved it" Eleanor commented. Sabrina, fully dressed and holding Clementine, walked toward her cousin and continued to speak.

"This cathedral room has been vacant for nearly a hundred years" she said. Eleanor widened her eyes at her cousin's words and looked around the dark room, admiring its antiqued design.

"If it's been empty for that long, then how did you get the organ to work?" she asked her.

"Sabrina fixed it" Clementine said softly. "It's her favorite instrument in the whole house, and it belongs to her now." Eleanor smiled at Clementine, and gazed around the room again, as she began to walk around it slowly. Sabrina followed in her own leisured fashion. Their footsteps made lonely echoes across the floor in the air as they walked.

"This place is so huge…I just can't get over it." Eleanor admired. "I wonder how long it took to build this place…and how much it cost.

Probably millions of dollars."

"Sabrina's ancestors were the richest people in the whole town" Clementine added. Eleanor nodded again and laughed.

"Heh, yeah…I know. Very rich" she said. She stood by one of the large windows of the room, and watched the snow fall lazily in the air. Ice was forming on the windows, and it blocked Eleanor's view of ground below them. All she could see was the sky and the snow seemed to disappear below the window frames into white nothingness.

"Sabrina…I need you to promise me something" Eleanor said faintly, as she watched the snow.

"What do you want Sabrina to promise, Eleanor?" Clementine asked. Eleanor turned around and slowly gave her cousin a gentle hug. Sabrina's eyes widened at first, but she slowly returned the hug to her cousin, and only friend.

"That we'll always be together…no matter what happens" Eleanor said quietly.

"We will" Sabrina replied.

As the morning dawned, the LaMore family members each woke up from their night sleep. Across the spacious lawns of the mansion, the sun's rays of light made the snow sparkle gently, and the ice on the tree branches gleamed in reflection. It was Christmas Day, and the world was dressed in a white wonderland, giving the overall feeling of soft relaxation and joy. This had been Sabrina's favorite time of year. The winter was special to her, and the snow was always gorgeous in northern states. Eleanor, never liking the feeling of being cold, rather despised winter most of the time, but the snow *did* catch her eyes. LaMore Manor was warm with comfort, and the large Christmas tree stood elegantly in the living room, near the large windows facing the side lawn. As the snow outside fell genially, it gave the illusion as though the tree was standing outside with it. The tree itself was adorned graciously with many ornaments and tinsel garland, as the electric lights glowed around its branches.

Everyone in the home was now all seated in

the room, getting ready to give and receive their gifts.   Victor handed everyone their gifts individually, while he held his meerschaum pipe in his mouth.   Erika and Gabriella sat on the loveseat, drinking their morning coffee, and chatting with one another as they opened their presents.   Even Meredith's mood had been lifted, and was in conversation with Rosario and Dmitri, sitting on the couch.   Sabrina and Eleanor were both fully dressed and sat together in the second loveseat across from the first one.   Victor was happy to see the household together, and not worrying about the past for once, and smiling.   Sabrina never smiled, but continued to open each of her gifts, while holding Clementine beside her, and thanking them quietly.   Victor was pleased to hear his daughter's own voice, even if it was only mumbles.   Even though Rosario and Dmitri worked for the LaMore family, Victor and Erika considered them both "family" as they lived with them, and gave them gifts on Christmas, and their birthdays.

After everyone had opened their gifts,

Rosario and Dmitri went into the kitchen and dining area, to prepare for Christmas dinner. The LaMore's never traveled on Christmas, preferring to stay home and celebrate in the mansion. It was the same with New Year's, and also Easter and Thanksgiving Day. Victor had gotten a phone call the day before Christmas Eve from his parents who lived in Greenwich, Connecticut. They were going to be visiting on Christmas and staying for New Year's too, and wanted to call ahead of time to let him know. They were also eager to see Sabrina and Eleanor again, since they were their only grandchildren. It had been years since their last visit, but Victor kept in touch via phone and letters. With Meredith and Gabriella now living in the house, it would be a good time for everyone to catch up. Erika had talked with her parents, Isaac and Shirley Ishtar, via phone the same day. They lived in the Erie county area of the state, but weren't coming to visit due to other plans. They usually only traveled in the warmer months.

Dmitri opened the front door, as Victor's parents rang the doorbell. Victor and Erika stood at the doorway, and soon saw a tall man standing there, gently hugging a shorter woman beside him. They both had dark hair, just as Victor's, and the man was wearing a long dark blue coat with a matching hat.   He looked up at Victor and smiled warmly with his green eyes seeming to gleam from beneath the porch light.   His wife wore a gray and black mink coat, which bundled her up cozily from the winter wind.   Her matching fur hat covered her entire head, and she too gave a delighted smile with her brown eyes fixed on Victor.   She was the first of the two to speak, and soon reached out her arms to hug her son.

"Victor!   So good to see you, my darling!" she said, taking him into her arms.   Victor returned a smile, as he was happy to see them after so long.

"Merry Christmas, son"   his father said with a deep voice full of heart.

"I'm glad you both could make it this year. We made some changes around the house since you moved out last time"   Victor replied.   Erika focused her attention on Victor's mother, and greeted her inside.

"Hello, Whitney, Merry Christmas to you" she said, leading her into the grand hallway.

"Erika, dear, it's been so long, and I love what you've done with your hair!" Whitney said with glee. She leaned close to Erika, speaking into her ear as she made a joke. "And I hope my son has been *behaving* himself" she said with a short laugh. She removed her coat and hat, handing it off to Rosario immediately, and began browsing the house in curiosity before Erika could reply. Jeremiah, Victor's father, came up to Erika and gave her a gentle hug.

"Good to see you again, Erika. I hope you've been well" he said kindly. Jeremiah was much like Victor at heart, and more soft spoken. Whitney was more outgoing, and often reminded Erika of her sister, Meredith, only much older and…happier.

"We've been doing great, Jeremiah, and I can't wait for you to see how much Sabrina has grown. I know it's been a while for you and Whitney since you last saw her" Erika said to him. Jeremiah took off his hat and coat, and hung them up himself, after politely dismissing Rosario from the task.   The maid gave a bow, and silently walked everyone toward the living room area.

    Whitney gazed at the Christmas tree with wide eyes, and lightly looked at most of the ornaments, as though she couldn't get enough of their sparkling beauty.

    "My word!   What a lovely tree!"   she exclaimed.   Gabriella walked up to her mother, tapping her on the shoulder for attention.

    "Hi mom, glad you could make it"   she said to her.   Whitney turned around, smiling wide at the sight of her daughter, and hugged her quickly.

    "Oh, Gabby!   So good to see you!   Are you living back up in the north now?"   her mother asked.   Gabriella nodded lightly with a smile, and gestured to Eleanor to come over and see her grandmother.

    "Yes, mom, I am.   It didn't really work out down in Florida, and Victor said I could stay with him as long as I like.   It's better for Eleanor too.   We needed a change"   she said.

    "Ah, good then.   Nobody wants to live down in that muggy, tropical swampland anyway"   Whitney said, disgusted by the very thought of being there.   She turned her head, and soon saw Eleanor standing nearby quietly.   Whitney's eyes lit up again, and she came over to hug her granddaughter.   "Oh my, how you've grown! Such a fine young lady you are now, Eleanor."

Eleanor looked at the woman with a slightly crossed glare, but soon returned the hug, uncomfortably.

"Nice to see you, grandma"   she said with a bland tone.   Jeremiah came into the room with Victor, and looked around for Sabrina.

"So, where's my lovely granddaughter at? I haven't see her in ages"   he said allowed.   To everyone's surprise, the door from the dining room opened slowly, and Sabrina stood there quietly in the arch.   She held Clementine in her arms, facing the room, and held her usual serious expression.

"Merry Christmas, grandpa"   Clementine said happily.   Sabrina's face was pallid and made no effort for attention as her grandparents gazed at her.   Her grandfather slowly made a smile, and nodded to Sabrina, who in return, did the same to him.   Whitney gave a look of confusion, and narrowed her eyes slightly.

"Why is she holding a *doll*?" she asked with a sarcastic tone. Victor chose this moment to speak up, before Sabrina became too annoyed.

"Well, mom, Sabrina had decided to become a ventriloquist not long ago, and has mastered it rather well in fact" he explained. Whitney's smile returned, and she looked back over at her granddaughter.

"Is that so? What rare talent that is. You must be very proud" she said. Victor and Erika exchanged looks, and nodded lightly.

"Yes…very proud indeed. She also does well in school" Victor added. Jeremiah and Sabrina stared across the room at each other, as though to be exchanging their thoughts. Jeremiah knew already that Sabrina had the "power" just as Victor had inherited it from him, and he sensed it was different within her. He soon summoned for Dmitri to retrieve Sabrina's gift he'd gotten for her, and continued to smile. Sabrina raised an eyebrow, and looked at her grandfather with interest. Dmitri soon brought in a large white box, slightly narrowed, and handed it to Jeremiah quietly.   Everyone was surprised by this, except for Whitney, for she knew about the gift beforehand.   Jeremiah walked up to his granddaughter, handed her the box slowly, and whispered lightly.

"This is for you" he said to her.   Sabrina took the box carefully, and opened it in silence. Her vibrant green eyes widened slightly at the sight of what it was.   Inside the box, sat a bright red dress, with a black belt to match it.   On the belt, several garnet stones were engraved within the lining, and she could see a matching necklace and set of earrings.   All made with garnets, being Sabrina's birthstone.   She looked up again, nodding to her grandfather, and soon left the room quietly, to change into her new outfit.

By the time Sabrina had gotten back, everyone was just getting ready to sit down to Christmas dinner, and eat the stuffed duck that Rosario had prepared.   Sabrina's short red dress fit her perfectly, and the belt graced her waist fittingly.   She wore her tall black dress boots to match, and let her long black hair down freely. Her necklace and earrings sparkled lightly from the chandeliers in the dining room, and everyone turned to look at her when she entered.

"Oh Jeremiah...that's a beautiful dress you bought her"   Erika admired.   Everyone nodded in agreement as Sabrina joined the table. Meredith looked at the dress in jealousy, but said nothing.   Eleanor smiled at Sabrina's gift, knowing how much she loved wearing black and red together.   Clementine sat on Sabrina's lap in front of her at the table, and soon the food was served.

All seemed to go well during the evening meal.   Jeremiah and Whitney talked of past times in the LaMore family history, and their journeys overseas, while Victor would tell his parents about the progress of his teachings at the private college and studies.   Meredith and Gabriella each told about how they came to live at LaMore Manor, and what their future plans were.   No one brought up any topic of Sabrina and Eleanor's paranormal abilities, nor any topic of the recent events that had occurred earlier in the year.   They felt it was best not to tell Victor's parents, especially due to the fact that his mother would be highly un-accepting of it.   Whitney had been much like Gabriella on this fact, and not wanting to admit their family had the telekinetic trait passing on.   Even though Eleanor had not received the trait by inheritance, her pyrokinetic ability still had a strong impact.   The trait had skipped Gabriella, lying dormant within her, and awakening in her daughter instead.   She knew, that if Eleanor were to bare any children in her future, they would likely inherit telekinesis, or pyrokinesis, or possibly both traits.   The same would happen for Sabrina's children as well, if she were to have any.

       Rosario calmly cleared away the dinner plates from the main course of the meal, as Dmitri rolled in the dessert on a dinner cart.   The dessert for Christmas dinner this year, consisted of caramel flan and lemon sorbet.   The large flan sat upon a glass cake dish, which Dmitri set in the middle of the table for all eyes to gaze at before he served it.   Sabrina was a big fan of flan.   It didn't really matter what kind it was, she would always eat it.   Tall wine glasses now adorned the table, and were being filled with a fine chardonnay.   As the butler passed by Sabrina, on his way to the other end of the table, he walked for half a second before falling to the floor after tripping over one of the dining chair's legs.   The wet chardonnay fell from his hands, making a splash in Sabrina's lap in what seemed a dramatic scene from a movie.   With widened eyes, the dark haired girl stared down at her new dress, as the wine merged quickly with the fabric in a pool, and dribbled off the dining table in front of her as well.   Everyone was silent.   They stared at the girl for a reaction, but there wasn't any.   She seemed too surprised for words as Dmitri quickly found his footing again, and apologized several times for his accident.   Eleanor put her hand over her mouth, and stared at Sabrina in silence, as she knew this wasn't going to have a positive outcome.   Dmitri briskly grabbed a cloth from the dinner cart, and started wiping up the mess.   His hands reached in front of her, attempting to soak up the wine rivers that were flowing gently across her dessert plate and the table.   She stared at his hands with hatred…

'How dare he do this...' she thought to herself. Clementine too, had some of the mess spilled on her, and Sabrina felt her anger rising inside her nerves. Her familiar sensation that her ability quite often loved to feed off of, was speaking to her. It wanted out. It wanted attention from her mind. *"Go on...teach him a lesson...he deserves it"* it said to her. *"It was your favorite dress...and he RUINED IT!..."*

Several pieces of glass soon dashed through the air, as each of the wine glasses shattered abruptly. The women screamed in alarm, covering their faces as best they could in the sudden danger, and stood up quickly. Sabrina's eyes gleamed as the tall glass serving dish that held the flan began to spin in a constant circle on the table. Its constant speed and friction was leaving an ugly indent with the wood, and the glass was cracking quickly from the tension. Eleanor's face held actual fear this time when she looked at her cousin. She backed away from the table as the flan dish soon flew across the room, colliding with the wall in a strident crash. The dining table drifted above the floor, hovering in place and acting like a seesaw.   Dmitri yelped in severe pain, as Sabrina broke the bones in his hand mercilessly.   Everyone in the room could actually seem them lifting and snapping under his skin with no other physical contact.   Jeremiah and Whitney, looking at their granddaughter with cautioned expressions, soon started running out of the room.   Sabrina wouldn't allow this.   The walls of the room moaned and the chandelier vibrated loudly.   As they ran through the living room to exit the house, Whitney made an alarming cry as the Christmas tree ornaments and bulbs shattered, followed by the entire decorative fixture falling to the floor in front of them; scraping across the carpet roughly.

"Stop it Sabrina!"   her father yelled from across the room.   He wanted to shake her. Knock some sense into her.   He wanted to discipline her terribly, but couldn't even look at her directly in the eyes for ten seconds.   Eleanor quickly ran up to Sabrina, and shook her lightly, telling her stop.   Sabrina's eyes returned to their normal state, and she gazed at her cousin in shock.

Eleanor had actually stopped Sabrina from raging any further, and this caught everyone else's attention.   Victor and Erika ran into the living room nearby, to see if Whitney and Jeremiah were safe from any wounds.

"I knew it!"   Whitney declared, shouting out across the room.   "I knew she'd have that terrible power!   That devilish little witch child!"

Erika spoke through her tears in response to Victor's mother.

"I'm so sorry Whitney!...We should've told you, but..."

"But nothing!   If you wouldn't have had any damn children, then this never would've happened!"   Whitney interrupted.

"Stop it mother!   It is not our fault, and you know it"   Victor chimed in.   "It's a trait...it's passed on through our family line, and we cannot control it."

Whitney threw her arms up in the air in disgust, and gave up the argument, leaving the room.   She slammed open the front door of the mansion, not bothering to close it again; continuing to yell out "witch child" and other such comments on her way to the car.

"The power is uncontrollable in her, son...she shames our family name" Jeremiah said with a hoarsened tone. "*She*...is not my granddaughter"

Victor stood there after hearing his father's words. Erika covered her mouth in a gasp, and looked to her husband. Victor's eyes were glassy, countering his father's, and he slowly pointed toward the front door in the main hallway.

"Then you're no longer welcome here" he said to him with a quiet, stern voice. Jeremiah's face lifted a bit, and he began walking away.

"Don't come to me, when she tears your lives apart...that's exactly what she'll do" he uttered. The front doors of the mansion slammed shut, followed by a few squealing tires on the front driveway. Victor looked out of the window, and watched his parents drive away in their expensive black Cadillac coupe. Rosario walked out of the dining room, and sat down on the couch with her hands shaking lightly from the disruption that just occurred. Dmitri held his hand in pain still, and came up to Victor.

"I fear I may need a hospital right away, Victor" he said to him with a shaken voice. Victor nodded quietly, and placed his hand on Dmitri's shoulder.

"My friend, you know you don't need to ask me permission to leave for such things. I'll drive you there, myself." he told him. He looked over at his wife, whom was now sitting with Rosario on the couch, offering her comfort. "Will you be alright until we get back?" he asked her. Erika nodded lightly.

"I'm...fine. Gabby and Meredith are here" she replied. Gabriella and Meredith soon came into the room, and Sabrina passed by in silence; carrying Clementine in her arms, with Eleanor following behind. Her expression was emotionless as always, and she made no eye contact with any of her relatives. She and her cousin walked up the spiral staircase, and disappeared for the rest of the night.

"What a fuckin' Christmas this turned out to be" Meredith muttered sarcastically to herself. Victor sighed deeply, wanting to react to Meredith's comment, but said nothing. He didn't have the energy for it.   He left with Dmitri out to his car with no further words.   Gabriella looked into Erika's face, seeing her crying lightly, and she gently pulled her into an embrace.

"I'm so sorry Erika…I never thought it would be…like *this*"   she whispered to her. Meredith stood up, walking over to the window, wiping tears from her face as she watched the snow, and Gabriella soon felt her own saddened emotions of hurt overwhelm her body in unison. They knew this was a situation that was never really going to go away.   They would have to deal with it straight on for the rest of their lives, no matter how much they wanted to avoid it. Sabrina and Eleanor were the ones in control, no matter what the outcome may be.

Part Three

Enter Hanako: Kyoto Princess

Chapter Fifteen

Love Never Fails

The flow of the northern winds invoiced by nature have started to dwindle now. Early spring loomed upon the earth as the flowers and trees started to bloom, and gain their leaves again of greenish vibrancy. Mid to late March, and early April was a time of change in the northern states. Snow flurries rarely shown themselves now, and the sun would wake up early morn of dawning beams across the sky. It had been almost a full a year, since the time of Gabriella and Eleanor's arrival to the LaMore family mansion.   From that time, a lot of their lives had changed.   Thrown out of proportion, and even turned upside down as one might say.   Death had followed the flaming girl's arrival to the small city of Warren, and new reputations were bestowed upon.   The once well known LaMore family, for their kindness, generosity, and wealth; now floated down a steady dark river of sorrow, hatred, and paranoia.   The townspeople had a completely different view of them, for they "knew" that Sabrina and Eleanor had been responsible for "all" notably random uncanny occurrences in the area.   Although, it could never be proven.   Without physical proof, the residents of the town were fixed upon the "seeing is believing" concept.

      It angered Victor.   So much in fact, he thought about leaving his family estate, and moving to another place in time.   Though, he knew he couldn't.   Just simply leaving the mansion that his ancestors took so long to build and place their effort of existence in the world, after arriving to America in hopes of freedom would be an insult to the LaMore name. He too, had put a lot of life into his home. It was a true, one-of-a-kind architectural wonder from the 1800's still sitting strong on its foundation, and that was rarely seen in these times of modern life. Erika hadn't wanted to leave either, despite her not liking how the town viewed them as people now. She had many memories in this house. Victor and Erika had even had their wedding there, with guests of over two hundred who gathered for the event. Even so, Sabrina had been born in this town, and if the mansion were put up for sale, it would probably never sell. It would be auctioned off, only to be torn down for land use of a ridiculous mini-mall, and that would be shameful. Victor would never let that happen as long he was alive, and the estate would eventually be owned by Sabrina after inheritance for further living use of her future family.

     School times were even harder for Sabrina and Eleanor. Students didn't just avoid them, but would immaturely whisper many comments about them, even when they were looking at them.

They still feared them, but only to a certain extent now. Some of the students were also intrigued by the fact the two girls were deemed as social outcasts and murderers, by "unknown means" in use of "powers". Not even half of the student body in the school had ever seen Sabrina or Eleanor using their said powers on anything, yet still believed it. For the ones who *had* seen them...those were the ones that *truly* feared them, and would stay clear as much as possible. Sometimes avoiding them in ridiculous ranks as to turn around in the hall they were walking in, and walk around the exterior of the building, just to get to class. Others would laugh at this; mock them for fearing the "freaks of nature" only to be silenced again by Sabrina's darkened glare. Her very eyes, with their solid glassy effect, would silence any being in her way. Much like the "Medusa effect" except they remained alive. Eleanor always found this amusing, and would feed off of it, by taunting some of the other students. On rare occasions, she'd even light a flame in her hand, and stare at them quietly, while their jaws hit the floor, and their eyes became the size of dinner plates.   This never helped anything, except increase their reputations.

   Sitting in her desk quietly, Mrs. Baker rummaged through some files and papers while her class did another weekly math test for her. Sabrina worked steadily in silence, finishing the assignment before the other students could barely look over everything on it.   She stood up, slowly walking toward her instructor's desk, and laid paper down without words or contact.   Mrs. Baker was always thrown off by the girl's demeanor, and still would make a scowl at Clementine being held in her student's arms.   She felt the need to scold her, but would always hold back.   She could never find the effort and need to go through with it, especially when Sabrina looked at her.   The girl went back to her seat, which was behind Eleanor's now, and indulged herself in a book for study and enjoyment.   Tammi and Lois watched them from afar, at the other side of the room.   Eleanor was too busy on her work to notice them watching, but Sabrina seemed to "know all".   One glance from the silent girl, made the only girls flinch, and turn back to their work unwillingly.

"She's psychotic..."   Tammi murmured to herself.

"Probably a slut too..."   Lois added with her own mild whisper.   Her vacant insult was meaningless to Sabrina, but she wouldn't let it go unnoticed.   Her glare tightened, as her eyes pierced at her from a short distance.   Lois couldn't help but feel Sabrina's presence, as though she were standing next to her, edging into her mind.   Sabrina found this girl to be utterly annoying and repulsive, but she wasn't going to just kill her off.   If Lois wanted to toy with her, she was going to give her a taste of her own game.

She noticed Lois holding her green colored pencil in her right hand freely, writing down the solutions of the math problems.   Lois's desk was located by the wall on the right side of the room, behind Tammi's.   Sabrina narrowed her eyes, and wasted no time, taking a hold of the desk's exterior.   Lois soon found herself sliding into the wall quickly, and hearing the bones of her hand crack fiercely between the wall and the desk's side.

Her graphite pencil pierced through her skin without mercy; wedging through a bone, only to come out the other side, and severing in half. Lois's screams of pain woke the class out of their studying trance, and looked at Lois with shock and surprise.   Mrs. Baker immediately stood up and went over to aid her screaming student, whom by now had her hand free, as the blood squirted across the floor in trails.

    "You fucking bitch!"   Lois cried out, pointing to Sabrina with her free hand.   "She did it!   That bitch, she did this!"   she declared through her tears.   Mrs. Baker took her arms around her student, and lead her out of the room quickly toward the nurses office.   Tammi was speechless as she stared at the dark red trails of blood lying on the linoleum floor of the class room, and felt disgusted as her stomach churned.   She gasped and held her hand up to her mouth, turning away.   Sabrina simply raised an eyebrow in silence, and turned back to her book without a change of expression.   Eleanor grinned to herself, at her cousin's action, and lightly chuckled.

    "It isn't funny, Eleanor, Lois is seriously

hurt!" another girl said directly. Eleanor beamed at the girl, and straightened her face when she spoke.

"Well now, whose fault is that? If she would've just shut her mouth, she'd still have a few veins left in her hand, wouldn't she?" she asked the girl with a sarcastic tone. Sabrina went on reading as though nothing had happened, and Eleanor still returned a menacing grin. The other girl looked at Eleanor as though she were insane, and got up from her seat, leaving the room.

"You're sick, Eleanor…" she muttered, walking away. Eleanor's grin slowly faded after the girl left, and she went back to her work; dismissing the girl's insult. Bryson Blackwell, looked over at Eleanor with interest. His interest in the girl had first started when she moved to Warren, and started going to school with Sabrina. He honestly found her to be attractive, and her overall appearance everyday of nothing but black clothing caught his eyes. Bryson was a Goth, and he too, always wore black, and often many silver necklaces that adorned his neck. Most of them skulls and crosses, with a few rings to match.

Eleanor noticed Bryson staring at her, and she made a small smile, for she found him interesting as well.   Sabrina had noticed this, and felt as though she needed to watch it from afar.   She felt protective over her cousin, and wanted to be sure everything would be alright for her.   She glanced at Bryson, but returned to her book again with her own thoughts.

After class, Bryson walked up to Eleanor and Sabrina in the hallway, lightly taking Eleanor by the arm to get her attention.   Eleanor turned around, and looked at Bryson in surprise, and wondered what he wanted.

"Hey.   It's Eleanor, right?"   he asked, referring to her name.   Eleanor nodded lightly as Sabrina stood with her dominating presence from the side of the conversation.

"Yes" Eleanor said.   Bryson ignored Sabrina's glare, and looked directly into Eleanor's eyes.

"I hope you don't think of me as weird...coming up to you in the hall like this, but would you maybe want to go do something later? Ya know, like go to the mall or something"   he said her with a softened tone.   Eleanor smiled lightly, and cocked her head to the side while looking at the boy.

"You mean like a *date*, Bryson?"   she asked timidly.   Bryson returned the smile, and Sabrina's glare faded lightly.

"Yes…like a date"   he said to her.   "How does this weekend sound to you?"

"Sounds great"   Eleanor said, widening her smile.

"Cool.   I'll pick you up around four"   he said to her.   His dark brown eyes seemed to enchant Eleanor from behind his brown hair bangs, and he started walking to his next class with the other students.   Eleanor turned to her cousin and kept her smile.   Sabrina nodded, but said nothing, and they soon went their separate ways to their other classes.

Sabrina's next class for the day, was her World History class.   As she sat in her desk quietly, her teacher, Mrs. Shumen, soon entered the room.   Behind her, walking shyly without speaking, was a girl.   She was Sabrina's age, and slightly shorter than her in stature.   Dressed all in a rose colored pink and white outfit; a short top, with a ruffled dress, and her short black hair in bob-like cut, held two white barrettes which accented her clothing.   She was of foreign ethnicity, mostly likely Asian as Sabrina could tell by the shape of her face and eyes, and she held tightly to a gold chain necklace with a humming bird decoration hooked to dangle.

    "Everyone, I'd like you to meet our new exchange student, Miss Hanako Kajima.   She just recently moved here from Japan, and will be joining us for the rest of the school year"   Mrs. Shumen said with a smile.   The girl made a slight waving gesture to greet the class, and forced a smile through her shyness.   The teacher then pointed to an empty seat toward the back of the room, for Hanako to sit at.

    Sabrina watched as the girl walked toward her seat, almost serenely, as she caught her attention.   This girl fascinated her for some reason.   Sabrina didn't know why, and it wasn't just because she was from the one country she'd always wanted to go to. No, this girl caught Sabrina's attention for another reason, and she couldn't understand it. Something about her was simply so intriguing, and she felt the need to find out. Hanako sat down at her desk, setting her books in front of her, and looked around the room. Her dark eyes met with Sabrina's, and she seemed to gaze at her with the same thoughts. To Sabrina's surprise, the girl actually smiled at her, and made the same waving gesture to her, as she did to the classroom when she first entered. Sabrina quietly nodded to the girl, and turned back to facing the front of the classroom. Hanako did the same, and the class began.

For the rest of the school day, Sabrina and Eleanor went about their daily classes as though nothing was different. Tammi McVay completely avoided the girls, after what she'd seen earlier in the day. Lois Platte has been taken to the hospital, for surgery to be done on her hand, since the severed pencil had been stuck inside, and her veins and bones were broken from the impact of

being crushed.
 As Sabrina walked slowly from her last class through the hallway, she could faintly here voices just outside one of the hall windows. After catching her attention, she peered out of the open window at the back parking lot alongside of the lawn, which surrounded the backend of the high school. Standing on the pavement, surrounded by three other boys, was Hanako Kajima. The expression on her face was something of being terrified, and Sabrina could easily see that she was being bullied, for not being able to speak enough English properly. One of the boys backed Hanako up against one of the cars, and placed his arms on both sides of her, as though to show dominance. He taunted her with words; a poor show of expression, and Hanako turned her head to the side, shouting out in her native language as a response.
 "Yamete! Watashi o kinishinaide!" the girl cried out. *"Stop it! Stop bothering me!"* She fell to the ground, scraping her leg on the side of the car, forming an open wound cut.
 Sabrina didn't know what came over

her...but for some reason her anger wanted to explode, and she swung open the door that lead to the parking lot briskly, capturing attention as the hinges creaked and broke off from the strain. The door flipped and fell to the pavement with a crash, and the boys looked over in her direction in surprise, along with Hanako.   She didn't use her hands, and neither did she care if anyone saw her displayed use of power.   The three boys silenced themselves quickly in Sabrina's presence, and soon started to run when they viewed the menacing glare from her face.   She didn't even have to speak.   One look, and they were gone; running like frightened young children.

      Hanako stood up slowly, looking over in Sabrina's direction, and brushing her hair bangs from her eyes gently.   Not only was she surprised, but still shaken up from the experience. Her arm trembled as she held it, and the cut on her leg bled a small trail of blood down to her shoe, soaking into the sock's fabric.   Sabrina's expression softened now, and she looked over at the girl, holding Clementine in front of her. Hanako opened her mouth, and made a slight gasp, before speaking in a hushed tone of voice that gently drifted over toward Sabrina.

"Arigatou..." she said, facing Sabrina head on. *"Thank you..."*

"Dou itashimashite" Sabrina replied, forming a small smile. *"You're welcome."*

The girl made her own smile in return, lowering her arm to her side as it no longer trembled. Sabrina walked up to her, closer than before, and stood in front of her as she spoke.

"Eego ga dekimasu ka?" she asked her. *"Do you speak English?"*

The girl shook her head slowly, and looked to the ground with a sigh.

"Iie. Eego ga sukoshi shika dekimasen" she voiced. *"No. I only speak a little English."*

"Daijyoubu desu" Sabrina said, nodding to her. *"No problem."*

She gently took Hanako's hand to comfort her, as if by second nature. She had no problem speaking in Japanese, and she felt comfortable with her. The two girls looked into each other eyes and faces, and at that moment they seemed to have a bond. A rare bond, just as Sabrina had with Eleanor, only it was different. Hanako turned her head away slightly, and seemed to blush from embarrassment.

"Anata wa totemo shinsetsu desu" she said quietly. *"You're very kind."* She turned her head back to Sabrina and broke through her shyness with a question.

"Onamae wa?" she asked. *"What's your name?"*

"My name is Sabrina…and this is Clementine" she said, as she held up her doll for Hanako to see. The girl lifted up Clementine's hat, and smiled at her, despite it having only one eye. Hanako had a general politeness and overall feeling of positivity toward Sabrina. She was also happy to meet someone in her new home that actually spoke her language, and could understand her.

"Dochira kara desu ka?" Sabrina asked her. *"Where are you from?"*
Hanako focused her attention on Sabrina again, and replied happily.

"Kyoto nihon kara kimashita" she said. *"I'm from Kyoto, Japan."*

Hanako slightly flinched as she put her hand on her wounded leg.   It wasn't a deep cut really, but still stung in pain nevertheless.   She slowly slid her hand up her leg, to wipe off the long thin blood trail, only to soak her hand slightly. Sabrina quietly reached out, taking hold of Hanako's wrist and stopped it from moving. Hanako was surprised for a moment as Sabrina stared at her in silence, while holding her bloodied hand.   She then took out a small handkerchief from her pocket with her free hand.   She handed the cloth to Sabrina with gentle movements, as though she were fragile.   Sabrina seemed to understand Hanako's every thought, and she softly wiped up the blood from Hanako's hand.   She then bent down, carefully wiping up the trail on Hanako's leg.   The cut was starting to dry now, after being exposed to the air, so Sabrina didn't bother with it.   Hanako was quite content in Sabrina's presence, which was rare for anyone other than Eleanor.   In fact, the girl with the fiery soul was now standing just outside the doorway that Sabrina had dismantled earlier, watching the two girls in the parking lot.   She hadn't said any words, just simply stared at them with curiosity.   Eleanor had never seen Sabrina so comfortable with anyone before the entire time she'd known her.   Most of all, she wondered who exactly the other girl was.   She wanted to know.   She felt she must know who the person was that her cousin was associating with.   It boggled her mind as she stepped out onto the pavement, walking over the broken door pieces.   Sabrina hadn't turned around, even when Hanako looked over her shoulder to see who was approaching them.   She simply spoke quietly, gently letting go of Hanako's hand to its rightful owner.

"Hello Eleanor"   she said to her.   "Glad you could join us."

Eleanor stopped in her tracks, and smiled lightly at her cousin.   Hanako's curiosity engulfed herself again, and she pointed to the other girl.

"Do…you…know her?"   Hanako said slowly, but clearly.   Eleanor gave a look of confusion at the Asian girl when she spoke out English words.   Soon realizing she couldn't speak much of America's language, and decided to be patient with the girl, since she seemed to be Sabrina's new friend.   Sabrina nodded lightly in response to Hanako's question.

"Hai.   Kanojo wa watashi no itokodesu" she said to her.   *"Yes.   She is my cousin."*

Eleanor gave a slight bow to the girl, for she knew it was a proper Asian greeting.   Sabrina had been teaching her about Japanese culture for quite some time now.   She then   introduced herself.

"I am Eleanor"   she said patiently. Hanako's face formed another smile, and she giggled to herself lightly.

"O ai dekite koeidesu"   she said, returning a bow to Sabrina's cousin.   Eleanor kept her smile, but looked to Sabrina for a translation and raised her eyebrows.

"She says, it's nice to meet you"   Sabrina said quietly.   Eleanor then gave a look of relief, while replying to the girl's greeting.

"It's nice to meet you too.   Welcome to America"   she said pleasantly.   Sabrina then translated Eleanor's message for Hanako, and soon the LaMore family's white limousine drove up

beside them in the lot.   Dmitri sat in the driver's seat patiently, looking through the windshield as he waited for Sabrina and Eleanor to enter the car. Eleanor was the first, as she opened the rear door, and got in.   Sabrina walked Hanako over to the car, and made a gesture for her to get in with them.
    "Would you like to see my home?"   she asked the girl.   Hanako gave a shy grin, speaking quietly to her new friend.
    "Watashi wa kitai"   she replied.   *"I'd love to come."*
    Sabrina led her new friend into the long luxury car, soon sitting herself down beside her. Hanako lightly stroked Clementine's hair with her fingers, making a positive comment quietly with a smile.
    "Kawaii..."   she said.   *"Cute..."*
    Eleanor was rather surprised into shock that Sabrina had let another human being touch her doll.   In fact, she was entirely surprised by this whole situation.   Sabrina was actually making an effort to communicate with someone she didn't even know that well.   Yet, she acted as though she'd known Hanako for years.   She knew

something was happening with her and this girl, and she knew it was for a reason. She sat across from Sabrina on the other end of the limo, smiling at her cousin. In a way, she was glad to see her talking with another person, rather than just her and Clementine. Sabrina still kept her usual emotionless state, but let out more expression across her face when she was with Hanako. Even Eleanor was now relaxed in Hanako's presence, but that was mostly due to the fact that Sabrina was comfortable around her. If Sabrina was comfortable with someone, then Eleanor knew, that person must be special in Sabrina's mind.

"Head to the home, Dmitri. We have a guest tonight" Sabrina said mildly to the butler. The man obeyed the girl's command, and soon drove off to LaMore Manor.

Chapter Sixteen

The Introduction

    After arriving back to the home where the rest of Sabrina's family was located, Victor's face soon shown his bewilderment after he watched his daughter exit the limo with an unknown girl to follow.   He walked away from the living room window, and met up with them at the door.

    "Well now, who might this girl be?"   he asked slowly.   In front of him, Dmitri stood, shrugging his shoulders and giving a look of confusion in his pale eyes.

    "I don't know, sir.   Miss LaMore requested

her as a guest for this evening" he said to Victor. Sabrina raised an eyebrow at her father while still keeping a stern expression, as though her mind was already made up and never to be changed. Eleanor too, said nothing, and the Asian girl bowed to Sabrina's father formally.

"Konnichiwa. Hanako Kajima desu." she said to him with a gentle smile. "Hello. *My name is Hanako.*"

Victor returned a bow to the girl, and stepped aside, allowing everyone to enter. He said nothing, for his head was filled with curious thoughts on why Sabrina had brought her back with her. He lead them all into the living room, where Erika, Gabriella and Meredith were seated quietly, watching a game show on TV. Victor caught their attention with a wave of his hand, and immediately spoke.

"We have a guest tonight. Sabrina's brought a friend over, so let's all help her feel welcome" he announced. Erika smiled and turned off the TV, receiving a mild look of disappointment from Meredith's face as she'd been watching it. "Everyone, this is Hanako

Kajima."   Victor announced again.   Hanako bowed once more, saying hello in her native language, and Meredith gave a scornful look.

"We speak English here"   she said shortly, staring at the girl.   Erika and Gabriella ignored Meredith's remark, and both made a gentle bow to the girl to greet her.   Sabrina slowly walked up beside Hanako, and looked upon Meredith with a solid face; miffed at her aunt's display of poor manners.   Meredith turned her eyes away slightly, and let her longish blonde hair fall to the side of her face, as though to hide.

"Welcome to our home"   Erika said finally with a delighted smile.   Hanako smiled as well, and soon took Sabrina by the hand as she began to walk about the room, feeling curious in the large mansion.

Erika was thunderstruck.   Sabrina actually had let another person touch her…and seemed completely fine with it.   Gabriella and Meredith were just as surprised.   Victor came up to his wife and whispered to her as they watched their daughter from afar.

"I'm just as surprised as you are.   Dmitri said Sabrina just requested her to come here"   he said.   Erika turned her head to him.

"Maybe she's finally coming out of her shell, Vic.   This is good.   I'm actually happy about this" she said softly, wearing a warm smile.   Victor nodded, but Gabriella still wasn't sure.

"Let's not assume so much right now.   We should just wait and see where this goes.   After all...I don't think she can just suddenly change so quickly like that"   she declared.

"Gabriella's right."   Meredith spoke up. "What if it's all an act or something.   Remember how many people she killed?   Her *and* Eleanor?" she added.   Victor sighed deeply, rubbing the back of his head with his hand in thought, and looked over at the girls again.   Sabrina seemed completely relaxed in Hanako's presence, along with Eleanor.   He didn't want his daughter to be a killer.   He didn't want her to be so withdrawn. He wanted her to be sociable.   Make friends.   Go out and express herself with the world.   Most of all...he wanted her to be *"normal"*.   Even though he knew she'd most likely never change.   She was who she was.   He needed to accept this, and so did everyone else.   He wanted her to be happy, and if she was making a new friend in Hanako, then he saw no harm in it.

"Let's let her decide for herself"   he said at last.   The others stared at him in silence, and he turned and walked out of the room without another word.

Dinner that night, held a feeling of comfort at the LaMore's dining table.   Hanako proved to be quite polite and well mannered, and she'd even learned more of the English language while talking with Sabrina's family.   They adored her. Everyone was in a good mood, and even Meredith had accepted the girl's arrival in respect for Sabrina.   Sabrina, herself, had spoken hardly at all, but Victor still got the feeling she was pleased with her family's acceptance of her new friend. He looked at her from across the table with a quiet smile as everyone socialized around him.   His eyes met with Sabrina's vibrant green hues, and they stared at each other.   As though the noise from the family's voices seemed to fade out, and all they could focus on was each other.   Victor gave a nod to his daughter, and Sabrina did the same without speaking.   It seemed to be their way of showing communication toward one another.

      No matter where they went in the house, Hanako would always be by Sabrina's side.   Still holding her hand off and on, and showing interest in everything at her new friend's home.   By nightfall, Sabrina took Hanako up to her bedroom, and they stood together out on her balcony that led off of the room itself.   Sabrina's balcony was a large, half circled shape terrace that was made of the same gray stone as the mansion.   It was attached along the exterior, while held up with three tall gothic styled pillars to match the mansion's design.   Hanako walked out to the end, and let her arms rest along the balustrade as she stared up into the starry sky with awe.   Since the town of Warren was located in an area far from major cities, it was easier to see the stars and constellations at night.   Sabrina quietly stood beside Hanako while a night zephyr blew around the two girls, carefully aligning their bodies with its invisible presence as it passed by.   The moon glowed steadily above them, and Sabrina found herself gazing upon her new friend easily. Hanako was content as she smiled up at the sky, and took hold of Sabrina's hand again.   She turned to her, speaking with a soft tone and looking directly into her eyes.

"Thank you.   You're the first…to be so kind to me" she said.   Her words were quiet, but Sabrina knew she meant what she said.   She opened her mouth lightly, as though to speak, but then stopped herself.   Back in the bedroom, Eleanor watched the girls from a distance with her own curious eyes.   Hanako tilted her head, expressing her innocence, and calmed her smile.

"What's wrong?"   she asked her.   Sabrina closed her mouth again, and lowered her eyes to the balcony floor as her doll spoke up.

"Sabrina is different than others" Clementine said lightly.   Hanako was surprised by this.   What happened next, was something she knew she would always remember for the rest of her life as she stood on that balcony with Sabrina in front of her.   Sabrina set Clementine on the railing ledge beside them, and slowly lifted her arms up at stomach length while closing her green eyes gently.   One by one…Hanako watched as red rose petals drifted their way up to the balcony from the garden below them in a row.   They moved quietly through the air, as though completely weightless, and began to circle her and Sabrina in an elegant loft into the silent sky.   The rose petals kept the position in a row, moving in a slowing motion, and creating a long chain to the air above them as Sabrina breathed in deeply and tilted her head gently upward.   Hanako was amazed by this effect that her friend was doing for her, and widened her eyes with a smile as the flower petals circled them in a genial dance.

     In the Japanese language, Hanako's name translated to "flower child", with "hana" meaning "flower".   In her own way, Sabrina was expressing the meaning of her friend's name, and Hanako realized this.   She let out a giggle as she reached out and touched the floating petals that surrounded them.   She then noticed Sabrina opening her eyes and letting a small tear roll down her cheek.   Hanako straightened her face…slowly walking up to Sabrina closely, and wiped the tear lightly from her skin with her finger and whispering to her.

"I do not mind. It is beautiful" Hanako said to her.   Sabrina made a sudden quick gasp, and all the petals fell to the ground below them. Staring into her friend's dark brown eyes, Sabrina felt motionless.   What was this feeling?   It crept up through her body like a snake, and yet it felt good inside.   It was every time Hanako was close to her like this.   She couldn't ignore it, and the feeling overtook her body in a slow and dominating way, as if she needed to give into a random urge.   Hanako understood her.   She felt Sabrina's inner pain…and the loneliness.   The girl slowly leaned in further, remaining silent, and gently touched her lips to Sabrina's delicately. Sabrina's eyes widened for a moment and she breathed in her own breath quickly, along with Hanako's at the same time.   It was so sudden.   A new experience for her, and the awkward feeling shooting up through her body like tiny rockets along her nerves.   It didn't hurt…it felt wonderful to her.   It was a natural instinct, and Sabrina gave in, despite her state of mind being split. Right now...it felt together. A whole mind. Nothing out of place, and completely serene. Hanako's arms lightly held the sides of Sabrina's body when this happened, and slowly and steadily, Sabrina did the same. Clementine...lay silent and still on the railing...ignored indefinitely.

Back in the bedroom, staring in surprise, Eleanor's eyes remained fixed on the situation. She, however, soon turned her head away to the side, and walked out of the room. She wasn't disgusted, and nor was she upset. She held a quiet smile to her face, and felt her cousin needed some time alone with her new friend, Hanako. She was glad for her. Glad she was able to finally experience a side of life, that she knew she hadn't felt yet. Eleanor, herself, had been with guys back in Florida, but none of them ever lasted long enough to be with her permanently. Either burned to a crisp, or meeting some other form of fiery fate along with her fatal personality.

Sabrina opened her eyes again after Hanako pulled back from her kiss. She was speechless, and tried to find something to say, but

Hanako simply smiled, and walked back into the bedroom.   Sabrina picked up her doll, and carried her back inside, looking at her grandfather clock ticking in the background.   It was nearing nine o'clock pm, and she knew that her friend needed to go back home soon.   With a sudden knocking on Sabrina's bedroom doors, Victor gently opened one of them.
  "Dmitri has the car waiting.   I hope you had a pleasant evening tonight with us, Hanako" he said.   Hanako bowed formally, and returned her smile.
  "Thank you for letting me visit.   Your home is beautiful"   she said slowly, but clearly.   Victor was impressed with how well the girl's English speaking skills were developing, and after bowing in return, he closed the door to wait for them.   Hanako walked up to Sabrina, and gave her a soft hug.
  "Arigatou, Sabrina-chan"   she said to her.
"Thank you, Sabrina."

Chapter Seventeen

Obsession

Throughout her life, Dr. Roberta Stein had always wanted to study the human mind. It fascinated her, and the paranormal side of her studies were no exception. She was drawn into the mystery of it, like flies were to honey. After meeting Sabrina LaMore, and her cousin, Eleanor, she'd been captured by their states of mind. Their "powers" of their energy flowing through their brains like electricity. Even though she had discontinued her ongoing visitations with the two girls, the thoughts of their unique abilities were still boggling her mind.   It wracked her brain to the point of her staying longer work hours in her office at night, and skipping meals here and there. She'd never met anyone as strong and lively current as Sabrina, and Eleanor's ability was like a volcano waiting to burst the top of her head. Both girls were truly gifted, and Roberta wanted to know more about them.   She wanted to see them in action;   know their thoughts, and feel their emotions.   Why they are…they way they are. However, despite being overly curious in them, Roberta was slowly failing to see the reality of the situation.   Both girls were in all honesty, human beings, whom only were able to use more of their brain's internal uses on a different level.   Roberta was starting to view them as science experiments, rather than people.

      On this late hour, and sitting at her desk within the darkness of her office, Roberta reviewed her studies of Sabrina and Eleanor LaMore.   Her small desk lamp, barely giving enough light to shine the tabletop, glowed dimly over her papers with a tiring feeling to the room.

Behind her, the moon shown in the sky through her window as she carelessly threw one of her notebooks to the floor in frustration.   She held her hands up to her face, gently smearing some of her makeup as she was in deep thought.   It was true, that Sabrina and Eleanor, as rare as they were, actually scared her to some degree.   On most accounts, though, she was more intrigued.   She was now debating with herself, on whether or not to call Victor LaMore the next morning, and start scheduling appointments again.   Outside her office door, came a soft knock as someone had heard the noise.   Roberta blinked her eyes, and wiped her mascara off of her hands quickly, and answering the door with a call of her voice.

"Its open, come in"   she said.   The door opened slowly, and a man stood there quietly, peering inside the dark room.

"Roberta?   Why are you still here?"   he asked her curiously.   "It's late.   You should be home, getting your rest."

Roberta sighed deeply, and held up one of her notebooks with part of her study work in the pages with one hand, and raising an eyebrow to the man.

"Darren, I have work to do" she said plainly. "I can't just leave it. It has too many questions."

The man then walked into the room, gently rubbing his hand on the side of his head, as though the situation was frustrating to him as well.

"Roberta, I've seen what you've been doing. You're coming into work at eight in morning, and going home around eleven in the evening. You're skipping meals, you're ignoring other clients…you're acting like nothing else matters" he said sternly. "You've got to take a break."

Roberta stared at Darren with a snide look across her face, and folded her arms.

"Darren…this case is too complicated. It can't just be dropped. These two girls…I've never seen anything like them. Especially Sabrina…the girl could bend a school bus in half without even touching it!" she said, raising her voice and grabbing the file papers. She threw them down in front of Darren, as though telling him to look at them.

"Roberta…you dropped the case…it's no longer your concern anymore, and the LaMore's haven't even come back here! Let…it…*go*" he spoke directly. Roberta rolled her eyes in hostility, and grabbed her books and files as she stood up from her desk.

"You know what? Forget it. You're right. I'll just sit here, while some demon girl and her little cousin tear this town apart, like they did at the Laramie Circus that one night" she said in sarcasm. Her voice gave a flat and dry tone as though she knew exactly what to do, and no one could tell her different.

"Just leave them alone, Roberta. I'm your friend…I *don't* want to have to report you" Darren said, as he watched her walk out of the building. He followed her to the parking lot as she opened the door of her Mercury Capri convertible. She threw her belongings in the passenger seat, and got in just as Darren approached her. He looked in through her window, and she lowered it to speak.

"Someone has to do something about them. The people of this town have no idea what they're up against.   These girls…they're stronger than anything I've ever studied or seen before"   she said to him.   Darren gave a stressed sigh, and after a minute of silence, he finally gave an answer.

"Just…I hope you know what you're doing. Don't get yourself into trouble you can't handle" he said.   His voice was more soft in tone this time, expressing his care for his friend, rather than his stress.   Roberta looked back up at him with quiet eyes, and nodded gently after starting the car's engine.

"I won't.   I just think I need to do something about this…before all hell breaks loose" she said mildly.   She then backed her car out, without another word, and drove off.

As Sabrina slowly walked down the hallways of the high school, many of the students stopped and stared as she went by them. Alongside her, Hanako walked casually, holding her textbooks in her arm as she noticed everyone's faces.   She couldn't help but wonder why they were all finding it so surprising to be walking with her new friend.   Sabrina spoke not a word, and keep her eyes facing front as she neared her next classroom.   Some of the students whispered amongst themselves along with the teachers. Hanako turned her head toward Sabrina and smiled lightly at her, feeling comfortable in her presence.   Eleanor walked behind them, smirking lightly to herself at the reactions of the other students.   No one said anything directly to them, but for the rest of the day, no one would even think about going near Hanako for anything.   For fear that Sabrina may "do something" to them. Hanako was in most of Sabrina's classes, just as Eleanor was, and whenever she was there with her, she'd sit in the nearest desk available.   It would always be empty of course, as no one in their right mind would ever go near the girl with the talking doll.

    Mrs. Baker looked across the room at the Japanese girl, sitting next to her friend, and gave a puzzled look.   Sabrina raised an eyebrow at the old woman, and soon the teacher moved her eyes onto something else.   She called for one of her students to come up to her desk, and handed a pile of worksheets to him, to pass around the classroom.   She soon had the class hard at work on some math problems, as she sat at her desk with her laptop computer.   She sent an email to Mr. Castle in his office, asking if he would talk to Sabrina about her carrying her doll with her every day.   She told him it distracted her from doing her work, and she would speak with it during class period, as it was bothersome to the other students. David Castle believed the small lie, and said to send her down to his office right away.

Mrs. Baker smiled to herself, and stood up from her desk.   She called across the classroom, interrupting everyone with a voice to break the silence.

"Sabrina LaMore.   Mr. Castle wants to see you in his office"   she spoke out.   Her serious tone drifted over the students' heads, as Sabrina stared blankly at her teacher.   She narrowed her eyes slightly, and stood up with a calmed motion, slowly walking down the aisle of desks between the students to the front of the room.   She left silently, and Eleanor decided to speak.

"What's that about?"   she asked in hard

tone. Mrs. Baker turned her attention to Eleanor, and said nothing. She simply sat down again, with a smug face, and went back to her computer.

    Sabrina entered David Castle's office with steps of silence as she stared directly at him. The elderly, African American man looked up at the girl from where he sat, and formed a welcoming smile.

    "Good mornin' Sabrina. How're you?" he greeted pleasantly. Sabrina stood in the doorway, saying nothing, and held Clementine close to her body. The man nodded his head once in gesture as he spoke again. "Have a seat."

    Sabrina then sat herself down in one of the brown leather chairs that were placed in front of David's mahogany desk. The two held a silence between them for about a minute, and David looked at the girl a few times, while rummaging through his work on his desk. In the background of the main office area, Sabrina could hear faint sounds of the secretaries, councilors, and other random people's voices talking about various things in which she could not make out, due to the distance of the hall.   A fax machine was busy printing a message in the next room over, and the antique wall clock in Mr. Castle's room ticked softly as it counted the minutes of the current hour.   Sabrina let her eyes wander about the room while David fell quiet.   He seemed to be in no rush to speak with her about anything too important.   Outside the window, graced with white color blinds, a small bush was bending its branches sideways as the wind blew over it. Sabrina could feel a change in temperature even through the glass.   A storm was approaching, possibly within the next hour or sooner.   She felt it in her body as the wind moved along.

"I believe you know why you're here" David said, breaking Sabrina's wandering daze over the room.   He looked up from his desk, to capture Sabrina's face.   "It's about you and that doll of yours."

Sabrina didn't like the tone that spilled from David's lips.   In fact, she knew the man didn't like her either, and felt she was a nuisance since all her teachers would complain to him about her "unusual" behavior.

"Sabrina knows you don't like her.   She knows you want to take me away"   Clementine said softly.   David widened his eyes slightly, and formed a serious expression.

"Young lady...I will not tolerate such childish behavior in my room...nor in this school. Is that understood?"   he asked her with stern voice.   His dark brown eyes were piercing as she stared right back at him.   She knew he was trying to be intimidating, but Sabrina held her ground. It looked as though they were both in a staring contest, and neither one of them were giving up.

"She belongs to me"   Sabrina said, in slow and dry articulation.   The wall clock on the side of the room sounded its aged chime for 9:30am after she spoke.   David leaned back, upright in his chair, and gave a sigh in frustration.   He then stood up, and reached his arm out to Sabrina.

"Hand it over, please"   he said to her. "You can reclaim it after the day is over."

"No"   she said blankly.   David was now getting angry, and he swallowed hard, to fight it back.

"Give it to me, or I will keep it for the entire school year" he said again. Sabrina narrowed her eyes, and stood up quickly from the chair. For a half a second, David felt himself being thrown backward, before hitting the bookshelf behind him with immense force. Several books fell from the selves, along with other objects to the floor beside him. He held his back in pain, and looked over at the girl in surprise.

"Sabrina doesn't like you, David. You better stay away...or she'll get maaaad..." Clementine taunted, dragging out her light, child-like voice on her last word. Sabrina turned quickly, walking out of the room, and David watched as his office door shut itself with a short blare after she left. It was clear, that Sabrina found no threat in Mr. Castle. He still stood against his bookshelf, staring over at the door and breathing heavily from being thrown backward so abruptly. He now knew why so many seemed to avoid her in the school, and why so many people in town would talk about her and Eleanor. He ran his hand through his graying hair as he thought, and slowly approached his desk again, sitting back down in his chair.

"That girl's insane…" he muttered to himself.

Chapter Eighteen

Brewing Hatred

Since the day of her "accident", Lois Platte had remained out of school after reconstructive surgery on her right hand. She'd been told that since the impact of the crush on her bones and veins was so extreme, she would no longer be able to use her hand correctly ever again. Lois had been home from school for about two and a half weeks after surgery, falling into a depression over the loss of her writing ability. She could still use the hand, but her written signature would never be the same. She merely wrote scribbles now, and felt no reason to ever try anymore.   As her most trusted and loyal friend, Tammi McVay made several visits to Lois in the hospital every day, until her arrival back home.   Lois didn't even want to think about going back to school again, even though she knew that she had to.   A thick bandage wrapped around her hand was the topic of much conversation the day she went back to school.   Many of the other students would ask how the surgery went, and if she was healing properly.   Lois would give short answers, not really wanting to talk about it, since she still, daily, had to take pain killers for her injury.

"I hate her..."   Lois said scornfully in a deep voice.   She was staring over at Sabrina and Eleanor during their lunch period in the cafeteria, with a look of constant odium.   Tammi paused for a moment, holding her fork that held the few pasta noodles that had been stabbed onto it, near her mouth.   She looked over at Lois's expression and spoke with a quiet voice.

"Lois...I've never seen you like this before. Its kinda...scaring me"   she said to her friend. Lois narrowed her eyes darkly, projecting her vision across the room at Sabrina.   With her other hand, she slowly bent a plastic spoon until it cracked in half.   A small tear rolled down her cheek, despite her emotion being angered.

"It's because of her…that I can't even write my fucking name anymore"   she replied with grisly tone.   Her voice slightly shook as though she were about to sob any moment, but it was clear that her anger was the dominate reaction this moment.   Tammi dropped her food, and slowly began to hug her friend.

"Don't worry…we'll think of something" she said to her quietly.   "She won't get away with this."

Lois felt her long blonde hair fall gently to the side of her face when Tammi hugged her.   She let the broken spoon cut lightly into her skin, making it bleed a bit without even noticing.   She was lost deeply in thought.   She looked upon Hanako sitting close next to Sabrina, and soon whirled an idea inside her brain as she remembered some previous information about the Asian girl.   Giving a slow grin, she spoke just above a whisper to Tammi.

"No...she won't. I have an idea."

  Later that day, Bryson took Eleanor to one of the local restaurants in town for their date. Eleanor was glad to see that he hadn't taken her to anything fast food, and the evening was going well. She was surprised at how polite he was to her, and even showed his romantic side by buying her some roses. She could tell he was nervous, and this made her smile, knowing he was trying his best for her to have a good time. She lightly held onto his hand as they walked slowly through the park after dinner, just talking about whatever came to mind and letting their bond grow. Even though Bryson was an outgoing person with everyone else, Eleanor thought it was cute how shy he was with her. As they strolled through the park, they came to a small playground that seemed to have been abandoned over the years. Most of the play area was worn down, and even the seesaw was broken. Eleanor gave a short laugh at the sight of the place, but soon sat down on one of the swings nearby.

"I guess kids don't like coming here anymore" Eleanor said, make a joke. She held a smile to her face as Bryson sat beside her on another swing, chuckling at her remark on the playground. However, his smile soon straightened as his brown eyes softly gazed over at her.

"I want to ask you something" he said her. Eleanor's smile faded lightly too, as she noticed Bryson's sudden seriousness.

"Like what?" she asked him.

"How come you hang around with that Sabrina girl all the time? Everyone at school talks about how you both have psycho powers or some shit like that. I just wondered" Bryson said. His voice was quiet, but still direct as he looked over at the girl. Eleanor's smile was gone completely now as she narrowed her eyes. She turned her head away, standing up from the swing, and beginning to walk back to Bryson's car parked along the street. Bryson stood up quickly, following her from the swings.

"What? Its true though...the whole school talks about you and her" he said. Eleanor rolled her eyes as she walked briskly over the grass to the street. Her harsh tone expressed her anger now as Bryson ran up beside her.

"I can't believe you actually took me out, just to ask me that." She turned herself around, staring at Bryson in the eyes with her own. Her gaze gleamed at him from under her large black hat. "Sabrina is my cousin. I care about her…even when no one else does. I don't expect you understand that, seeing how everyone else doesn't."

Bryson was speechless for a moment, staring back at Eleanor's reaction to his prior question.

"I…never said I didn't understand" he said to her slowly. His voice held slight caution now, as he knew he had upset her, and wondered why she was defensive so quickly. Still, he wanted to know why Eleanor preferred the company of her anti-social cousin, rather than other people her age. She slowly shook her head at him, and turned to walk away again down the sidewalk.

"You'll never understand…" she muttered from a distance. "…and don't follow me. I'm

walking home alone."
    Bryson stood beside his car as he watched Eleanor walk away down the street until finally disappearing around a corner.   He wanted to follow her, but if he did, she might only be more reluctant to leave with him.   He sighed to himself deeply, getting into his car and began to drive home again.

    As Eleanor arrived at the main gate of LaMore Manor, she was surprised to find Sabrina standing there and waiting for her.   She held her doll in front of her with a placid, yet still emotionless kind of look, seeming like the gate's guard.   Eleanor stopped a few feet in front of her, and remained silent.   Sabrina's eyes viewed her cousin in such a way, as though she already knew what happened.   Eleanor seen this, and slowly put her arms around her cousin in a gentle embrace of comfort.   It was just the communication they both shared.   Almost knowing exactly what the other was thinking, even when apart.

"We'll never be normal…" Eleanor's quiet whisper drifted in Sabrina's ear when she hugged her, and she closed her eyes slowly in return.

"We are who we are." Sabrina replied softly. The sound of Eleanor's muffled cry merged with the fabric of Sabrina's shirt as they stood together in the chilled night air. She knew her cousin would probably never trust another person as much as she trusted her. Eleanor's life was just as lonely as Sabrina's, except for each other's company. That was how it was for them, while living in a world of control and misjudgment.

Chapter Nineteen

The Cats of LaMore Manor

As Sabrina walked down the hallways of the school the next morning, she noticed many of the girls staring at her, and making mocking giggles as they whispered with one another. Eleanor had noticed this too, but none of the girls seemed to be paying any attention to *her* this time. All their attention was on the girl with the long black hair, who carried the doll, and she wondered why they weren't avoidant as usual.   The girls didn't say anything directly, but watched as she walked down the hall toward her locker.   This was when Sabrina noticed it.   She stopped, dead in her quiet tracks, and stared over at her locker door with a slightly surprised gesture.   Eleanor noticed it too, and her mouth almost dropped completely.   In a bright red color, several words had been printed loosely over the locker door like a child's finger-paint session.   The other students in the hall began to laugh as the girls stared at the words of "slut", "lezbo", and "murderer" gracing the exterior of Sabrina's locker.   Eleanor scowled at the other teenagers surrounding them, muttering to herself of their childish action toward them.

"You fucking assholes…"   her breath whispered.

Sabrina, still standing in the center of the hall, moved not an inch as her green eyes narrowed slowly.   She could hear them.   All around her, their laughing voices as the sound slammed into her ears.   She stared at the red paint that had dripped down in messy drops to decorate the linoleum floor in fractured appearance.   Such fools they all were…to pull a stunt like this, and test her anger.   She could feel it inside.   Her powerful mind wanting to react and let loose a wave payback on them.   How *dare* they laugh….and how *dare* they mock her.   She felt the energy rise all around her, while staring at the metal slender door.   It was shaking now. The bolts and hinges were bending quickly, and the students' laughter was fading away.   She heard the hall go silent as the locker door bent directly in half, and flung itself across the room, and slamming into the wall on the opposite end. The sound of the metal colliding with the wall was almost deafening to everyone watching.   Lois and Tammi, the culprits behind the situation, both viewed from afar with horrified looks, as two of the students both fell to the floor.   One of them, having a hole through his neck now from an airborne broken hinge, when Sabrina ripped it off the wall with her force.   He now lay on the floor; his hand trying to hold in his flowing blood that was escaping his wound rapidly.   He crawled on the floor sluggishly as a few of the other students aided to his rescue in attempt to help.   The other student met her fate when the door had flung across the room, and hit her forehead directly as it passed by.   She two, now lay there, but a lifeless body for everyone to see.   Her forehead displaying a deep dent within her skin, as her nerves in her body still kicked around, letting her arm bounce aimlessly beside her.   She looked like a puppet without a skilled puppeteer.

    Many of the students had fled the scene as the faculty rushed over.   By this time, the injured male student was now dead, after losing too much blood, and Sabrina still stood there, staring at her empty locker.   Her reflection gazed back up at her from the dark red liquid pooling on the linoleum below her.   Eleanor was speechless.   She was standing against the wall, as the scene of high emotional tension filled the air.   Lois and Tammi ran out of the building and into the parking lot where Lois's car was.   She sat in the passenger's seat, her arms folding around herself, and shaking. Tammi sat beside her in the driver's seat, trying to catch her breath after what they both just witnessed.

    "Did you *see* that?!   She fuckin' *killed* them!"   she exclaimed through her rapid breaths.

Lois had caught her breath already, and was staring quietly at the car's dashboard ahead of her.

"By accident" she muttered. Tammi looked at her friend, and spoke with a calmer tone this time.

"What do you mean?" she asked her.

"She killed them by accident." Lois said, lifting her head up, and turning to look at her. "She was pissed off, and the other students were just in the way. She wasn't aiming at anyone in particular."

Tammi's face became confused, and somewhat fearful now of her friend's words. Lois had changed almost completely after the day Sabrina crushed her hand. It seemed by now, Lois was enjoying the reaction she created after painting those words on Sabrina's locker door earlier. Like it hadn't mattered that two people were just killed in front of their eyes.

"Lois…I…" Tammi started to say, but soon cutoff her words with a hard swallow. Lois gave a small smile out of nervous tension and handed Tammi the car key. In the distance, the sounds of police and rescue sirens dawned closer as they rushed toward the high school.

"Let's just...go home. School is most likely canceled now anyway" she said softly. Tammi didn't speak now, but took the key, and started the engine. They drove off just as the sirens approached the school and stopped, followed by the medical technicians and police officers running toward the main entrance. Back in the hallway, Mrs. Baker looked over at Sabrina with tearful eyes, as she watched the girl slowly walk out of the building. Eleanor quickly followed, and they both disappeared out one of the side entrances of the building.

The classes for the day, and the next, were indeed to be canceled, and several of the students were too afraid to even come to the building for the rest of the week. The LaMore family stayed hidden once again, as the town of Warren mourned the loss of young life after mysterious and tragic deaths. No one could physically prove that Sabrina killed those two students, even just by accident. Although, all the eyewitnesses were already set on no other explanation.   Victor and Erika didn't want to leave Warren, but it seemed that they may have to since Sabrina and Eleanor were creating a terrible reputation for themselves. It wasn't fair to them though.   Victor knew they were extraordinary, and still deserved to be treated as people.   However, he also knew that other people would never do that.   Especially after what they'd already done.   Even Gabriella was feeling ashamed of her daughter and niece, and wondering if she should just leave the mansion to another place.

"It was a mistake for me to bring her here. Eleanor is dangerous, and being with Sabrina makes everything worse"   she told her brother. Victor gave a look of disagreement, even when seeing where his sister was coming from in this. He too, felt ready to give up entirely on trying to have his daughter "fit in" with everyone else. "She's just too different.   They both are, Victor, and you know it just as well as I do"   his sister spoke again.

"Yes...they're different.   But that doesn't mean they should be cast aside like trash in our society.   Sabrina has managed to make a friend in school...and to me...that's progress.   This other girl, Hanako, sees something in Sabrina that we don't.   And I highly respect her for that.   She is welcome in my home anytime she wants"   Victor said.   Gabriella buried her face into her hands as she sighed deeply.   Erika didn't know what to say to this really, but decided to agree with Victor.

"I don't want Sabrina to be known as a killer...I want her to be normal"   she added.   Meredith gave a short laugh of frustration at Erika's words.

"Don't count on it.   She'll never be *normal,* and neither will Eleanor.   I'm afraid to even go near them, much less go out in town anymore with them.   God knows what they'll do next"   she declared.

"So then what are we supposed to do?!   Just leave them somewhere?!"   Victor said, raising his voice.   Meredith jumped slightly as this happened and glared at him.   "I refuse to do that to my own daughter!   She is all Erika and I have as our child, and she will be treated with respect.   No matter what she can do with her mind" he announced. Meredith turned away, leaving the room, and Gabriella viewed her brother with shock.   Victor's face was dominant and set upon his words, as though they were his last.   No one was going to tell him different. Erika let a few tears roll down her cheeks as she put her arms around her husband slowly.

       "If that is what you want…then I agree with you" she told him in a whisper.

       "She is our daughter…I won't just tell her to leave" Victor returned.   Gabriella then nodded to both of them, and left the room with her own personal thoughts, saying nothing else.

       In the distance of the house, Victor heard the doorbell ring, and Dmitri went to answer it. Victor hadn't moved from his spot, and simply hugged his wife, as he had no care to see who just arrived.

       "Probably just another reporter…"   he mumbled to himself.   "…I'm locking the front gate again tonight."

       Dmitri soon entered the living room, followed by the guest, and announced quietly.

"Miss Kajima is here, sir. She'd like to see Miss LaMore" he said. Victor turned his head to see Hanako standing there with a small smile and bowed lightly to him.

"Konbanwa" she said pleasantly. *"Good evening."*

Victor nodded to her with a smile, and pointed toward the staircase down the front hall.

"She's up in her room. You can go see her if you want" he said, referring to Sabrina. Hanako bowed again, and followed Dmitri up the stairs to Sabrina's room in silence. In the distance, she could hear the sound of music playing from down the hall. Dmitri left her there, and went back to his duties after leading the girl to Sabrina's room. Hanako lightly knocked on the doubled doors of the entrance to the room, and soon the music stopped. After a short silence, Sabrina opened the door, and took Hanako by the hand to lead her in the room. It was as though she was expecting her to be there. Hanako gave Sabrina a gentle hug before speaking.

"I know…about everything" she said to her. Sabrina immediately knew Hanako was talking about the incident at the high school one week prior.   "They were cruel to do that…to you." Hanako's voice was serene as she stared into Sabrina's eyes with a calmed stance.

"You're English has gotten better"   Sabrina said softly.   Hanako smiled and nodded again.

"Thanks to you"   she said with a giggle. Sabrina returned a similar small smile and lead Hanako over to her bed.   The Asian girl's eyes lit up as she saw what was there.   On the bed, all nestled together like a pack, were several cats, all sleeping.   Each one was different in color and breed, and all seemed to be near in age as well. They laid there, clumped together like kittens on a lazy afternoon.   A few of them poked their heads up as Hanako sat down on the bed beside them. She picked up the nearest one, snuggling it closely and giggling more to herself.

"They are so cute!"   she said happily.

"They're all my pets.   Selene is the eldest. She's the black one on the far side of the bed" Sabrina said quietly.   She too, sat down on the bed beside them and began to pet a solid white cat, with brown ears.   "This one is Natalie.   She's the youngest." The white cat opened its blue eyes, and curled into Sabrina's lap beside Clementine for attention with a delicate "mew". The other cats soon woke, and all began to surround Hanako, for she was the newcomer, and full of interest. They sniffed her clothing lightly, and with little mews, as they all seemed to greet her in their own ways. Selene, the sleek black cat, still lay in her spot, but kept her eyes open dimly to view the commotion of the others. In her old age, she hadn't done much but sleep and eat, and as a result she became very lazy. Her light green eyes looked upon her master when she spoke a quiet meow, and stretched her paws out from slumber. There were twelve of Sabrina's cats all together, and Hanako was delighted to see each one. She almost didn't know who to give attention to next, for there were so many in one place. Each of them, loyal companions to Sabrina and Clementine.

"What are all their names?" Hanako asked her. A reddish brown tabby cat with long hair, was now laying in her lap. Sabrina pointed to each one, starting with the one Hanako was holding.

"That one is Roxanne.   The others are: Misty, Aki, Rose, Sybil, Cheshire, Isabelle, Priscilla, Cleo, and Phoebe" she explained.   Phoebe, the silver-gray Siamese cat, had been Sabrina's third cat after Selene and Roxanne.   Hanako found it easy to remember all of their names, since they were all truly different breeds and colors.   Aki turned out to be a male white and orange Japanese bobtail cat, which Hanako recognized right away. Priscilla, being a fluffy white Persian cat, was now relaxing again beside Selene.   Cheshire was completely dark brown, and his breed was somewhat mixed between short and long hair, somewhat like a Turkish Van or a Maine Coon in appearance.   Misty was the most vocal one besides Phoebe.   A lively calico of many colors together, as she continuously pawed at Hanako's leg.   Sybil was a Russian blue, whose fur color shown clearly from the light of the windows gleaming in from the evening sun.   Rose was mostly a bright orange tabby, resembling a small chubby pumpkin with legs, a face, and a tail.   Cleo was an elegant female, softly licking her paws of white fur as the rest of her body gleamed in black. Her ears were the only other spots with white patches on them. Last of all, was Isabelle, a gray striped cat with softened white undertones on her belly.

"They are all very pretty" Hanako said, observing each one.

Sabrina stood up, taking Hanako by the hand, and began leading her over to the other side of her room quietly. Hanako watched, as her friend opened a tall antique armoire, that held some of Sabrina's finest clothing inside.

"I have something to show you" Sabrina said in gentle tone. She reached instead the wardrobe, and took out hangers that held two different colored Japanese formal kimonos. This made Hanako's expression light up again, at the sight of fine clothing from her home country. Sabrina handed one to her, as Hanako held it up to her body, running her hand over the fabric lightly in awe of the coloring. She could tell they were both well taken care of. Sabrina held the other in her arms as well; a solid white kimono with light blue butterfly prints decorated across it in many areas.   It was rare that Sabrina wore white, but she was able to support the color in clothing rather well, with her long black hair hanging freely behind her.   Hanako's kimono was a puce colored one, with many yellow flowers adorning its design. Sabrina had given her this one, due to her name actually meaning "flower".

"Go ahead and try it on.   I want you to have it"   Sabrina said to her.   Hanako was surprised by Sabrina's words, immediately accepting her gift, and soon began to change into it.   Sabrina did the same with her white kimono, and the two girls were now standing in front of Sabrina's tall dressing mirrors, observing their appearances.   Hanako held her usual cheerful smile as she gazed at herself, and Sabrina at the same time in the reflective glass in front of them. Hanako turned, and cocked her head to the side as she complimented her friend.

"You look very beautiful, Sabrina"   she said in softened voice.   Hanako's deep brown eyes stared direct and deep into Sabrina's green spectrums.   She stepped forth, taking hold of her hands, and began to lean herself against Sabrina's body lightly, speaking with a whisper.   "Thank you…"

Sabrina could feel the breath of her friend on her face when she whispered, and felt the urge to hold her again.   The night Hanako had kissed her made her feel unnatural at first, but yet she'd fallen into it, as though second nature.   She knew that it was right, and she knew that ignoring your true inner feelings and who you were was wrong. So she went with herself, and placed her lips to Hanako's once again.   She pinned her against the wall, sliding her hands up her body gently as she gave into her care for her.   Sabrina had never felt this way about anyone before, and she knew what it was now.   What the exact, overwhelming good emotion that shot up through her body was. Over the course of time of knowing Hanako…Sabrina had fallen in love with her.   She wanted her now.   Her mind had never felt so sure of it.

Hanako felt the same.   She already knew of her own sexual interests, and was comfortable with it.   She also knew, that Sabrina was new to it, but was accepting herself rather easily.   And so she fueled the emotion with her own movements, and took Sabrina over to the bed, where she laid herself down, pulling Sabrina along with her.   By this time, the cats had left the blankets, while Hanako sprawled upon them.   They shared no words, for it was as though they already knew their thoughts entirely.   Exactly who they were, and what they wanted from each other.   It came so quickly to Sabrina, that she couldn't stop.   She switched off the lighting for the darkness, locking the doors, and dropping Clementine to the floor with no regard to anything else.   The moon shown high into the sky now as the night approached, glowing over their naked bodies, and for the rest of the night…Sabrina gave all the love she could to Hanako…her one and only.   There was no one else more important in her life than her.   She wanted her to know this…and forever remember it.

    By the next day, as the sun shone through

the old glass balcony windows of Sabrina's room, she realized that she and Hanako had slept well up past noon.   She felt Hanako's embrace over her body in the warm bed, under the blankets, and she smiled at her.   Hanako's brown eyes soon opened slowly, and Sabrina gave a small kiss, speaking in quiet tones.

      "Ohayou gozaimasu"   she said to her.
"Good morning."
Hanako stretched and moved lightly under the blankets and she nestled up to Sabrina happily. She returned the morning greeting in mumbled voice, and smiled back to her, remembering the long night they had both shared recently. Sabrina's emotions seemed to carry a balance now. She would still hold Clementine in her arms wherever she went, but would very seldom use her voice.   As she dressed herself, she looked over at her shoulder; seeing Hanako was busy looking at several of Sabrina's vinyl records that were stacked beside her gramophone turntable. She seemed intently curious about them, and trying to read over the famous recordings of music from the American 1950's and 60's eras.   She

remembered Sabrina telling her at an earlier time, that she liked older music, and Hanako had not known much of it from America.   Sabrina walked up to her casually, and took the record that Hanako was holding.

"Do you want me to play them for you?" she asked her.   Hanako grinned, and nodded in response.

"I have never heard it before" she answered.   Sabrina smiled, and placed the record down, starting the power switch.   Hanako listened as the upbeat sound flowed through the air of the room from the speaker horn, as the song "Little Honda" by The Beach Boys began to play. Hanako seemed to like it right away, as she soon started moving her body in matching motion to the beat and giggled to herself.   She seemed so high spirited, and full of energy, that Sabrina could never ignore her.   Hanako grabbed Sabrina's hands, wanting her to dance with her, after she placed the second record on.   The song "Come On, Let's Go" by Ritchie Valens, gave a certain spark in the room, that Hanako just couldn't ignore.   She had never heard music such as this before, from older times when rock n' roll was very popular among many. It still was to this day, but obviously had changed over the years with the times. She didn't even know all of the words to each song, but it didn't matter to her. One after the other, as Sabrina played songs from her thoughts, Hanako grew a liking all the same. Sabrina's fondness for her was strong, and she knew it would never end. She would be there for her, love and protect her, and no one would ever take that away.

By that night, after Hanako had gone home again, Sabrina stood in the middle of the large glass conservatory of LaMore Manor, sharing a quiet serious conversation with Eleanor. She told her of everything that had happened between her and the Asian girl, and about her deep feelings toward her. Eleanor was the only other person in the world she could trust, besides Hanako, herself. She warned her not to tell her parents, for Sabrina knew that may not approve or take it well in their thoughts. She felt that her family was just too close-minded, just like most of the world truly was. Even though their ultimate opinions would not matter to her, Sabrina didn't feel it was their business to know her personal life. Eleanor simply gave her cousin a genial hug in response to her words.

"Don't worry, Sabrina. I will always care about you. I knew Hanako had a special place in your heart. I could tell, just by looking at both of you together" she told her. Sabrina breathed deeply, calming her mind as she looked back into her cousin's eyes again.

"I'm glad I have you here with me, Eleanor" she said to her.

Chapter Twenty

A Vengeful World

Revenge.   It consumes us like a drug. Takes over our mind and soul, making us feel good along the trip...until it kills us in the end.

With school back in session by the next week, the students of the area high school were highly cautious of their surroundings now.

Especially those who'd witnessed the deaths of two other students after Sabrina had shown her anger.   They could hardly concentrate on their schoolwork whenever Sabrina and Eleanor were nearby.   It was the same with Hanako now too. Although the Asian girl hadn't possessed any paranormal ability to show, the others still avoided her.   They made sure not to contact, for fear of meeting a gruesome fate from her lover, Sabrina.   Hanako was well protected…no matter where she went.   Sabrina was always nearby…watching from shadowed silence.

However, Sabrina wasn't the only one who'd been watching and observing.   Dr. Roberta Stein had taken keen interest in the fact that Sabrina was so close with Hanako.   Due to the fact she'd been obsessing over the girl, and her rare capabilities, as well as her cousin, she decided that Hanako would be part of her thoughts now too.   She made it her business to know about them.   After reading about the deaths in the school a week before, Roberta had taken the initiative to investigate Sabrina and Eleanor at their school now.   She had followed them there, carrying with her, a bag full of the file papers with the information she'd gathered in the past about Sabrina and Eleanor's cases.   It contained everything about them, except their own personal thoughts, and since she'd decided to warn people of their abilities, she figured the school would be a good place to start.

She sat in the parking lot of the high school that morning, waiting as the students entered the main doors and got ready for their day ahead. She waited until every school bus unloaded their passengers even before leaving her car.   She wanted to be sure no one would distract her from her "mission" as she called it now, in her thoughts.

Making her way to the head principal's office to reveal her information, Mr. Castle was sitting quietly in his chair, reading over the files; each with intent viewing and constant thought. Roberta held a face of confidence and assurance, that this was something he needed to see and know, and that Sabrina and Eleanor must be taken seriously.   David raised his eyes up from the papers, and leaned back in his chair as he looked at Roberta in questionable silence, before finally speaking.

"What is it you'd like me to do exactly? You do realize this is highly confidential information, right? I could easily report you for showing me this" he said to her. Roberta gave a slight smirk, and leaned forward slowly in the brown leather chair in front of David's desk. She looked into his eyes, and responded with a soft tone directly to him.

"These girls…are dangerous. I'm only looking out for everyone's best interest and safety, by showing you this information. They've already killed before…and they'll surely do it again. You don't want the burden of another dead student on your hands, now do you?" she said slyly. David narrowed his eyes, and folded his arms while he looked at the woman in mild animosity. He didn't care for her sly tone and egotistical attitude toward him, as though overly confident that she could solve this problem. He did, however, not want to have anyone else die within the walls of his school, and nor have anymore danger come about the town they all lived in.

"Fine. I'll expel her. She won't be allowed to enter this building for the rest of the school year" he said to her. Roberta Stein rolled her eyes in frustration, followed by a steady sigh.

"That's not enough" she mumbled to him.

"Well? What would you like me to do about it?" he said, raising his voice a bit. "There is no physical proof that Sabrina LaMore, and her cousin killed anyone for sure."

Roberta widened her eyes slightly, and pointed her finger against the file papers on the desk between them.

"The proof…is here in these files. The *proof*…were the two dead adolescents that were laying in your hallway last week. Think about it, Mr. Castle. You'd be doing everyone a huge favor by helping me get rid of them. They've already got the Japanese girl on their side as well now" her persistent voice fumed. David took in a deep sigh and placed his hand up to his forehead in an attempt to relieve the stress headache he'd gotten from the conversation. Roberta had been right about most of her information, but to take matters into her own hands was a rather idiotic notion to him. He knew something had to be done about the girls, but he wasn't sure what to decide now. After what he'd seen, and heard about...Sabrina was a true threat to the lives of everyone in the school, and Eleanor, with her defiant personality and easily angered, would just make it worse.

"I'll see what I can do" he said to her, looking back over from across the desk. "But this information is just between us for now." Roberta smiled and nodded her head slowly in return, echoing David's words in agreement.

"Just between us."

As she sat in her plotting thoughts with Tammi by her side, Lois stared down at her writing hand with a disheartened face. Still angry and hurt by what Sabrina had done to her, she formulated another plan to even further pull the girl's life into fractured self-esteem. Or, at least try to. During the study hall class period before lunch, she quietly viewed Sabrina and Hanako from a distance of the other end of the room.   Her face was solid, working the form of her impending thoughts into ideas of something Sabrina would never forget.   With her left hand, she slowly swirled a pencil over paper in small aimless doodle circles at the same time.   She'd been practicing to learn to write again, since her right hand would never be sufficient enough now.

"Tammi…"   Lois started to say, gently getting her friends attention in the quiet room. "…do you remember what Mrs. Baker told us about the Japanese girl, when she first came to our school?"   she asked her.   Tammi looked up from her schoolwork, and noticed Lois's constant stare at Sabrina's girlfriend.

"No…what?"   Tammi asked in return.

"She told us…that Hanako had a bad allergy"   Lois reminded.

"So"   Tammi said dully.   Lois simply smiled, and turned to look at her friend.

"*So*…Hanako's allergic to peanuts.   We should give her some"   she proposed.   Tammi cocked her head, and slowly smiled in unison.

"We could put peanut oil on her food at

lunch.   It will make her sick, if I remember right. I know just where to get some too.   They keep it in the school's kitchen"   she said.   Lois nodded lightly, and grasped a hold on Tammi's hand.
"And we will…"

During the next period was the lunch hour. The entire student population was divided into three different lunch periods; to be sure that everyone got their chance to eat, while still having time for all their classes.   Every day, Hanako brought her own lunch to school with her, in Tupperware containers from home.   Her food mostly consisted of her mother's traditional Japanese style cuisines from their homeland country, as she was used to eating them.   Sabrina and Eleanor had learned that Hanako and her family had moved to America when her father transferred in his medical career.   Settling in small town, like Warren, Pennsylvania was rare for foreigners, but did happen occasionally. Hanako's father was actually hoping to work in nearby Pittsburgh, the state's second largest city, just south of Warren's location. Pittsburgh had a highly promising area for most medical careers, with several hospitals and colleges in it surrounding location. Hanako's living residence in Warren was to only be temporary, but due to the fact she'd fallen in love with Sabrina, she now never wanted to leave.

She sat close to her girlfriend, sharing some of sushi her mother had prepared for her. Sabrina enjoyed it very much, and would often listen to all the stories that Hanako would tell her about living in Japan. A place that Sabrina had always wanted to see and visit. She and Hanako had bonded on many levels, and Eleanor thought it was grand for her cousin. She was pleased to see Sabrina finding some happiness in her life. Hanako was special to her. She meant everything to her, and no matter what anyone said or done, she would always have that love for her. Eleanor didn't feel jealous, even though she *did* miss the attention that Sabrina used to always give to her in the past. Eleanor, in all honesty, wanted to find someone special for herself as well. She remembered her date with Bryson some weeks back. She remembered how good it felt to have someone want to be with her, even though it ended badly. She looked around the cafeteria for Bryson's presence, and soon found him sitting over at another table with three other girls surrounding him. Eleanor gave a look of sheer annoyance and great displeasure at the boy, narrowing her eyes and soon turning away from him. It seemed to her, that she'd never be able to have someone want to love her for who she was. It truly bothered her mind as she stared down at her food in disgust, suddenly losing her appetite and pushing the tray away from her slightly across the table. Sabrina and Hanako noticed this reaction and were now wondering why she did it.

"Is something wrong, Eleanor?" Hanako asked her. Sabrina's eyes looked calmingly at her cousin, when Eleanor raised her head up again.

"It's nothing. I just have some thoughts on my mind" she replied. Sabrina knew of course, as she could sense it, and Hanako simply smiled and nodded her head to the blonde girl quietly. She took another one of her many sushi rolls, and stuffed it in her mouth.   From the other end of the room, Lois and Tammi grinned to themselves after watching Hanako eat her lunch, unknowingly doused with peanut oil in heavy amounts.   They knew the salt and soy sauce on the sushi rolls would counteract the taste, and Hanako wouldn't notice right away.   Before lunch begun, they had sneaked the peanut oil to Hanako's food even before she took it from her locker.   Hanako had never kept a lock on her locker, so this task was simple.   They both then turned away, dismissing their sinister act and walked off to the auditorium to practice for their parts in an upcoming play. The Drama Club was soon to be hosting it on that night's schedule.

"An eye for an eye…Sabrina"   Lois whispered to herself.

Chapter Twenty-One

The Massacre

By the time the lunch period was half over, Hanako had eaten all but one of the sushi rolls completely. Sabrina noticed that she wasn't talking, and hadn't made an effort to speak for the last five minutes. Hanako held her hands over her stomach and gave a look of discomfort, while swallowing hard. She looked as though she would vomit soon, and had trouble breathing. Sabrina saw how it seemed that Hanako's neck was slightly larger than before, and she leaned close to her girlfriend, holding an arm around her for comfort. Eleanor eyed the last roll, and slowly reached for it while looking at Hanako.

"Can I have the last one? I've never had one before" she asked her. Hanako said nothing, but merely nodded in response. She then held one of her hands up to her throat, and on her chest, gently moving it over her skin as though trying to soothe it.

"This taste like peanuts..." Eleanor said then. Sabrina widened her eyes, and looked back to Hanako.

"Are you ok?" she asked her. Hanako shook her head while holding her hands pressed against her stomach. Her eyes dimmed quickly as she spoke murmured words, and falling backward in her chair.

"Sore wa...itai..." her words whispered, falling back against the floor, with her head colliding quickly with the linoleum beneath her body. *"It hurts..."*

Sabrina was soon kneeling on the floor beside her lover, watching in horror as Hanako began having severe convulsions.   Her arms and chest bounced up and down uncontrollably, and her eyes were no longer visible from rolling back into her head.   Eleanor ran over to help Sabrina try to steady her, and started shouting for help in the cafeteria room.   All the other students just seemed to watch in shock and surprise at what was happening, not even thinking to get up from their chairs.

"Get the fuck up and help us!"   Eleanor shouted in demand.   Clementine slammed against the floor with a loud thud as Sabrina dropped her carelessly.   It was the first time in her entire life, she didn't know what to do or think.   She held tightly to Hanako's hand, feeling her tears run down her face in flowing streams.   Hanako was completely out of it, unable to speak or look at anyone.

"What the fuck is wrong with you people!" Eleanor shouted again, this time causing a small flame on the lunch table, and burning one of the food trays into a smoking fire in no regard.   She couldn't help it, since her ability was linked to her emotions, just as Sabrina's was.   The flame was caused from her panic and anger.

    Sabrina could see Hanako's blood starting to ooze from the sides of her mouth through her gasps for breath as the convulsions went on, seeming to increase with every moment.   She yelled out Hanako's name through tears, gaining more attention from the others in the room, some too afraid to go near the situation even to help. She felt Hanako's grip in return on her hand, knowing that Sabrina was there beside her, but could not say or do anything.   Her grip became weaker as both Sabrina and Eleanor watched her shaking body slowly come to a halt…falling dead to the floor.   It was now…the room grew quiet…and Sabrina made a blank stare down at the girl who was now a lifeless corpse.   Just like that…her love was gone.   Hanako had died from an anaphylactic shock of her allergy…and was gone forever.   The blood that leaked from her mouth, formed a small river, lining along the cracks in the linoleum tiles as tiny canals around her head.   Eleanor's tears now came as she held her hands over her mouth, finding no ability to make a sound.   Hanako's eyes were hazed…a constant dimmed stare into

Sabrina's green hues, even after death.   The students in the room ran with following screams at the sight of the dead body on the floor in front of them, and Sabrina slowly stood herself up again.   Eleanor could see the emotionless state come over her cousin's mind again, as the walls of the room created a rattling sound of strain, like an approaching earthquake in the ground.   Her eyes were solid and glassy.   Her brows were narrowed and tight.   An empty stare into open space as the lunch tables soon slammed themselves against the walls of the cafeteria roughly, shattering into millions of splintering wood pieces.   Eleanor covered her ears from the impact vibrating around the room, and she knew then...nothing was going to stop her.   Sabrina's rage was overwhelming and strong.   With each small step that Sabrina took, large fissures snaked their way through the floor, and up around the wall's edges, making the entire room quickly unstable with the ceiling beginning to fall in several fragments.   Sabrina was only heading in one direction...and Eleanor could see the school's auditorium sign in the distance of the hall as her

cousin walked toward it.
"Oh my god…" she muttered to herself, knowing the Drama Club was still busy rehearsing for their play.

With Clementine in arms, Sabrina soon flung open the doors of the large auditorium with her mind. She hadn't touched anything. She simply moved her eyes, along with her thoughts, and chaos would follow. She could see them there. The ones that took the life away from her lover with no remorse. Tammi and Lois were up on the stage of the room, practicing for their lines in the upcoming play, with no regard to what had just happened in the cafeteria. They were laughing, and smiling. It made Sabrina's stomach churn as her hatred for them grew deep and powerful. She *knew* it had been them. They were the soulless whores that stole the most precious thing Sabrina had ever desired and truly loved in this world. It had been taken from her so quickly, that she hadn't even had time to grieve or say goodbye, even if she wanted to.

She would show them...

She would let them know how she felt, and the pain that now coursed through her veins so rapidly, that her heart was pounding for escape within her chest. She would let *everyone* know how she felt. Give back all the aggravation and hurt they all caused for her, and never let anyone in her path have a happiness...no matter who they were. She was fed up with this world. Deciding it not worthy enough for her compassion, or her thoughts of well being, or any promises of love. They took it all from her...and now she would take it all from them.

Lois sat at the grand piano behind Tammi on the stage, watching as Sabrina walked slowly down the aisle to the stage front. In the first few rows of seats, a few other students and the Drama Club teacher along with Mrs. Baker, watched Tammi recite her lines. No one but Lois realized that Sabrina was there, and her eyes widened quickly with fear at the sight of the extreme hatred over Sabrina's pale face. She clutched her doll tightly, and looked up to the ceiling at the studio lighting hanging along their wires on the catwalk. She quickly bent the metal, and unscrewed the bolts that held them up as Tammi announced one of her lines proudly.

"...and if I be lying, then may lightning strike me from the clouds above!" she shouted, and pointed toward the ceiling as the heavy studio lights came quickly crashing down onto her tender body. Metal rods and glass protruded her skin in several directions as her neck twisted and broke from the weight, and her body literally crumbled into a fractured pile below the catwalk light setting. Tammi was dead instantly, and Lois soon screamed from the site of her friend lying in gooey pile. The other students and the teachers began to scramble out of their seats, now after realizing just who'd entered the room with a grand entrance.

Sabrina wasted no time on her next attack, not even bothering to let Lois stand up. She slid the piano abruptly over the floor with swift movement, and the screaming girl soon felt her entire body crush against the stage wall behind her from the weight of the piano pushing to her front.   Her eyes bulged quickly as her chest became a flattened dismemberment.   She gave a loud gasp until collapsing to the jagged keyboard in front of her.   The blood that rolled out of her mouth, created a stream down her body to the floor.   Her loss of life gave a wave of relief through Sabrina's mind and body, and she could not stop.   No one was allowed to ever be happy again.   Not after what they've *all* done to her. She threw one of the broken metal rods from the catwalk through Mrs. Baker's back, as the sharpened end vaulted out the front of the woman's chest in a show of gore.   By this time, Eleanor had been standing at the entrance doors, watching the grotesque scene unfold.   As much as she loved her cousin, she knew she had gone too far now, and needed to be stopped.   She couldn't even find the courage to approach her.   Sabrina was stronger than Eleanor, even with her pyrokinetic ability at full force.   Nothing would stop her now.   Her rage was just too great in strength.   Her emotions were torn apart again. Her mind…a divided state of right and wrong;

happiness and sorrow; hatred and compassion...all forever off-balanced in uncontrollable actions. The joy and normality of her state of mind was now diminished.   Lost with Hanako's life when she died.   For most accounts...Sabrina was a vacant being now.   Clementine had returned...capturing all of the girl's inner thoughts, passions, and emotions.   Locking them within her porcelain-wood head for eternity.   Sabrina was the dominant personality now, and would soon unleash herself.   All those in her way...would be consumed by her fury.

The flames from the damaged studio lights soon engulfed the lifeless bodies laying around the room on the stage.   It burned toward the ceiling on the tall curtains, causing sparks in the electrical equipment.   Sounds of pops and buzzing were heard about the room, and Sabrina's soulless facial gesture gleamed darkly over Lois's burning corpse. The fire reflected hauntingly in her pupils while her sweat drops trickled down her face. She made her doll whisper a soft, child-like phrase into the smoked filled air.

"An eye for an eye, Lois..."

Chapter Twenty-Two

A Dangerous Mind

What happened next, was something that can never be forgotten.   The day Sabrina sought her revenge upon the world, for the loss of her one true happiness.   A topic that many cannot discuss.   Not just for the horror she caused, but also for how she caused it.   The force so strong inside her mind…the power of the gods themselves.   Some say that telekinesis does not exist.   A hoax that people made for pure enjoyment of the unknown.   It's the reality of the mind that you should fear. The human brain, more powerful than any force of nature to ever plague the planet. A person can only take so much when pushed to their extremes. For in all things of nature...there will be something of the marvelous.

> Fear not the one who turns to run.
> Beware the one who turns to face.

    Sabrina walked slowly down the halls of the high school with circles of mayhem following her every step. The fire ate the building alive, like a brand new pile of dry wood. She locked the doors shut, not letting anyone escape until the walls began to fall and crumble over everyone inside. The falling ceiling was a finishing crush on whoever was trapped beneath it. Some of the students indeed escaped, breaking open the windows, or simply exiting the building without being buried.   David Castle and Roberta Stein were among the few, but Sabrina didn't care.   Her brain was only focused on what was on the path ahead of her.   Cars on the street flipped over completely with simply a gaze from her face.   The streetlamps bent in several directions as her body energy flowed out like an invisible fog to cover the area.   Even the plants and trees would sway as she walked by them, breaking from their trunks, as nothing went untouched in her presence. Eleanor, being one who could protect herself in a fiery scene, ran out of the demolished school to catch up to her cousin, but soon realized she couldn't get close to her.   The energy that poured from Sabrina's body was literally protecting her, as well as destroying her surroundings.   She wouldn't let anyone near even if she were possibly dying.

      Eleanor called out to her cousin, trying to get her attention, but Sabrina would never turn her head.   Nothing mattered to her anymore. Sabrina's vision was focused and impenetrable to the point where everyone's faces began to blur and look the same.   Having no regard to their lives, she merely cast them aside in death whenever they stepped in her way.

"You have to stop this Sabrina!" Eleanor's voice announced. "I know you're mad, but you can't kill anymore!"

Sabrina didn't even move the muscles in her face, let alone speak any words. The tears that rolled off her cheeks were the only movement on her skin. Eleanor didn't even see her blink as she walked down the center of the road, pushing objects out of her way like small toys. Eleanor was about to lose hope, when she suddenly saw Sabrina stop walking. The girl with the doll, and long black hair, blowing gently behind her in the wind, was now standing silently on a chain of train tracks that crossed over a short spot of the road she'd been walking on. Eleanor wasn't sure why she had stopped there, staring down the tracks at the considerable distance beyond them. Sabrina closed her eyes quietly, and slowly knelt down to the metal rails that crossed below her feet. With one hand, she reached out and touched the rail gently; holding it there, as though waiting for something.

In the distance, Eleanor could now faintly hear a train's horn approaching the area. Warning those in ahead of its approach. The train crossing bells soon starting to ring as the lights flashed and the gates lowered down. Sabrina stood back up again, still keeping her eyes closed comfortably as she felt the train's presence getting closer to town. At least two or three miles down the track, the passenger train in route from northern Ohio to New Jersey was busy carrying its cars full of passengers. Completely unaware of anything that had previously happened; the stewardesses were busy serving their guests in the dining car as the engineer kept his eyes on the tracks. Their course was set through northern Pennsylvania, and it was their unfortunate time that the train was about to pass through the small city of Warren. Sabrina could feel it coming. She felt its energy and heat. She could taste it…rolling down the tracks in a steady motion of progress, as though bored with its artificial life. And there it was…the item she'd been searching for on the locomotive. She could see it in her mind, as she pulled the speedometer lever forward quickly, and let the train pick up momentum.   The stewardesses standing in the hall of the dining car fell to the floor as the train gave a sudden jerk forward.   Sabrina had captured it.   Snatching control of its very existence, and pulling it toward her.   She let the engine build up in motion as the train starting reaching speeds over 70 to 80 miles per hour now. The passengers began to panic, and the engineer strained the breaks, only to have them wear and bend.   They were no match for Sabrina's mind of control.   The train was hers now, and the passengers were on the ride of the lives.

    People on the street began to gather around Sabrina now.   They weren't able to approach her, since she protected herself, but nevertheless they still tried.   They wondered why she stood on the tracks as the train came ever closer now, blaring its horn of warning.   It smashed cars and trucks here and there while barreling down the line.   Eleanor saw the train come into view, feeling ground vibrate like an earthquake.   By now, the locomotive had reached its top speed, nearing over 100 miles per hour with Sabrina in control.   The passenger's screams could be heard as it rushed down the rails and barely staying on track.   It seemed to float lightly over the rails in some points on the long stretch. The people whom surrounded Sabrina were now running away from the impending danger of the runaway train.   Some fleeing in cars for a faster getaway.   Pedestrians shouted out for warning to others as the train finally reached the intersection. Voices were drowned out by the thunderous vibration.   It sounded like a tornado rushing through the area.   Eleanor covered her eyes in dismay, hoping Sabrina would be alive after it hit her.   She fell over on the pavement in a panicked scream as the train rushed in.   The ground cracked apart and the trees blew over the ground. Sabrina opened her eyes in a sudden glare and the entire locomotive flipped up into the air.   The front end lurched toward the sky and blocked the sun's view.   The passenger cars buckled together in utter chaos of smashing glass and straining metal as they collided together in a mass of destructive force.   The locomotive hit ground behind Sabrina with such a strong impact, that the fleeing people all bounced into the air.   The pavement tore up from underneath it in a crazed noise of flying machine particles.   It tore in half from the collision of roadway.   Anything and everything on the street was plowed over like bowling pins as the train cars slid down the road in a high-pitched scrapping destruction.

       An explosion soon followed that could be heard from around town.   The darting pieces of jagged metals, rods, and glass, puncturing into innocent objects and people near the scene.   Sabrina stood on the tracks with her hair blowing wildly in the wind from the explosion, yet the pieces soared around her body as though she were immune.   The cries for help within the burning damaged train cars was horrifying to the ears around the area.   So many were either dead, or on the verge of dying when the speeding wreckage finally ceased.   Eleanor slowly lifted her head up from the ground, watching as the survivors of the wreck were burning alive.   Some fell to the ground in front of her.   She stood up quickly in alarm, and looked over at Sabrina; whom was now walking on down the street again.

Sabrina had no thought. She merely continued walking toward the downtown area while the disaster burned on the ground around her. By this time, the police were making an attempt to stop the girl from her murderous acts. Firing bullets and rushing police cars weren't enough to stop her. Sabrina knew to protect herself at all costs, and nothing would faze her. Not now…and not ever. Hanako was gone. Taken from her life, and she was grieving. She would show the world that it was no match for her anymore, and she had no remorse for it. To her, the society that surrounded her had no right to be happy, since they took it away from her. Why should they? They would never understand. They go about their daily lives, with eyes staring full of careless judgments over what was different and unnatural in the world. She was the difference, and they didn't accept it. It didn't matter what she did now, for they would never accept her for who she really was. It wasn't her fault being born with such power of the mind. It was her gift.   She chose how to use it.   People weren't going to choose for her.   She wouldn't let them.

"I will give you something to fear…"   she mumbled, as the sirens blared around   her on the street.   She was now standing by the town square, staring up at the clock tower bank building in silent thought.   The tower was the tallest building in Warren, of eight stories high in bricks and terracotta in the center of downtown.   At one in the past it was struck by lightning, and nearly burned to the ground due to the lack of a lightning rod.   Police cars rushed around her, attempting to box her in.   She heard the policemen giving her commands and warnings while aiming their guns at her.   Telling to her to stop all actions, and place her hands on her head.   She assumed they felt brave and noble as they stood there.   Such foolish orders…   Sabrina was no barbarian to be *handled*, and nor would she ever let people touch her without permission.   The windshields on the cars began to shatter randomly, and the metal doors and hoods started to bend and break around them.

She gave the policemen fair warnings to leave her be as she stared up into the sky.   Something new was happening in her body, as her energy increased.   She felt her eyes becoming hot, although it didn't hurt.   It felt good in fact.   Her green irises formed a constant glow of crimson red and she took in a deep breath.   The electrons of her body buzzed around inside her brain, and she gathered several dark storm clouds in the sky above the square.   The sun was quickly faded out as the thunderheads soon boomed overhead the clock tower with angry tones.   The policemen watched in awe and fear, as several lightning bolts shot through the clouds in rapid bursts.   Sabrina could feel it all.   Her heavy breathing grew with every bolt she made.   Her long hair floated in the air around her as she captured all the wind currents.

      By this time, Victor was playing a round of golf with Dmitri in the side lawn of the manor.   The men stopped when the train explosion occurred, and the clouds above them rolling by in strange movements.   This made them both curious about the random phenomenon. Dropping his club on the grass, Victor clutched the sides of his skull and let out a loud yelp from sudden pain shooting through his nerves.   Dmitri immediately ran over to him, taking hold of his body and helping the man to stand.   Victor's eyes, wide with surprise...could feel his daughter's pain. His psychic brain suddenly linked with her own...and for the first time, he could *feel* her thoughts.   They so powerful...so scattered and angry.   Tears rolled down his face and gasped for breath.   Dmitri was horrified by the sight of this, and he quickly urged the man to go inside the home.   Victor shook his head and broke away from the butler's arms.

"I have to go to her!"   he shouted.   Erika came running outside as her husband ran passed everyone, knocking over objects in the room as he fought to steady himself.   "She's going to destroy everything!"

The LaMore family all gathered together as they lead Victor to his car.   They knew it was useless to try and stop him, and something very wrong was happening with Sabrina. Eleanor was standing in the downtown area, still following Sabrina and feeling worried of what she would do next. With the storm looming above, Victor ran up to the police chief after arriving on the scene. He explained to him a few words of advice about his daughter. He had no clue how far she would go with her capabilities. The chief of police was a stubborn man in this situation, giving no care to what Victor had to say, and not wanting to get him involved. Yet, with the crowd of people standing around them, and the storm continuously gathering in the sky, he gave no order to fire any bullets. He feared they would hit pedestrians instead. He'd seen how Sabrina could move them around her body with ease, and he wasn't going to take any chances. He didn't know who, or *what* she was. In his mind, he only knew he had to stop her somehow.

     Sabrina stood calmly in the street, raising her hands up slowly into the air at waist length. She closed her eyes in a gentle fashion and the sky above developed a swirling appearance.

Everyone now knew what was about to happen. Roberta Stein watched from a distance in awe at the show of power Sabrina was displaying. It was clear to everyone, that she wasn't going to let up. She and David Castle had followed the girl into town, completely astonished at everything she'd done so far. Eleanor slowly advanced toward her cousin now, coming close to her and softly saying her name while standing by her side.

"Sabrina...that's enough. You have to stop now" she told her. Sabrina ignored her cousin's request, opening her eyes again to unleash her might of the tempest. The wind soared around them in roaring currents as the funneling clouds formed a twister overhead the clock tower. The sound was almost deafening to everyone, and the wind was so powerful, they could hardly look toward her. Lightning bolts struck the building harshly in several loud plunges of electricity, shattering the windows and bricks into falling debris. Parts of the building's exterior was thrown to the ground from the damage. They crashed cars, people, and other random objects in the way. Eleanor could barely stand up as the tornado gained its ongoing power over the building.   It quickly ate it apart.   In all directions, flying parts of the façade were colliding into everything.   With people running about the area, sheer turmoil unleashed around them.   The tornado tore into the building like scissors with paper, generating a menacing roar of noise to fill the ears.   Eleanor shouted out to Sabrina through the powerful winds as the six sided clock tower came crashing to the ground in a pile of devastation.   Eleanor opened eyes to find the tornado spiraling in front of them as Sabrina controlled it.   For a moment, all she could do was stare at the force of nature beside them.   Sabrina was protecting her cousin from any damage the storm gave off as they viewed it.

"They…took her…from me…"   Sabrina whispered.   She was staring up into the vortex with glowing eyes.   Eleanor watched Sabrina's tears trickling down her face, and most of them blowing off her skin from the immense wind force. Slowly…and carefully, she placed her arms around her cousin, holding her into an embrace.   The tornado began to lose power and die into a dwindling wind.   Sabrina's arms fell to her sides, and she collapsed to her knees on the street. Eleanor dropped with her, still holding her arms in a tight grip to never let her go.   She could feel her pain, shooting through her body like knives cutting deep into the skin.   Sabrina's pain of losing her love, and only real happiness in life.   She had taken it so hard, and the sadness was incomparable.

"It's over now, Sabrina…"   she whispered through a shaken voice.   "…she's gone.   You can't bring her back."

As Clementine lay quietly on the ground, Sabrina's father slowly stepped up to her in cautious movements.   He knew what had happened, from what her mind had told him.   He listened to Eleanor speak softly to Sabrina as she held her close in her arms, both closing their eyes tightly in tears of pain.

"I'm sorry they took her from you…"   he murmured to his daughter.   Sabrina didn't respond, and nor did Eleanor.   Victor gently placed his hand over his daughters head, stroking her long hair as he tried to comfort her.   The three of them were alone in the street.   Everyone around them was dead now.   Distant sirens were echoing as he knew they were coming for her.   They were coming to kill her.   He turned his head to his family sitting in the car down the street, and Erika motioned for him to bring them back.   In the opposite direction, he could see the police lights coming into view.   Soon, they'd be surrounded once again, and more death would ensue.   He couldn't bear to let that happen.   He had to protect his daughter…ironically…from those who were meant to protect *them*.   Reaching down, he took his daughter by the hand carefully and swallowed hard before speaking.

"Come on, Sabrina…let's go home."

Chapter Twenty-Three

Black Umbrellas

Black umbrellas fill this time
As they surround my ancient mind

Our feelings torn as raindrops fall
They cannot hide my anger's call

To soak my hair in drowning voices
The winds of change have made their choices

You were taken from my hold
The love we shared in nights of old

The pain they've caused is unforgivable
I will show them I am unforgettable

The storming skies cry out above me
I ache inside from words that burn ye

You are gone, I can't commit
Acceptance is not a choice to fit

These black umbrellas surround your grave
I lay you down; I could not save

I need you standing by my side
My love for you will never die

Black umbrellas hold this rhyme
Tell the world, the sun won't shine

Death did not change the fact that she loved Hanako.   Sabrina had loved only once, as she was loyal.   That love was now gone.   Taken from her grasp… and she knew…that she would never love again.   Her emotions were torn.   She had no care of anything else, and her mind would forever be split in half of its sanity.   Distraught from her loss in which her powerful mind could not bring back.   She would hate the world forever now.   It did not deserve her compassion, and so, she discarded it eternally.

Sabrina stared down at the royal black casket laying just above the hole in the ground, where Hanako Kajima would be laid to rest.   The funeral was small and done in high honor at Sabrina's request on the grounds of LaMore Manor.   Everything done professional and formally respected.   Her grave was to be placed at the base of the unicorn statue at the far end of the manor's hedge maze.   It would be thoroughly protected from outsiders, as the maze would distract them long enough from finding her. Hanako's parents stood across from Sabrina on the other side of the coffin, both still grieving as much as she was with blank stares filled with silent tears.   No one spoke a word as the priest read off the eulogy in softened tone, which now, was a blurring drone as Sabrina blocked out the world. The constant rainstorm above them was soaking her long black hair as she stepped away from the large black umbrella that Dmitri had been holding over her head.   She didn't even notice the cold, wet sensation of nature's waters rolling down her face and body.   It aligned the shape of her physique, and her fear of the rain seemed to melt away completely.   She clutched Clementine in her arms tightly while slowly kneeling down to her deceased lover, placing an elegant pink rose upon the coffin's lid.   The entire scene seemed to lack color, as everyone was dressed in formal black clothing, and holding white roses on this rainy afternoon.   The world around them was saddened and gray, lacking all joy and happiness as Sabrina mourned.   The air wouldn't move as her green eyes gazed ahead of her.   Nothing but the rain fell, and no one even dared to speak throughout this scene.   Even the priest had stopped reading, and noticed the kneeling girl beside the casket...and as Sabrina spoke...her words came out languid and melancholy.   Just loud enough for those standing nearby could hear. It would be the last time...in a long time...that people would hear Sabrina's true voice.

"Watashi wa anata o wasureru koto wa arimasen...Watashi no Kyoto no ojo."

Hanako's mother gasped slightly at hearing Sabrina's words, and in turn, made a low formal bow to the girl after drying her tears away.   Her father, also bowed in quiet response, as Sabrina stood up again after leaving the pink rose on Hanako's coffin.
"I will never forget you...my Kyoto princess."

The priest then finished the eulogy as Sabrina remained standing.   She watched Hanako being lowered into the earth until the grave diggers' began to cover her with dirt.   She felt her own tears forming again, and didn't bother to stop them.   Her face may have been half emotionless...but she was not afraid to cry for her love.   This had been the first time she spoke with her natural voice, since the day of her destruction throughout the town.   It'd been a week since then, and many residents of Warren were in grief. It was true…Sabrina had shown them her sorrow, and anger, and capabilities.   Although, it didn't seem to be enough.   She felt alive when Hanako was with her, and now, her mind was ripped apart again.   In a way, Hanako had actually saved Sabrina.   In every way a person could be saved. It was during the wake of her death and sheer hatred for the world now, that Sabrina would no longer function in sanity completely.   She allowed her own mind to rule her.   Control her every move.   To let Sabrina show herself in constant…while Clementine was to be locked away, and buried deep within the darkness. Sabrina may have used Clementine's voice to communicate, but her fragile mind was always overpowered by the nothingness.   The abyss of Sabrina's lack of compassion for almost anything. Eleanor still remained in Sabrina's mind.   The only person the girl would ever care for and accept.

Eleanor hadn't said much. In fact, she was still in shock at everything that'd recently happened. She had mixed feelings toward Sabrina's actions. The destruction from her cousin's power was both surprising and also fascinating to her. Both terrifying, and yet awe inspiring at such strength. She felt Sabrina's pain and overwhelming sadness, and felt the need to comfort her. Knowing she was the only person who could now, with Hanako being gone. Eleanor knew that Sabrina would need her by her side. Not only for trust and loyalty, but also support in times of emotional need. She loved her cousin very much, and Eleanor needed Sabrina just as much in return. Since the time of their bond, they knew they'd always have each other to lean on, and be there for. They certainly could not rely on their parents. Nor anyone else.

Meredith and Gabriella were surprisingly respectful on going to Hanako's funeral for Sabrina, although they never spoke to her. Victor and Erika had been there as well, as they both wanted to be sure this was something that pleased Sabrina's request.   They knew their daughter would be grieving for a quite some time after this, even though they were both upset about her reputation.   There had been talk of Sabrina's want for arrest, and also death in spreading rumors over the town.   Many feared her, and hated her existence, and wanted the LaMore's gone from their lives.   Victor didn't want to hide anymore.   Even his teachings at the local private college was now dwindling, as his class members stopped coming.   Even though he had no need to work, he still loved his career and had no desire in retiring yet.

	After the funeral session ended, everyone was speechless and Victor couldn't stand it. Sabrina and Eleanor immediately went up to their rooms without conversation after Hanako's parents drove home. Victor's deep sigh caught his wife's attention as he stood at one of the large living room windows. He was staring out at the specious side lawn of the grounds. Erika slowly put her arms around her husband and stood beside him in silence.

"I want her to smile again" Victor spoke up. Erika leaned her head against his shoulder.

"So do I" she replied. Her voice was so quiet, that only Victor could hear it. Meredith and Gabriella sat quietly over on the sofa, talking between each other in the same manner.

"She was so happy...I could see it. Every time she was with that girl...Sabrina could be herself. She actually spoke" Victor said again. Erika lowered her head now, and began to cry lightly as Victor noticed this. He tilted her head up and looked into her eyes. "I'm sorry. I know this is hard on all of us. We don't have to talk about it right now if you don't want to" he said to her. Erika nodded and Meredith and Gabriella soon approached them standing at the window.

"We should all do something. Anything that will calm our minds...or at least try to" Gabriella suggested. "Sabrina probably won't come down for a while anyway. She probably wants to be alone."

Victor nodded, and Meredith's stomach

growled suddenly in the quiet between them all. They all realized they hadn't eaten anything since yesterday, and even then, it wasn't much. Erika formed a gentle smile as she looked at her sister.

"What are you hungry for?" she asked her. Meredith smiled back, holding her hands along her stomach.

"Pizza...but not just any kind. Homemade pizza. The deep dish kind." she said to them. Gabriella and Victor managed a smile as well at the idea, as it sounded so good to them right now.

"Then let's go to the kitchen. I'll tell Rosario to get everything ready" Victor said.

As Eleanor knocked on Sabrina's bedroom doors, she could feel a small breeze drifting slowly through the cracks in the frame. It brushed against the skin of her face with a cooling effect, and she turned the knob softly. To her surprise, the doors were unlocked and she entered the silent room carefully. The gentle zephyr floated in the room more frequent now and she found Sabrina standing out on balcony in the distance.

The glass doors were wide open; one of them softly swaying in the windy presence as the lace on Sabrina's canopy bed lightly blew in delicate fashion.   The girl's long black hair swayed a bit behind her body as Eleanor looked out through the doorframe.   Her own blonde hair was drifting around her face.   She looked up into the sky, noticing the swirling clouds, and small flashes of lightning in the far distance.   Sabrina was most likely creating a storm from her thoughts, but not as powerful as the day she wreaked havoc upon the town.   It was a quiet storm.   One of sorrowed voice, just passing around the sky as if dreaming.   Sabrina's gaze stared ahead of herself, looking into the black forest of the night that surrounded the outer limits of the mansion's grounds.   They had a clear view of the hedge maze below, which seemed to go on forever as the walls disappeared before the forest area, creating a merging effect.

      Eleanor's steps on the balcony floor were unhurried when she walked up to her cousin. Sabrina knew she was there, even without turning to look.   She knew who'd entered her room to check up on her.   Eleanor was the only person now, who was allowed to do so.   She willingly let her cousin stand beside her in the night air.

"I miss her, Eleanor..."   Sabrina's voice said softly.   Clementine was in her arms, as always, even though she would lie on the balcony's ledge before.   She hadn't let go of the doll since arriving to her room again.   Eleanor calmly placed a small dish on the balcony's railing that held a slice of the pizza that was made.

"I um...figured you might be...hungry" Eleanor said.   Sabrina turned her eyes, and then slowly her head as she stared at the food lying beside her.

"Thank you"   Clementine said to her. "Sabrina isn't hungry much, but she will eat it."

The blonde girl made a smiling gesture, and then sat down on the ledge beside her cousin, knowing she would at least eat something.   The cooling effect of the night wind from the storm far off, gave a relaxing feel to Eleanor.   There were no trees aligned against the backend of LaMore Manor, due to the large hedge maze the covered the entire back lawn.   The flowing wind approached them easily, and the smell of the roses below filled the air with a sweet aroma.   This scent...made Sabrina's grief worsen, as she remembered the night that she and Hanako first kissed on her balcony.   It made her remember how the floating rose petals danced around her body.   Her tears streamed again, lightly dripping to the railing below her, and Eleanor pulled her into a caring embrace.

"I miss her too, Sabrina.   She was a good person, and I know how much she meant to you" she said to her..   She didn't know what to do. She'd never seen Sabrina so upset before, and the pain was hurting her just as much.   She held her close, gently patting her back, and whispering to her that everything would be alright.   Even if she didn't know for sure.   Sabrina's head sank into Eleanor's arms as a crash of thunder boomed overhead through the sky.   The lightning lit up the area like daylight, even only for a brief second and made Eleanor slightly jump.   She continued to hug her cousin, despite the loud sound nearby, and closed her eyes slowly.   Another loud thunderhead made the mansion vibrate for a moment before dwindling.   Eleanor knew Sabrina wouldn't destroy the house, for it was her home, but she knew that she would be grieving this way for a long time to come.   Storms would become common here.   No matter how many towns Sabrina would destroy, or how much destruction and death she caused, Eleanor promised to be there for her.   For she knew that Sabrina would always do the same for her in return.

	The glass balcony doors slowly moved in the wind, lightly banging against their hinges inside and Eleanor noticed the swirling angry clouds were only covering the sky of the mansion itself. As she looked off to her side in the distance toward the town, she could see the view of the damaged clock tower, and the sky remaining clear. The mansion vibrated again, and Eleanor slide herself off the railing, holding close to Sabrina.
	"I will find a way to make you happy again, Sabrina. I will always be here for you." she said to her.

Part Four

A New Dawn

Chapter Twenty-Four

Wrathful Judgment

With much talk and rumors throughout the small city of Warren, it was no surprise that the LaMore's would receive hateful glares whenever they were out. Even the occasional trip to the supermarket with Rosario, would result in feeling of discomfort. Erika often did her food shopping with the maid, and Gabriella would sometimes join her. The three women simply only wanted to stock up some goods for the home, and as they walked down the aisles of the store, many other residents exchanged their expressions of hatred. Some would stop in the middle of the aisle, as though not to let them pass through. Erika began to feel very uneasy as the old woman ahead of her glared darkly from behind her thick bifocals. Never had such an innocent looking small woman been so threatening to her. Although short in stature, the grandmother accompanied by her two grandchildren were fearsome. The children weren't moving an inch and resembled zombies just standing there in silence. Erika then watched the woman reach into her shaggy old purse and pull out a can of mace. She clanked it against the handle of the shopping cart as though to say *"Just you try and come near me whore...I dare you"*. Erika dropped the box of noodles she'd been holding into her own shopping cart without a word. She turned around to leave the aisle after Rosario and Gabriella grabbed what they needed off the shelf.

"We should leave here. I don't like how they keep looking at us" Erika said quietly. She walked close to Gabriella with Rosario on the other side of her. Everyone was looking at them, and had even stopped what they were doing after realizing their presence in the store. Erika pushed her cart into a small checkout aisle, waiting for the cashier to ring up their purchases. The girl behind the register, seemingly seventeen years of age, stood there in silence as Erika loaded the food onto the counter beside them. The girl blew a few bubblegum bubbles with quick sounding pops as she stared at Erika. Her long hooped earrings slapped against her neck as she chewed loudly. Reluctantly, she began to ring up the food with a snide expression from behind her make-up covered face. Gabriella noticed the girl's reaction and narrowed her eyebrows at her. She very much disliked her disrespectful attitude toward them. Rosario looked around cautiously, feeling very uncomfortable in the quiet room. No one but them was moving. Literally every person in the store was standing there around them in a crowd. They resembled a forest of mannequins.

Waiting over by the exit doors, a man was lightly tossing a glass jar of pickles back and forth in his hands. His eyes were piercing and bright, and he never blinked.   Standing beside him was another man, slightly taller and holding long and heavy snow shovel with an eager tightened grip. A woman on the other side, held her hand on her hip as she clutched another pickle jar.   Rosario assumed these people either knew each other or were related.   Either way, they gave off an uncaring vibe from across the room.

      Rosario took Erika's hand and held it with a shaken grip.   After the checkout girl had rung up all the food and bagged it as her job intended, Gabriella quickly took as many bags as she could with Erika and Rosario's help.   Refusing to use the shopping cart for a faster leave, they left the building through one of the vacant exit doors. The Lincoln was thankfully parked nearby.   They threw the bags aimlessly into the back seat and quickly locked the doors after getting inside. Erika started the engine and a random car quickly stopped in front of them.   It was clearly preventing their escape, and the three women knew they were in danger now.   Coming to the store was a mistake.   The man in the car in front of them sat there with a determined stare.   He slowly shook his head "no" without moving his lips, as though to tell them they weren't allowed to leave.   Gabriella noticed another car drive up behind them, sidelong just as the one in the front.   Both vehicles were preventing any movement for the Lincoln.   With parked vehicles aligned beside them, the women had no way of escaping easily now.

"Oh god…"   Erika whispered to herself.   She was staring back over at the store's entrance.   The two men with the woman from before were looking over at them.   They still held the jars of pickles and the snow shovel.

"We have to get out of here!"   Rosario panicked.   "They're going to kill us!"

Gabriella was startled into a sudden scream when a loud crash of breaking glass slammed across the hood of the car.   The impact cracked the windshield as well, when the jar hit the car forcefully.   Rapid lines snaked their way through the glass, and Erika knew it wasn't going to hold together much longer.   She had to make a decision for them now.   Their lives were in danger, and these people weren't going to stop attacking them.

"Drive now!" Rosario shouted out. Erika put the car in reverse and stomped on the gas pedal. Quickly slamming into the car behind them, the slanted trunk crumpled as the collision came together. The man in the car behind them fell over in his seat as the driver's side window shattered onto his face from the impact. He never expected the women to panic and try such a desperate escape. The second glass jar had better aim, as it shattered through the rear passenger window on Rosario's side. The maid luckily ducked her head down far enough to avoid most of the flying pieces of glass that surrounded her. The man with the shovel was near them now, and wasted no time in giving a heavy swing into Gabriella's door. Her screams were almost deafening through her fear as she held tightly to Erika's body for protection. With every swing the man took, he became more accurate in breaking the window, and denting the door severely. The man was raged in his desire to get to her. Erika's tears fell over her face as she switched the Lincoln's gear again. The car advanced forward quickly.   This time she veered the hood to the side as it slammed into the car ahead of her.   She pushed it out of the way, scraping the parked cars beside her with screeching metal and sparks.   The Lincoln's powerful engine had torn them through the blockage to safety, and out onto the street.   Gabriella held her arm in pain as a flow of blood leaked out through her fingers.   She'd been cut in several places from the protruding broken glass of her window when they were attacked.   Erika soon sped down the street nearing over seventy to eighty miles per hour, dodging traffic flow, without even thinking to break anytime soon.   Her only thought was to get away.   Her initial thought was to go home, but not they needed the hospital.   Erika only even began to slow down when the parking area was in plain view.   She couldn't say anything, and nor could she think and focus her thoughts properly.   She left the car's engine running after stopping by the hospital's emergency entrance.   She ran inside with Gabriella and Rosario.   To their relief, the people inside would be much more humane, and quickly aided to their injuries.

After hearing about what happened to his wife, his sister, and the maid, Victor soon drove his Mercedes over to the hospital to meet them from his workplace. He'd left the classroom without thinking twice, and after seeing the condition of his Lincoln sitting in the parking lot, his worries only worsened. He ran into the hospital, pushing a few people out of the way and demanded to know where his wife and sister were.

Gabriella received over twenty stitches in her arm, and had bandages on her cheek when Victor rushed in. Erika and Rosario had only some minor cuts and bruises, but the doctor told them they would all be fine. Erika was still very shaken, and quickly ran into her husband's embrace. He cried at the sight of them. He hated how ruthless those other human beings had been to his family. How could they do this to them? Just because they were different...and all because of their daughter and her cousin. Suddenly normal life turned out to be a challenge, and Victor wouldn't accept that. They didn't need to fight for their right to live. The police had already been called by his sister, and several policeman were all standing in the recovery room for their protection.

Later that night, Victor made the necessary arrangements to have a high security system installed around the mansion's grounds. He had the men install it the same night, refusing to wait for service to come the next day. He paid them double for their work and made sure they installed it properly. The tall iron fencing the adored the mansion's outer limits was now set up with an electrical shock device, that would kill anyone who attempted to enter without authorization. The main gate of the manor had always been guarded before, and it would remain that way. Under twenty-four hour surveillance. Victor's guards would walk their trained canine companions around the outer grounds and iron fence every half-hour to an hour in shifts. He told them if they were to catch any perpetrators, to let him know about it, so that he could deal with the matter in his own personal way. His anger was enraged at the town he lived in, soon developing his own hatred for the residents that surrounded them.   His family should not have to live in fear, just because of other's ignorance.   He would make sure of this, with every power at his disposal.   Being one of high wealth on his side, he was capable of many things, including his own telekinetic power that coursed through his veins. She may be well stronger than him, but he would still use his ability to his advantage.   After all, she got it from him.   He fantasized about snapping the necks of the people who attacked his family, and the thought was all too relishing.   Of course, knew it was wrong to think of murder…but at this moment it felt like the best solution.   If someone approached them again with hostile intentions, he would do away with them.   Simple as that.

After staying inside the mansion for a week and grieving over the loss of her lover, Sabrina was feeling the need to get out for a walk.   She too, was quite angry at the fact that her family was attacked, even though they didn't pay much attention to her.   She knew about the rumors, and she knew that many people feared her as well as hated her.   She was not afraid.   They had no real threat to her.   She would leave the house if she so pleased, and would go wherever she wanted.   She was not afraid of some meaningless people that may attempt to kill her.   She could easily protect herself.   If anyone would make any advancement, she would give them a reason to never do it again.

"Be careful out there tonight, Miss LaMore. You father will be worried about you."   one of the guards said to her, standing in the control booth beside the gate.   Sabrina paid no mind to the guard, and walked out of the gate's entrance with Clementine in arms.   It was nearing two in the morning, and settling fog was covering the area now.   It blanketed the streets and lawns in delicate fashion.   An distant owl hooted calmly in the darkness of the wood.

Walking down the center of the silent road, Sabrina stared her gazing green eyes ahead of her as she recalled her constant various thoughts.   It was a cooled night, but she felt warm.   The cold never bothered her really.   It was Eleanor that despised it.   Sabrina was dressed in a long black gown that made her skin glow palely in the moonlight.   Her heeled shoes tapped gently as she walked on the pavement below her.   It was the only sound in the night air.   The darkness felt so calm and collected, like an old friend greeting her after a long separation.   She was in no hurry, and her pace was slow and natural.   Her long black hair swayed a bit as she strolled through the fog, and she could hear the owl off in the distance. This night reminded her of those nights in old horror films, during the month of October. Though she wasn't bothered by it, and she found it to be relaxing.   She took in a deep breath as she stopped.   Standing in the middle of the street, she looked up to the sky above her at the stars.   Most of it was covered in by the fog, but her vision was a perfect 20/20.   She could faintly make out the celestial bodies, as they tried their hardest to gleam through the clouds.   The world was lost in a taciturn sleep, and only she was there.   A lone human standing in the middle of nowhere it seemed, making her own existence on the planet that everyone inhabited.   She missed Hanako so dearly, and wanted so much to share this moment with her...but couldn't.   She read about Heaven and Hell in old books, and wondered if they both truly existed in the realm of the afterlife.   She was a very open minded person, and believed there must be something more...to just one life.   It seemed too pointless to her...to only live once...and never exist again.   Sabrina's thoughts about her own death sometime in the far future would come to her now and then, wondering about how it would be.   As long as she could be with Hanako again...it did not matter when or where.   She would die for her...even just to see her again.   She knew Hanako would want her to live on, and it was true that Sabrina could easily destroy herself in many ways if she wanted. Despite the thought of suicide, she was going to respect Hanako's choice and live on until a natural death succumbed her.

    Shortly in the distance, Sabrina heard the sound of a car's engine coming toward her in the fog covering.   She could see the light of its headlamps glowing through the darkness as it approached her.   From what she could hear, the car wasn't driving very fast.   Probably due to the fog layer and the driver was being cautious on this late hour.   Sabrina stepped herself off to the side of the road as the car came near, allowing it room to pass.   To her surprise, it slowly came to a halt beside her.   Inside, the driver had recognized who she was.   He stepped out of the car slowly, and with a turn of his head, he looked back at the silent girl with a small smirk.   Sabrina knew who he was, and she didn't like him.   The young adult boy walked around his car and to the backend, with his hands in his jean's pockets as he looked at her.

"Well…this is a surprise.   Tell me girl…what are you doing out so late?   And all by yourself…"   the boy said.   Sabrina stared right back at Bryson Blackwell with narrowed eyes of hate, only to respond with her doll.

"Sabrina is simply walking.   She would like you to leave now, Bryson" Clementine said lightly. Bryson gave a smug little chuckle, and walked closer to her.

"And what if Bryson *doesn't* want to leave?" he asked, referring to himself in third person.

Sabrina raised an eyebrow as the boy's sheer foolish determination to bother her.

"Sabrina has given a fair warning. Leave now, before you make her upset" Clementine suggested. Her delicate voice drifted in the night air clearly, breaking the silence between them. Bryson watched the fog around them begin to drift in circles near Sabrina's body as the wind current followed her command. The air was motionless in the area except for moving around their bodies. Bryson's smug grin and demeanor had disgusted Sabrina and she didn't want him near her. She had hated him the day she met him, and for what he did to Eleanor. Sabrina wasn't a person to just let anything slide easily. He was like an insect to her, and she would squash him if bugged.
"Ya know, Sabrina...the whole town knows about you...and your powers. It's only a matter of time before they catch you" Bryson said to her. Sabrina's eyes stared into Bryson's almost blankly, and with a confident gesture.

"The others are weak. Lost souls, trapped in their own world of close-minded right and wrongdoing" Sabrina said to him with low tone.

Her calmed, yet dark voice edged into Bryson's ears and he felt the need to retaliate. He came up to her face, looking deep and closely, and Sabrina stood her ground. Her dominance was clear in this situation.

"It's too bad you're a lesbian. That Asian slut couldn't satisfy you like I can....Hanako is dead now. Get over it already" he whispered to her. His voice was menacing...and Sabrina felt the hate enraged inside of herself. How *dare* this boy speak in such a manner of Hanako. He clearly had no clue who he was dealing with...but she was about show him.

With one turn of her eyes, Bryson flew backwards with immense speed, slamming against the backend of his car as his spine cracked in half within his back. He flipped over his car quickly, hitting the rear window as it broke, and landed on the ground in front of the headlights. His body made two short bounces on the asphalt before stopping completely. His eyes were wide open in the fear. He felt the intense pain coursing through his body like knives ripping through his muscles. His gasps for breath were severe as he lay on the ground, motionless and staring to the side at his car's front-end.   It happened so fast, he didn't even have time to think, much less yell for help.   He couldn't move his legs to get up, and his arms barely slid on the road when he tried to move them.   He felt a river of his blood leak out of his mouth as he felt helpless and ignored.   Sabrina walked up to him with glare of her eyes, standing over his body.

"You will now lay here…in a night filled with pain…to know what I feel…every day of my life."   Her words were strong, even though she spoke above a whisper.   She made it clear that he would never be the same again.   Bryson's tears filled his eyes from the immense pain that cut inside his body as he watched Sabrina walk away from him.   She was leaving him there to die alone.   His vision became blurry until finally blacking out in the night around him.   Sabrina's voice floated in his mind like a haunting memory even after falling unconscious.

Chapter Twenty-Five

Enemies

    The next day, many residents of Warren were stunned to see the news report of Bryson Blackwell's condition.   The boy who'd been left to die on a lone street, had been found the next morning and taken to the hospital for immediate care.   Many of the doctors were amazed at how he survived such terrible wounds to his body, and much internal bleeding.   He'd been paralyzed from the waist down, in courtesy of Sabrina

LaMore.   She made sure he would never be able to walk, or move any part of his lower half ever again.   This included making any future offspring or sexual performances.   Sabrina left him alive for only once purpose…to live the rest of his life in pain and grief, just as she would have to do the same.   Both of his arms were broken in four to five places, and wouldn't been healed for several months.   Even after then, he would have to take physical therapy in order to use them properly again.   His neck had been twisted to the side, but not completely broken.   For all accounts, the young Bryson Blackwell was now a disfigured being, who would spend most of his life laying in hospital beds with needles laced into his veins.   He could not speak.   His vocal cords were broken beyond repair.   When people would question him about who had caused his condition, and ask if it was Sabrina, he would merely cry at the sound of her name.   The people knew it was her, and they wanted her dead.   Bryson's parents intended to sue Victor and Erika for Sabrina's actions, but there was no way to prove she even touched him; and for all final accounts on the matter…she hadn't.

    The only person, who knew for sure that Sabrina wounded Bryson, was Eleanor.   After arriving back home that night, Sabrina told Eleanor everything that happened between her and the boy.   Eleanor was furious over what Bryson said to her cousin, and was determined to get back at him even after Sabrina already did. She didn't tell her cousin this though…she simply planned it in her own mind.   She gave comfort to Sabrina, and after making sure she was calmed again, Eleanor set out on her mission as planned.

    Staring out at the large and grayed façade of LaMore Manor, Roberta Stein sat in her car in profound thoughts.   She stared at the mansion through her Mercury's windshield, wondering about Sabrina and Eleanor.   About how she would approach them…and how they would be stopped.   She'd parked her small white convertible down the street from the mansion and watched it most of the day.   She felt the need to focus on their lives since the time of first meeting them.   After all, they were indeed such rare beings to hold the power that enveloped their minds.   After opening her window half way, she pushed in the small lighter in her car and waited for it to warm up.   She lit her cigarette and began to smoke as she watched Eleanor leave the mansion's front gate.   The girl dressed all in black and wearing her favorite hat to match, walked down the street in the direction toward the town. Roberta started her engine and turned down one of the side streets so that she could follow from a short distance.   The blonde girl didn't notice the white car as it followed her slowly all the way to the hospital.   Roberta was puzzled to see her come here.   After parking her car, she suddenly remembered about the story of Sabrina paralyzing Bryson Blackwell the night before.   She figured that Eleanor was there to see him, possibly due to the fact they used to date.

  She followed Eleanor into the hospital and waited for her to go to Bryson's room as a visitor. Eleanor's face held a look of determination, and also anger as she went down the hall.   After arriving to Bryson's room, she peered through the window of the door at the wounded boy lying in the bed. Eleanor was standing at the foot of his bed, staring at him while clutching a tight hold on the bed rail with her hands. Bryson slowly opened his eyes, seeing the blonde girl standing in front of him with a glare. He couldn't move, due to his condition, and felt his heart beat accelerate at the sight of her. Eleanor tilted her head slowly, letting her radiant blue eyes reflect the light of the room over their surface.

"Rise and shine" she said to him, her voice emitting a ghastly feel. She did not smile, or make an attempt to move. She only stared…a long gaze to his face and making him feel the discomfort of not knowing what she would do. He widened his eyes slightly, trying to speak, but his quiet words only came out as murmured tones of sound from his lips. He reached for his "call help" button, but Eleanor simply raised her hand to show she'd been holding it. "Looking for this? I thought you might try that" she voiced, tossing the small controller to the floor. She soon began to walk slowly around the bed, toward Bryson's side while watching him. "Bryson…we need to talk" she began. "You see…Sabrina is my family. Her well being means everything to me. And so I'm determined to protect her…just like she does for me."

Bryson started to panic as Eleanor came closer. He could feel the heat of the room rising fast, and the energy waves floating toward him from her body. Her hair softly moved in floatation, as though a wind stream was blowing indoors. He forced his words from his mouth in a dry speech as his tears rolled down his cheeks.

"Don't….h-hurt…me…" he said to her. Eleanor stopped for a moment, and slowly placed a smile to her lips. Snapping her fingers, a bright hot flame formed quickly in her hand, with the second soon to follow. She raised her hands up in a slow motion, letting her smile fade into a plastered glare of abhorrence. A solid whisper drifted toward Bryson's ears as he stared back at her, not finding the courage to look away.

"I believe the world is burning to the ground…we are a violent species." Her eyes gleamed liked ice as their gaze held a piercing effect. "Bryson…your fear excites me…"

The walls of the room ignited into bursts of flames as Eleanor held in a deep breath. Her burning hands grew in strength, sending blasts of heat onto Bryson's body, quickly charring the blankets over his skin, and melting into his flesh. The room was like an oven, as objects were melting into false liquid-like shapes, and the bed collapsed to the floor. Eleanor let out her breath again, releasing an energy force that consumed the entire room in a blaze of light. Bryson screamed at the pain of his body burning alive, and melting into the remains of the hospital bed as Roberta Stein stared in horror. She quickly backed away from the door of the room, falling to the floor as she tried to run. The smoke from the flames flowed out from the crack below the door, soon followed by the searing fire escaping into the hallway. Roberta ran down the hall, bumping into people right and left, shouting out in warning of the fire that was quickly taking over the building.

Bryson's window of his hospital room shattered violently as the glass fell to the ground below.   People now knew of the situation, and were rushing around in attempt to save the other patients of the building.   Eleanor stood within her blaze, feeling at ease as she tilted her head back slowly.   She closed her eyes and let the feeling of the heat surround her.   It felt so good to her...all the power and energy force in a constant flow inside her veins.   The flames cradled around her body, making her warm in the immense heat of room.   Bryson's body was now scorched completely, showing no sign of life within it.   The very shape and outline of his physique was destroyed and deformed permanently.   His skeletal structure was melting into the bed where he once slept.   The fire made her feel alive.   It put her mind at ease, like she'd just had sex after a long absence from pleasure.   This was her world...to exist within the flames.   She was a part of them, and they would never hurt her.   She was like a goddess...showing the world what she could do, and nothing would ever to stop her.   It had been a while since the last time she let her energy lose.   It felt like an erotic dream.   Relaxing her body in a deep slumber of refreshment, and restoring her mind to clarity. She needed this…needed to feel alive again. She smiled to herself at the thought of her power and ability to create such beauty of flames, regardless of the lives she claimed with them. The world viewed her as a destroyer of humanity…but the light of her soul could make an art. Fire was beautiful to her, and nothing would ever change her mind.

After escaping to her safety from the burning hospital, Roberta gazed at the inferno while the firefighters rushed in attempt to stop it. She let a few tears fall from her eyes, seeing Eleanor leave the building completely untouched.
"You won't put it out" she said quietly to herself, staring at the men with water hoses in rescue. "She wants it to burn…she won't let you save it." They couldn't hear the woman's words, but that didn't matter now. The incident was already out of control after Eleanor left her mark. She had succeeded on what she came to there to do.
Roberta watched explosions bursting from the building. They sent thousands of debris

particles flying through the air. Several of the firemen were thrown backward from the blast, and killed instantly. Roberta covered her mouth and eyes, feeling the need to turn away from the terrible scene unfolding. Any remaining survivors of the building were now dead, and Eleanor calmly walked away from destruction. Roberta opened the door of her car and spoke to herself again.

"Someone has to stop them...and it might as well be me."

Chapter Twenty-Six

A New Form of Travel

It was no doubt that as Sabrina and Eleanor aged with time in their lives, their minds would do the same. Becoming wiser and gaining strength and ability of power. Eleanor's pyrokinetic mind wasn't like Sabrina's. It was true, her ability had grown since early teenage years, but Eleanor's was stable. It did not grow into something else, or branch out into different "powers".   Sabrina's mind had been unstable due to her telekinetic energy growing in strength as she matured. Potentially limitless power wasn't out of the question, as her mind found newer ways to capture and manipulate other forms of energies around Sabrina's body.   This included the creation and control of weather patterns, by use of Atmokinesis.   Her ability to enter someone's mind, and fabricate illusory states, and also her ability to generate land based earthquakes due to Terrakinesis.   Often called "Geokinesis".

    Paranormal abilities have been present within the minds of humans since the dawn of our species, and even after years of study, we still don't know about them clearly.   Perhaps we are not meant to know.   Maybe the depths of the brain are hidden for a reason, and we've only discovered paranormal power by mere accident. Whichever the cause, mankind has always been curious about everything that surrounds them, and especially about our bodies that we inhabit with a soul.   No one is ever truly in a position to say how exactly something is or works completely. For everything with the unknown, and life itself, is all best guess.   Many will claim to know it all, showing off their "evidence" to prove their point of study.   However, when it really all comes down to it, they have no clue how something will all turn out in the end.   We humans seek to understand about what we do not know.   When something seems to be impossible, we want to *make* it into possible.   Nearly all forms of energy are found within the brain.   So it is not out of the question to say that our minds are able to harness those particular forms of energy around us. Giving us the ability to manipulate them according to our will, or control how it reacts to our surroundings.   Until you have entire proof, or have discovered everything completely from the unknown, and how it works right down to the very last form of fact; you cannot say it doesn't exist.

     Sabrina continued to mourn over Hanako's death for several weeks after the event.   The emotional stress from her loss began to cause her brain to develop once again, she felt something new happening with her body. Not only did she experience random headaches, but she could feel her body's weight shift around. Sometimes becoming lighter in mass of density. The reason for this was unexplained, and at first guess, she thought the headaches were from mental depression. Tension of her body's muscles would easily form a migraine, but this didn't feel normal to her. They felt like the first day her telekinetic ability took effect, even though the pain didn't seem to last long. It came in waves. Random flows of pain from her mind shivered down through her body, and then would dissipate. Eleanor had gone through a similar experience with her own ability years ago. After Sabrina mentioned the situation to her, she offered her support. It wasn't easy for people like them, especially when Sabrina's mind would take on a new "stage" or develop. The headaches were becoming typical...but the weightless feeling was not.

      Standing in the center of the hallway that

lead to her bedroom, Sabrina held Clementine closely as she felt her body seem to float.   Her feet were flat against the floor, although she felt like a feather aloft in the air around her.   With her breathing beginning to quicken, her heart beats accelerated and she had only one thought for the moment.   She must get to her bed for rest.   She felt nauseated, and held her stomach lightly as she closed her eyes.   With a sudden jolt of her body, she felt the air around her move like a fast breeze.   When she opened her eyes, she found herself standing in her bedroom with her bed positioned right beside her.   Sabrina's eyes widened in surprise, for she had no clue how she got there so quickly.   The nauseous feeling took over and she immediately threw up her breakfast food on the floor.   Her stomach felt terrible from the rapid trip from the hallway to her room.   She now realized what she had done.   She read about it before from a book on paranormal studies.   Sabrina's mind learned to teleport…and this had been her first jaunt.   She dropped Clementine on the bed and fell on the blankets.   The room was spinning and her vision seemed distorted, but after a few minutes the nauseous feeling wore off. She breathed slow and deep, calming herself before sitting up again.

"This is something I'll have to control" she said to herself. Staring at the undigested food on the floor, Sabrina turned her head away in disgust. She reached for her bedside telephone, and pushed the intercom button in request for Rosario's presence. After another few minutes, the stout maid knocked on the girl's doors and entered the room.

"Yes, Miss LaMore? Is there something you need from me?" she asked her. Sabrina nodded once, and pointed to the floor quietly. Rosario seen how Sabrina had been ill, and spoke again. "Right away ma'am, I'll clean it up for you soon."

Sabrina fell back against her pillows again, letting herself drift off into deep thought about what just happened. She remembered how she wanted so badly to go to her room and rest when feeling sick, and ended up transporting there by mere thought. She figured that was probably how this new ability worked. She also realized, that if she were to mastering it, she then could very well use it to her advantage in many ways. She would be able literally teleport herself to anywhere she pleased, as long as she thought clearly in her mind of where she wanted to go. She knew it couldn't be a place she never been to before, for she could easily end up teleporting inside a wall or solid object.   Thereby possibly killing herself.   This would have to be done very carefully.   Like her prior abilities of her mind, she accepted this willingly.   Sabrina knew she was becoming stronger every day, and she accepted who she was.   The energy flowing through her body was always good to her.   How she used it however, would determine her fate entirely.

      Later that evening, Eleanor sat in her quiet dark room, reviewing her studies on her laptop computer.   She liked the peace and silence of the large mansion and how she could escape the world.   It was something she and Sabrina shared in common.   She always kept her laptop on her bed when using it, and this was mostly in the evenings.   Several black candles in her room surrounded her with small dancing flames of dimming light.   They were lit to make her feel more comfortable and warm.   This was how she liked it.   Her body craved heat more than the average person, due to her brain being able to create it.   She rarely even used the electric bulbs of the lamps that were given to her for her bedroom.   With her natural ability of fire, she was more comfortable using it for light, rather than modern electricity.   Even her closet held several candles for when the others melted down over time.   She would also light her bedroom fireplace during the summer months, much to Gabriella's disagreement.   Her mother still would try and enforce her own opinions on the girl, regardless of Eleanor's capabilities.   She insisted the fireplace would make the home too hot, even though Eleanor's room was just one of many in the mansion.   Victor dismissed it, saying one fireplace would cause the whole place to burn down.   Eleanor would stop it before that happened.   Victor told his niece that he wanted her to be comfortable, but she knew his real thought was not wanting to cause any drama within the household.

On this quiet night, Eleanor was quickly surprised as her cousin appeared in front of her without warning.   She calmly stood at the end of her bed with Clementine in her grasp.   Eleanor gasped and fell back slightly as she stared at her. It wasn't the fact it was Sabrina, but rather how she entered her room without coming through the doorway.   It happened so fast, that she barely had time to react to her.   Sabrina noticed her cousin's reaction, and raised an eyebrow as though this incident was common.

"Good evening, Eleanor"   Clementine said gently.   Sabrina's doll viewed the blonde girl with her one eye staring ahead from under the hat. Eleanor caught her breath and smiled nervously.

"H-How'd you…do that?…"   she asked her, referring to Sabrina's sudden entrance.   "Did you just teleport?"

Sabrina, herself, gave a slight smirk, and then let it fade quickly with her vacant mind.

"I learned"   her uncanny voice emitted. Eleanor blinked a few times and sat up forward again, closing her laptop computer.   She opened her mouth to speak, but didn't know what to say. This was amazing to her. Never in her life, did she ever expect to witness a teleporting person. She then shrugged her shoulders, admitting to herself that she should've known not to put it past Sabrina on learning new abilities with a growing mind. She leaned toward Sabrina slowly, and whispered to her face with a fixed stare.

"Do you realize what you're capable of?" she asked her. "Your mind amazes me."

Sabrina said nothing, but simply nodded her head in a slow response. Eleanor's grin widened a bit, and she held her arms around the other girl in a gentle embrace. "I'm really proud of you, Sabrina" she murmured again giving her support. "We will show this world that we won't be taken lightly." The room fell silent as Sabrina took in the heat from every candle in the room around her. She absorbed the energy of each flame as they softly dwindled into tiny cinders, and dying out with a floating trails of smoke into the air. The darkness settled in on the girls, blacking out the light as Sabrina's voice drifted in the shadows.

"Yes, Eleanor…we will."

Chapter Twenty-Seven

Criminal Minds

When living in small cities or towns, news travels like fire burning gasoline.   With the events of Warren in the last few months, Roberta Stein knew it would be difficult to mention the names of Sabrina and Eleanor in public settings.   Being a professional in her fields of work, both Parapsychology and Psychology, she felt she had a responsibility to do something about that matter concerning the two girls.   She was not alone either. Since the time of Sabrina's attack on the public high school on the day of Hanako's death, David Castle had decided to help Dr. Stein. However, he was unclear on just what exactly they would have to do. He'd been meeting with Roberta a few times a week, since the times of the attacks on the town, as they would always need to meet in new places to discuss their plans. It was becoming more difficult each time, needing to meet where there weren't many people around to hear them. Roberta's choice of location this time around was a somewhat isolated pavilion located in Betts Park, just south of Warren's downtown area beside the river. The location of the park had once been a small airport, back when the town was more populous and a location of much travel. Since the removal of the airport, Betts Park would further be a location for recreational activities and the Betts Park Fair that came every year during Independence Day for a week.

   While sitting in her small Mercury convertible, Roberta watched a bulky luxury sedan drove toward the spacious parking lot near the pavilion area where she'd been waiting.   It was a typical clouded day on this late afternoon in Warren, and not many people were in the park at this time.   Roberta and David would be able to talk freely about anything, without being interrupted or overheard.   The silver colored Buick Roadmaster slowly drifted down the pavement, before finally parking itself in one of the spaces beside Roberta's car.   The driver's door opened and David Castle stepped out, holding a serious look over his dark toned face.   He looked as though he wasn't very pleased to be there in this moment, but came to meet up with her regardless.   Roberta put out her cigarette with a small smile, and exited her own vehicle as well.

  "I'm glad you came"   she said to him, as he walked up to her.   For a brief moment, David said nothing as he stood in front of the younger woman and folded his arms quietly.

  "You better have a good reason for wanting to meet all the way out here"   he told her.   Roberta nodded and started walking toward the pavilion in a short distance behind them.   There was no direct path with a grassy field and several trees nearby.

"Its peaceful here" she said, and stopped to look at David again. "We won't be interrupted, and besides, the whole town wants to kill Sabrina and her cousin. Just think of what they would do if we mention their names, and realize we have information on them." Roberta then walked over to the pavilion and sat down at one of the picnic tables inside. David sat across from her, placing his hands on the table in front of him and locked his fingers together in an attempt to look relaxed.

"So, what do you propose we do about them?" he asked her. Roberta looked back and forth, making sure no one was around to hear them and then leaned forward slightly, speaking with a mild whisper.

"We kill them off" she replied. "They've already caused too much death and destruction here." Her eyes were stern as she stared to David's face across from her. Her lips slightly trembling as she spoke, showing her nervous tension. David leaned back in surprise, raising his brows and staring at the woman with an appalled expression.

"Are you out of your mind? You're talking about killing two young girls...what the hell has come over you..."

"Two dangerous girls" Roberta interrupted, confronting David's seriousness. Her eyes held determination as he took in a deep breath. After thinking for a minute, he relaxed his face.

"How would you do this?" he asked again, showing some interest. Roberta smiled and leaned closer, deepening her whisper.

"Sabrina's in a state of mourning. She never leaves the mansion. Her cousin, Eleanor, often goes on walks because of her need to feel active. Sabrina is the same way, but since Hanako's murder, she hasn't been doing much of anything" she explained. David stroked the side of his head as he listened, holding uncertain thoughts in his mind of the situation.

"Where are you going with this?" he asked. Roberta sighed for a moment, but continued.

"With Sabrina being at the house, we could capture her cousin. Eleanor doesn't have telepathic ability like Sabrina does. She wouldn't sense our attack. The two girls protect each other, and with Eleanor being away from the house, she would be vulnerable to a certain degree" she explained again. David looked at the woman with curiosity and disbelief.

"There are many flaws in this. You do realize that...don't you? The blonde girl is able to make fires with her mind. Even if you wanted to "capture" her, the odds are against you" he told her. He sounded like a wise old man correcting a stubborn young child. Roberta's anger and impatience started to grow as she laughed a bit, and turned her head to the side.

"Eleanor is capable of burning down this entire town by her own will" she turned back to him again, raising her voice. "Do you want to burn to death, or finally rid this fucking problem at hand?! I need to know if you're with me on this...you're the only one who will listen to me."

Staring at the woman, the older man gave a look of disgust, despite being mildly interesting in her plan.

"You're obsessed aren't you? You've

thought about them so much, that they're all you can think about now.   Stopping them for good, as though nothing else matters to you"   he said to her.   "Have you even considered what would happen if Sabrina found out you kidnapped her cousin?   There would be nothing left of you."

Roberta rolled her eyes and stood up quickly, slamming her hands down on the table stressfully.

"Ya know what?   Fuck off then if you're not going to help me.   I'll stop them myself, since no one in this damn town seems to have the balls to do it but me"   she retorted.   Walking toward her car, she began to rant and David soon followed.   He grabbed her arm, stopping her from moving, and yelled back at her in his own anger.

"Now wait just a minute!   You can't just go off and act like some sort of *hero*, just because you know things that others don't!   This is a no win situation, and you know it."

Roberta yanked herself from David's harsh grip, and turned to face him straight on.

"At least I'm willing to do something about it!   You're all too afraid…every one of you.   I may be scared of what they can do, but I'm certainly not afraid to stand up for what's right in this world.   They must be stopped, and if you're with me, then help me.   If you're not, then stay out of my way."

After hearing the woman's words, David turned away and placed his hands over his head in deep thought to concentrate his mind.   This woman was stressing him to no end, and he was quickly getting tired of it.   Roberta slowly walked up to him again, speaking quietly behind his shoulder in a calmer tone.   "I can't do this without you, David.   I need someone who's willing to help me stop them"   she said.   David's sigh escaped his lips without opening his mouth. He knew it wasn't right to just kill the two girls because of the powers they wielded, and yet he also wanted them gone.   Everyone in town wanted their lives to return to normal again. Letting his arms fall from his head, he turned to face Roberta after a long pause of silence.

"No one is to know about this…ever.   As far as everyone is concerned, I never agreed to this.   If we're caught, then I never helped you.

We don't even know each other.   Agreed?"   he proposed while staring deep into her eyes. Roberta smiled again with a look of confidence and acceptance of David's will to help her.
"Agreed.   No one will ever know.   I promise that for us."

David nodded to her and swallowed hard as began walking toward his car.
"It will have to be done quickly and quietly. We cannot draw attention to ourselves, or to the situation.   If we do this…and take Eleanor away…no one can see it happen."   he said to her. He opened the door of his car, looking over at the woman across from him as she stood beside her convertible.
"Nobody will" Roberta added.   "There is only one way to do this, and I've already made the necessary arrangements for what we need.   Meet me at my place tomorrow morning around nine."
After nodding in agreement with Roberta, David soon started his car's engine and left the large parking lot.   Roberta sat for a minute in her car, thinking over the situation as it was planned.

She knew this would be dangerous, and she knew both her and David's lives were at stake. Although, so were the lives of everyone else that lived in Warren.   She held tight to the steering wheel in front of her, clutching the rubber as a few tears streamed down her cheeks.   She felt the tension creep throughout her body.   She wanted everyone to be safe again, and wanted the girls gone from their lives; and most of all…she wanted to live through this experience in which there was no turning back from.   Her determination and hopes would help see her through this…no matter what the outcome may be.   It was time she took a stand against them, even if it meant her last chance.

Chapter Twenty-Eight

Criminal Intent

    The sun of the early morn shown dimly over the hills of the forest that surrounded the town of Warren.   It was nearing nine o'clock am, and already the residents of the area were getting ready for their day ahead of them.   Roberta had been awake since the rise of dawn, and was staring at the sunlight from her living room window as the curtains draped on both sides of her body loosely. She hadn't blinked in well over a minute as she stared at the natural light peering through the trees in the distance. She'd been thinking about her life, and everything she had done up to this point. All the people she'd met, and places she'd gone to after her years of college. It seemed her whole life was coming back to her now after making this decision to stand up against two very powerful people. Lives would clash on this day...she could feel it. In her hands, she held tight to a small photograph of herself, standing beside a man she once knew. It had been some years ago, after college graduation, and her mother had taken the picture. The man that stood beside her was her former lover, long since deceased. Over time, after his death due to an illness, Roberta had grown bitter to her life. She indulged herself in her work to drown out her thoughts of sadness and being alone. Before meeting Sabrina and Eleanor, she had searched for something of real importance in her life. Something she could accomplish in her belief that it was the right thing to do. Now, after taking on the responsibility to put an end to the suffering of people in the town she lived in, she made it her mission to stop the girls from harming others.   Completely disregarding the facts of Sabrina and Eleanor's own tragic lives.   Their powerful abilities were fascinating to her, and yet she believed they should be stopped.

    David Castle parked his Buick in front of Roberta's house right on schedule.   After ringing her doorbell, she opened the front door without speaking, only simply gesturing for the man to enter her home quickly.   David stood in the middle of the room and observed the surroundings.   He quickly noticed a few wooden crates sitting on the floor in front of the sofa. Seeing how they were already previously opened, most likely by Roberta, he wondered what was inside them.   They appeared to be very deep boxes, and looked like they'd been delivered from a military warehouse.
    "You weren't followed here, were you?" Roberta spoke up.   David looked up at her and shook his head."
    "No, I wasn't.   What's in the boxes?"   he asked her.   Roberta knelt down in front of the

boxes without moving her eyes from her guest.

"What's in the crates, is why I wanted you to come here first.   To prepare" she said, lifting off each lid and tossing them aside.   "You told me you had some background in handling guns, right?"

David widened his eyes slightly at the mention of weaponry, and answered the woman with a slow tone.   He was starting to catch onto what she was planning.

"Well…yes, but not for several years now" he answered.   "I was in my twenties the last time I fired a gun."

Roberta took out a long and heavy metal object that reflected the morning light on it's shiny body, and handed it off to him.   She rummaged through the second box for the added accessories and parts that went along with it.   David was speechless at the sight of the tranquilizer gun that laid in his hands now.   Roberta stood up slowly, and held the darts and silencer piece for the gun.

"Where'd you get this?…"   he asked her, not even looking up from his hands at this point. She answered with a vague response, and handed him the silencer.

"I have connections, David." She left the darts sitting on the coffee table as she walked toward the door. "Load it up while I go get the car ready. We're using yours, since mine is too small."

Eleanor calmly walked toward the front doors of the mansion, and soon felt a gentle touch to her shoulder. She turned around to find her mother there. Gabriella stood behind her in stillness, and the girl she gave a sigh at the sight of her. The woman flinched, but forced herself to speak after gathering the courage.

"Going out?" she asked her. Eleanor said nothing and made a slow nod in reply. Gabriella eyes drifted away as she held tight to her purse that she previously was holding. Feeling impatient, she wondered why her mother was stopping her from leaving.

"What do you want?" she asked. Gabriella looked at her daughter again, and forced more conversation.

"Would you mind...if I went with you? I would feel better if I did...and besides, I haven't left the house for a little while either" she proposed. At first thought, Eleanor was reluctant to let her mother go with her, but then felt it wouldn't really matter. Even though Gabriella was fearful of her daughter's fire starting ability, Eleanor still cared about her to a certain degree. It was most other people in the world that she felt little compassion for, since they'd always avoided and disregarded her emotions in the past.

"Alright then" she answered, and then opened the doors to leave. Gabriella was surprised at her daughter's reply, and soon followed from behind in a subtle fashion. Eleanor placed her large black hat over head and let her golden hair drape down over her shoulders. She took in a long breath of the morning air to refresh her lungs, and assumed her mother was following without looking. It was a long path down the front driveway of LaMore Manor to the gate. The home was positioned far from the street privately, and with recent events, this protected everyone inside. The sun was brighter upon reaching the sidewalk in the neighborhood they lived in.   Its warmth was gathering, and Eleanor closed her eyes from the delicate feeling. Unicorn Acres was mostly quite serene, since many of its residents had long since moved out. Knowing Sabrina and Eleanor lived nearby had made them flee.   Some of them, however, stayed in their homes, believing the rumors of the two girls had to be fantastic lies.   Although, how one could come to this conclusion with all the recent news was rather surprising.   Some people just don't believe until they see it with their own eyes.

      They reached the long stretch of road that lead toward the town, and Eleanor looked up at the bluish sky though the leaves of the trees.   The weather was warming up now, and calmed, since Sabrina was at home asleep.   No storms plagued the area until she woke up again.   It was always a sure sign.

      Scattered cumulous clouds floated high above them in the sky, as the spring winds blew gently through the air around them.   It was the middle of May now, and the end of equinox was nearing with summer not far behind.   A time of transition into warmer weather for the northern states.

"My, it certainly is a beautiful day" Gabriella observed, breaking the silence between her and her daughter.   Eleanor turned her head a bit, watching her mother walking behind her but not turning completely.

"Yes, it is"   she replied.   Her voice was distant in feeling, but loud enough for her mother to hear her.   As she stared down the long sidewalk ahead of her, she started to get a feeling deep inside herself.   She wasn't sure what it was, but she felt as though something wasn't right. Like something was about to happen and it wasn't necessarily a positive thing.   She stopped abruptly with Gabriella bumping into her from behind.

"What's wrong, Eleanor?"   she asked her daughter, confused by her sudden change. Eleanor stood in the middle of the sidewalk, shifting her eyes back and forth.   Viewing her surroundings in a paranoid way.

"I'm not sure…something's not right."   she answered.

In a short distance down the sidewalk and hidden behind a large shrubbery bush, was David Castle.   Previously, he and Roberta had chosen this spot for their eager attempt to attack Eleanor. They knew she'd be walking this way, for it was the only exit out of the Unicorn Acres neighborhood.   This quiet, and somewhat desolate location, before merging out into the main streets was the perfect place for their plan. There was no one to see them.   Nothing but the walkway, the road, and surrounding trees were present here.

As the older man knelt behind the shrubs for a hidden shot, he held the tranquilizer gun in his grip with shaking hands.   He felt a wave of nervous tension come over him, after seeing Eleanor standing on the sidewalk.   He realized she was not alone, and this would create a problem.   Looking down at his watch, he knew that Roberta would be driving by any minute now and he would have to temporarily paralyze the girl into a dazing sleep.   Their plan was to kidnap her, and with Eleanor's mother standing nearby, he knew he would have to deal with her now too. This was added stress he didn't need for this moment.

Advancing slowly from down the street in David's silver Buick, was Roberta.   She kept a steady pace of the car as she drove closer, realizing the situation that David was already fretting over. While breaking the car, she took in a deep breath to relax herself as she slowly let the car drift toward them along the curb from behind.   She would have to change her plan a bit in order for it to work.

Turning around, Eleanor and Gabriella noticed the car stopping beside them on the street. Confused to see it there, Gabriella spoke up after recognizing who was driving it.

"Dr. Stein?   Is that you?"   she asked the driver.   The woman in the front seat lowered the window on the passenger side, and smiled in a cheerful manner.

"Afternoon, Gabriella.   What a surprise to see you here"   she told her.

"Likewise.   What brings you to the neighborhood?"   Gabriella replied, forming a smile of her own.   Roberta never answered within the split seconds of the situation.   Eleanor soon found herself falling toward the car, as her head slammed against the passenger door with a thud.   A large tranquilizing dart pierced through the skin on the back of her neck, and Gabriella's smile faded.   She quickly moved to grab hold of her daughter, whom was now unconscious and began to cry out for help.   David came out from his hiding spot nearby, and with one strong swing, he stuck the side of Gabriella's head with the gun. The woman crashed to the ground, further silencing her calls for help as David tossed Eleanor's body into the backseat of the car. Gabriella, regaining her consciousness in a dreary and slowing manner, was forcing herself to get up. Her vision was blurry and she felt the aching pain through her head from where the man struck her. Her attempt to sit up again was foiled, as she watched the car's rear tires spin a screeching sound of rubber against the street.   The escaping car barreled down the road, slamming another car out of its way as it turned down a side street.   In less than a minute, Gabriella's daughter was gone.

Taken from her life by people she barely even knew, and had no idea where they were going. She fought the dizziness to stand, only to fall again to the sidewalk with tearful eyes of despair.   The driver of the other car ran quickly over to the woman, helping her to stand again.   His questions of what happened to her, and if she was alright, were drowned from Gabriella's mind.   She cried out with slurring speech, telling him they took her daughter away.   Over and over, and repeating the same phrase as he lead her over to his vehicle.   He was not sure what to do, except drive her to the hospital in nearby Youngsville, since the one in Warren was destroyed.   The distraught woman could barely focus for anything, and he knew he needed to get her to safety.

     Back at LaMore Manor, as quiet darkness surrounded Sabrina's room, the girl's   vibrant green eyes opened slowly.   Staring out her windows as the balcony doors opened quietly by themselves, she sensed the pain and danger of Eleanor's capture from afar.   She gazed out the doors without blinking and narrowed her eyes darkly. Standing up from her bed and clutching her doll, Sabrina dressed herself casually. She was in no hurry, for she could sense where her cousin was being abducted. Roberta and David had underestimated Sabrina's mind, for it was more powerful than they could ever imagine. She already knew of their location without even leaving her bedroom.

As Eleanor sluggishly opened her blue eyes, she stared up at the ceiling above herself weakly. The room was dark, only emitting enough light from an aging yellow bulb on a lamp somewhere near to her. She felt a pain on the back of her neck where the dart had pierced into her, and as she started to move her arms, she realized they were belted down. Her arms and hands were restrained with metal cuffs and buckles while laying on the bed she woke on. Quickly becoming afraid, she looked around the room, not being able to move very much within her state of capture. She soon felt a pinch against her neck as Roberta Stein stood above her, poking a long needle against Eleanor's skin.   The woman stared down at her with a hateful expression and whispering in an angry tone.

"You start one little fire, and I'll jam this needle in your vein quicker than you can blink" the woman voiced.   Standing beside Roberta, David peered down at the blonde girl with eyes holding an apology, yet he never spoke.   Why he did nothing, actually confused Eleanor in this situation even further.   She was terrified and held immediate hatred for them both as she glared at the from the bed she lay on.

"Where the fuck am I…"   she growled at them.   Roberta pinched the needle more against Eleanor's skin, until the girl made a small sound of alarm from the pain.   Eleanor's eyes turned away, filling with tears.

"You watch your tone.   You belong to me now, Eleanor."   Roberta said, holding sadistic vibes within her speech.

"Sabrina will come for me!"   Eleanor cried out, keeping her head turned to the side.   Her tears rolled over her nose and cheeks, making a tiny drops.   "You won't get away with this!"

Roberta leaned close to Eleanor's face, and spoke with haunting murmur, letting her victim know that she was no longer afraid of her.

"I'm counting on it."

The woman's further speech was soon interrupted by another voice in the room, as she and David turned their heads quickly to a darkened corner.   Eleanor too, moved her eyes in the foreign direction, soon feeling some relief as Sabrina slowly stepped forward from the blackness.   She was holding Clementine in her arms, and the looked at them with a grisly expression.

"Such fools you are...to try and take my family."   she said to them, stepping forward. Roberta's eyes widened slightly and she smiled at Sabrina's surprise entrance. She wondered how she entered the building without using the door. David backed away from her in horror, almost stumbling over a small table sitting behind him. He leaned against the wall, hoping for an escape. His hands wildly moving as he slid himself away.

"H-How did you...get in here?"   he asked

her.   Sabrina paid no mind to the man to the side of her, and focused solely on the doctor.

"Don't even try it, Sabrina.   You make one false move, and Eleanor's life becomes mine" Roberta expressed in bravery.   Sabrina stood calmly at the foot of the bed that held Eleanor down, staring deep into Roberta's eyes.   She spoke not a word, as she felt the woman's fear and tension slowly building inside.   Sabrina had this situation under control, whether or not the doctor believed it.   She could feel the woman becoming weak from the silence and Sabrina's constant glare.

"You're very unintelligent...to think you can control me.   To think...that you can stop me..." Sabrina's words floated into Roberta's ears with a drifting ghastly effect, letting her know this was one mistake she was about to regret.   She felt the walls and floor of the room beginning to shake as Sabrina tilted her head slowly, staring directly at her with the long black strands of her hair falling to the side.   The yellow bulb flicked in tiny buzzing noises.   Objects in the room were rotating and lifted aimlessly in the air.   They floated around Sabrina's body while Roberta's mind began to drift.   It fell into a lost daze of Sabrina's vision.   She held up her doll slowly, letting the pale face gaze deep into her soul.   Its solitary eye flashed quickly with a gleam of red light as the mouth began to open.   It creaked in the wood hinges and it made David cover his ears. Sabrina's voice merged with Clementine's and it floated through the air of the room in pulsing waves.   Roberta was terrified to see the room becoming black, letting only the stare of doll shine through the darkness in horrifying gesture.   The doll's wooden mouth cracked slowly, forming sinister grin as the teeth fell out of the mouth. The face of the doll began to melt, mixing the paint in a ruined state over the wicked smile; pieces falling to the floor in a gooey puddle as it laughed with a deep chuckle in the throat.   The murmured voice captured Roberta's fears as her heart raced inside her chest, beating her blood through the veins of her body as it overworked itself.   The doll's voice was grotesque and creature-like, echoing through a gargled bubbling mess…and it threatened her without remorse.

"You're mind...belongs to me..."

Roberta's mouth opened widely in a long gasp as her heart exploded inside her body.   The skin of her chest began to bend, and her ribcage broke fiercely.   Her blood oozed out of her mouth in streams around her chin.   It trailed down her neck, soaking into her clothes and dribbling to the floor by her feet.   The body of Roberta Stein fell victim to Sabrina's illusory gaze, until finally stealing the breaths of her life away with forceful heart attack.   Her body collapsed to the floor with eyes fixed open and bloodshot.   David screamed at the sight of the woman lying by his feet and her blood floating out of her mouth.   He started to run from the room on a frantic flee for his life, only to be stopped by the needle that was held to Eleanor's neck.   Sabrina simply turned her eyes toward him, and the syringe jabbed into his eye, further ceasing his movements.   Both the doctor, and the principal now lying together in death. David was lucky with a quicker death, but his body made little convulsions as Sabrina stepped over it. She unlocked the restrains on Eleanor's body, and the blonde girl quickly hugged her cousin. She felt safe now, and glad that she had come to rescue her. The light of the room came back as the darkness dissipated. David's muscles finally ceased their movements, and he was dead.

"I'm so sorry I worried you, Sabrina" Eleanor said through tears. Sabrina slowly placed her arms around the weeping girl, closing her eyes in her embrace.

"You have nothing to be sorry about. I will always be here for you." she said to her.

As the two girls walked home together, they were soon discovered by Victor as he had previous set out to look for them. He quickly drove up to them in his Mercedes, and stopped it on the curb as he rushed toward them. He'd been so worried for their safety after hearing what happened to his sister, Gabriella and left Erika and Meredith at the hospital to watch over her. He had set out to find the girls himself, determined to stop the people who kidnapped his niece. He embraced his daughter and his Eleanor together, holding them close and feeling thankful they were both alive.   He did not care about their power, and nor did he care about the fact they didn't want to be hugged.   He was simply glad they were alive and in his grasp.

Chapter Twenty-Nine

The Past Revealed

After arriving home the next day from hospital in Youngsville, Gabriella laid silently in her bed to rest, as Victor, Erika, and Meredith talked quietly together.   Sabrina and Eleanor had long since busied themselves in their rooms to be alone after going through another stressful event.

"I don't want to leave her alone"   Victor said, staring at his sister as they stood in Gabriella's bedroom.   Gabriella had been asleep for several hours now, and Victor hadn't left her side much.   He only left to eat and sleep.   Erika held her arms around her husband to help comfort him with Meredith standing nearby.

"How much longer do we have to stay hidden"   Meredith said quietly, not making it sound a question.   She was staring out Gabriella's bedroom windows as she spoke, feeling trapped within her own home.   Victor was feeling the same way, but just hadn't mentioned it.   Erika too, was getting restless.

"I never said you couldn't leave the house, Meredith"   Victor added.   Meredith turned toward her brother-in-law, and gave a short smile until it faded.

"I know, Vic.   I'm just…worried…and scared.   About how people here will react to us" she said to him.   Victor nodded in silence, holding tightly to his wife's hand over his shoulder.

"We have plenty of food here and several rooms to go in.   Plus the lawns to go out on when we need air. We should just stay here for a while again" Erika suggested.

"Yes, I agree. And we'll leave Sabrina and Eleanor alone for a little while too. Let them keep to themselves. It's not easy for them, most of all" Victor said.

Meredith held mixed feelings over the girls. She didn't know whether to fear them, or feel empathy for them of their difficult lives. She walked toward the door of Gabriella's bedroom without answering Victor, and stopped to turn to them.

"I'm gonna get some playing cards. We'll all sit in here together, 'cause I know you don't wanna leave Gabriella's side, Vic" she said to them. Victor smiled, and nodded to Meredith as he pointed down the hall.

"Get my favorite deck then, from the desk drawer in my study. It's been a while since I've played with those" he suggested. Meredith nodded, and walked down the hall to Victor's study room to get the cards.

"Where will we play at? There is no table

big enough in here"   Erika asked him.

"We'll sit on the floor then.   It'll be fun, just like old times"   Victor replied, smiling back to his wife.

Off in her own bedroom, Sabrina sat quietly on the side of her bed, staring out her balcony doors at the early evening sun.   It was setting slowly over the horizon as she listened to a vinyl playing on her phonograph.   The alluring voice of Jo Stafford echoed through the room as she sang "Yesterdays" softly.   The bright orange and yellow light shone brightly into her bedroom, as the breeze for the evening drifted in with a genial touch.   Behind her, several small objects in her room were floating around her body in a slow and circular manner, as she held them aloft in that position.   They made no sound while rotating around her head, as though representing the moons of a planet in orbit.   They made a soundless dance.   Her thoughts were of Hanako, and the times they shared together.   She so badly wanted to feel her again.   Wanting to feel the light of her soul, reach into the empty darkness of her melancholy heart.   She didn't want to hurt anymore.   Despite her split mind of emotions, she was feeling them all at once.   All the pain, and sorrow, and the joy and love of Hanako's touch by mere memory.   The song was bringing back her yesterdays.   She felt her all the time.   She could still taste her in her mind.   Wanting so much to reach out and touch her again, but rather she was falling into a void forever.   A deep abyss with only memories for company.   Sabrina didn't know how to move on from her loss.   She held tightly to it, for it was the only comfort she found when she thought of her.   For Sabrina, it was the only way to keep her alive.

As Meredith opened the small drawer of Victor's desk, she rummaged through his belongings until finally seeing the playing cards he bought years ago.   She picked up the small cardboard box, and stood there for a moment as she peered into the drawer again.   There, lying on the bottom of the drawer, was a small photograph of a younger Victor.   He was standing with his arms held closely around woman she didn't recognize to be Erika.   Both people in the picture were happy, showing their smiles with confidence and love.   Meredith couldn't speak. She simply stared at the photo in sheer shock and surprise. She dropped the playing cards to the floor, and picked up the picture slowly to get a better look at it.   After turning it over, she read the faded writing on the back, dated shortly around the time when Erika was first pregnant with Sabrina. Meredith gasped at the words on the back after reading them, soon realizing what Victor had done just before Sabrina's birth.

"To Victor,

I love you, babe, always.

Love,
Marsha N.

Completely unaware of who "Marsha N."

was, Meredith became mortified at the fact her brother-in-law had cheated on her sister. She didn't even know if he still was seeing this other woman, or if Erika even knew about her. A wave of disgust and anger crept through Meredith's mind, as she held tight to the photo and walked quickly back toward Gabriella's room to confront him.

Back in her bedroom, Sabrina quickly turned her solid green eyes toward her doors, as the objects around her head stopped moving instantly. They fell to the floor around herself, and she knew something was wrong. She could sense Meredith's anger and betrayal that followed the woman's thoughts of Victor. While holding Clementine close, Sabrina opened the bedroom doors with her mind, and began to head down the hall toward Gabriella's room.

Meredith soon burst through the door where Victor and Erika were waiting, and they looked at Meredith with surprised expressions. Erika's sister soon struck Victor in the jaw with her fist, and he fell to the floor in alarm.

"You son of a bitch! How dare you do this to her!" she declared in a loud show of anger. Erika quickly grabbed her sister in an attempt to stop her actions, as Victor stood up again.

"What the hell is your problem, Meredith?!" he retorted.

"You fucking cheated on her, you asshole!" Meredith raved on. By this time, Gabriella woke up, and slowly sat up in her bed with a look of concern.

"What is going on?!" she asked them. Victor looked at his sister, and tried to walk over to her, but Meredith cut him off and placed the photo in her hands. Victor was surprised to see the picture, in which he thought he destroyed years ago, now resting in his sister's hands. He put his hand over his mouth in shock and turned away quickly, feeling both embarrassed and angry. Gabriella viewed the picture and gasped to herself when she read the writing on the back. She looked up at Victor, and gently began to cry.

"Oh victor...you didn't...tell me you didn't cheat on your wife" she said with a shaken voice. Erika quickly snatched the picture from Gabriella's hands, and stared at it with hatred.   She turned toward her husband with a scowl as he quickly responded to her.

"Honestly Erika, I didn't know it was there…I would've thrown it away, I swear I would have…"   he said to her.   Erika shook her head, repeating the word "no" over and over, and letting her tears slide down her cheeks. She ripped the picture in half as it fell to the floor.   Meredith embraced her sister, trying to stop her from crying and giving comfort as she glared at Victor.

Without realizing the door was left open, Sabrina was now standing in the door way and looking at the torn photo on the floor.   Everyone noticed her presence in the room, and suddenly the world fell silent.   The two halves of the picture floated in the air lightly like feathers, as Sabrina pieced them together again, viewing both sides.   Her radiant eyes dawned closely on the fact, that the woman in the picture was holding something in her arms.   Something small, wrapped gently in a blanket as the woman felt proud to show it with the man beside her.   And that something…was a child.   An infant child, born to both Victor and Marsha, when he had his affair some time ago during his argument with Erika.   Sabrina's mother had been still pregnant at the time, carrying Sabrina until the 3rd of January.   For years, Sabrina was under the impression that she was an only child.   That she would claim the LaMore heritage after her parent's death.   Now…seeing this child in the arms of another woman, *with* her father…she knew…she was no longer the only one.   She would have to share everything with her.   She would have to *know* her, and *accept* her presence in the family.   To be a sister…

    Victor's eyes held a look of fear as he stared at his daughter.   The picture fell to the floor again, as Sabrina glared darkly at him from the other end of the room.   No one could speak at the sight of her face….a face so angry and full of tensed emotion, that the very sight of it was haunting.
    "How dare you…"   she whispered to him. Her voice crept across the room like a snake, sending shivers down each of their backs.   The walls cracked quickly, as the lighting of the room

buzzed on and off...until finally dying in a dimmed darkness.

"Now Sabrina...that was a long time ago..." Victor began.

"Don't address me. You are NOT my father..." Sabrina sourly interrupted. With the flow of her voice, she moved Gabriella's bed across the floor until it slammed against wall. Gabriella quickly fell off of it, and looked toward her niece in terror. Meredith jumped as Erika held tight to her sister. She turned away from her daughter, and her panic was rising. She couldn't take it anymore. Victor was too afraid to move as his daughter blocked the only exit of the room. "You disgust me, Victor..." Sabrina's voice slithered. Erika soon starting building rage with her fear. She felt she might lose her mind in spite of the situation, feeling hatred toward not only her husband, for not mentioning the other baby...but also toward Sabrina...for being who she was. For *what* she was. A murderous witch-child. She held tight to Meredith's arms, allowing the climbing anger to surface when Victor spoke again.

"Sabrina...just calm down..." he repeated.

Sabrina no longer held patience as she yelled across the room.   The windows shattered violently into millions of jagged fragments blowing through the air.   Meredith screamed and fell to the floor with Victor, and Erika seized her chance to get away.   She physically shoved her daughter aside and ran down the hallway.   She ran to her bedroom, retrieving one of Victor's hunting guns from his closet, and loading it with the large bullets with murderous intension.   Sabrina turned herself toward her mother, and soon softened her angry face…into one of fear. Standing in the hall…Erika fired the gun at her daughter as the bullet pierced into the wall, shattering the wood into several tiny pieces. Sabrina flinched quickly, and stopped herself from falling.   She was not sure what came over herself, but her mind seemed to form into one mind again. Staring at her mother with the shotgun, and feeling the woman's rage and fear along with her own at once.   A show of emotion between them both, hitting each other in pulsating waves. Sabrina soon ran down the hallway in fear for her life, as Erika chased after her, firing the bullets at the walls in attempt to put a hole in her daughter's head.   It was her solution.   Her way to solve the "problem" that everyone had been talking about.   Now finally it would be gone.   *She*...would be gone.   The gun was the answer to her rage as Erika fired it again, enjoying the feeling that took over her mind in this moment of insanity.   Sabrina...would be no more.

    She knew she had to get away.   Her mother was trying to kill her, and she knew she must get away.   With Clementine in hand, Sabrina ran through the halls of the house.   The child-side of her personality took over for the moment, making her fearful and afraid of the situation developing.   Erika seemed to laugh when she fired the bullets, one after the other into the walls and objects throughout the home.   Victor, in fear of his wife's actions, ran after her in a frantic attempt to stop her from slaying their daughter.   He was horrified by her and everything that was happening.   Wishing and hoping that she would be okay.   That everyone would be okay.   He wanted their lives to start over.   He wanted to go back in time, and never meet Marsha Nelson.   To never have a child with her, and just live his life normally in the mansion that he inherited.   He wanted a normal daughter.   One that would laugh and play, and grow up to be a successful woman in the LaMore family line.   But no, reality was hitting him hard in the face as he watched his wife tear up the house with bullet holes of anger and wretched despair.   It was in this moment, Sabrina was standing at the corner of the kitchen, feeling terrified and having nowhere to go.   She was calling for her father to desperately save her.   He didn't know what to think.   Save his daughter? Or save his wife?...

    Being mentally unstable, and torn completely into two different personalities, Sabrina's mind suddenly jumped again.   All the emotion, and hatred, and sorrowful pains that enveloped her powerful mind were too much for her to bear.   Clementine was buried again, as Sabrina resurfaced, becoming the dominate one.

She hung her head low, as her long black hair dangled in front of her face.   Erika stood in the kitchen's doorframe.   She aimed the gun directly toward Sabrina's head with no regard to who she was, or what she was capable of.   Erik had gone mad, with her only thought to rid the world of the dangerous girl.   Before the woman could pull the trigger, Sabrina raised her head up abruptly, staring deep into Erika's eyes with a reddish white glow in her irises.   The ceiling fractured as piles of the pieces fell upon her mother, crushing to the floor as she disappeared into the rubble.   Victor was nearby, ready to cry out in sadness as he ran toward his daughter.   Before he could grab a hold of her, his daughter's body vanished in front him.   Completely into the air itself, as she teleported from the room.   Victor slid into the wall, and fell to the floor from the impact, nearly breaking his hands as they collided with the solid structure.   He laid on the kitchen floor unconscious, still seeing the image of his daughter in his deepest thoughts.   He mumbled her name delicately when his eyes reopened...staring at the hole above him where the ceiling had collapsed.

Chapter Thirty

The Journey Begins

Victor stood in the hallway in silence, leaning against the wall while Meredith and Gabriella stood beside him. They watched in saddened thoughts as the police inspected the remains of the kitchen's ceiling, and searched through the rubble of the piles. Victor suspected his wife was now dead, after Sabrina disappeared from the mansion. A search team was gathered by authorities to comb the grounds of LaMore

Manor, and search every room for his missing daughter and wife.   Since the time of the impact when the ceiling was fractured by Sabrina's telekinetic ability, Erika's body had not been found.   This confused Victor, and the others, considering they should've found her lying dead beneath the broken beams, plaster, and wooden remains.   His only hope, was the fact she was still alive.   Somewhere, out in the world, his wife was still alive…and so was his daughter.   He knew Sabrina would come back when she was ready to, but as for Erika…he was lost.   Being someone who was very wealthy, he would use his money to help him find his wife again.   Hiring some of the foremost detectives in the world, to search for and find Erika LaMore.   He would promise them a very handsome payoff to the one claiming to do so. He did not offer a reward for finding Sabrina…for he knew very well where she was going.   He would follow her from then on, to a place where he knew she could cause even more destruction and devastation.   Much more than where they were now.   He would find his daughter at all costs, no matter how far she traveled…he would follow.

Ultimately he would stop her for good, or bring her back home again where he felt she belonged.

      LaMore Manor Cathedral was always a darkened room.   The vast space and silence it endured was mind-numbingly differently from the rest of the mansion.   Staring up at the large and grand pipe organ, Sabrina had chosen this room to think for a while.   Her mind was trying to calm itself as she looked up toward the taller pipes of the musical instrument, feeling alone, raged, and melancholy.   The rising sun for a new day was glowing softly through the large windows, showing the dust particles afloat within the air in beams of light.
      After doing research, Sabrina discovered the name of her half-sister was Clair Nelson. She'd been thinking in this room since the time of the incident with her mother.   So many thoughts were coursing through her mind about her life now, and what she must do.   She hated this girl. This Clair Nelson who entered her family line like a stab in the chest, cutting deep into the flesh and

making a jagged, uncanny entrance.   Damn her father for making a half breed...

Her acceptance would never be shown for this person, for Sabrina was the heir to the throne. The true heir in the LaMore bloodline, and she would never consider welcoming someone born as a half-sibling into her life.   A dark, and wicked feud was now crawling inside Sabrina's body, capturing her mind with thought of killing this other girl.   Melting her off the face of the planet forever as she carried a mix of *her* blood, and another.

"How dreadful..."   Sabrina said to herself. "She will *never* be one of us."

Sabrina's damaged thoughts were soon interrupted as she felt the presence of another being in the room with her.   Although she wasn't angry, for she recognized the feeling of this person anywhere, even if she were sleeping.

"Good morning, Eleanor"   Sabrina said to her.   The blonde girl slowly walked up to her cousin, and put her arms around her in a gentle embrace.   She felt her cousin's sadness as they shared a telepathic connection.

"I don't want you to leave…" Eleanor said quietly. Her face held a mournful look of expression, as she realized Sabrina was leaving to New York City in search for Clair Nelson. Sabrina lowered her head from the gaze at the pipe organ, and spoke softly to her cousin in a kind tone.

"I have to, Eleanor. I must rid this world of the one who's entered our bloodline unwontedly. Clair Nelson will corrupt our family history" she said to her. Eleanor raised her head up, and stood herself in front of Sabrina with serious, yet radiant blue eyes.

"Then I will go with you. We'll destroy her together." Eleanor suggested. Sabrina shook her head slowly in disagreement with her cousin.

"I need you to stay. You must stay here and watch my home for me, and wait for my return." she said. Eleanor sighed deeply, but nodded to Sabrina. The feeling of own tears started welling up in her eyes warmly.

"And besides, I won't kill her right away. I'm going to bring her here. I will show this girl who I am. She will be intrigued, yet also fear me…and fear what I can do.   Eventually capturing her mind with such intensity, that she will have no choice…but to follow me here."   Sabrina informed.   Her voice was strong, and held confidence in every word she spoke, letting Eleanor not to worry over the situation.   This reassured her, that Sabrina would be back one day in the future.   Eleanor smiled and hugged her again, commenting on her last sentence.

"As they say…curiosity killed the cat"   she said with a gentle laugh.   Sabrina nodded to her cousin, and with a small, yet delicate smile, she disappeared through teleportation…leaving Eleanor there on her mission to guard the home. Eleanor knew what she had to do, and would never disappoint Sabrina for as long as she was alive.   She would wait for her arrival again, bringing the half-sister to the residence of the LaMore's, and Clair would soon know…what she truly was born into.

Being one of the largest cities in the world,

New York is the center of many things possible. A city with millions of inhabitants, all scurrying about in their daily lives. Their lives that were locked within the concrete walls of the skyscrapers dominating the horizon by the sea.   A cultural gathering of many spoken tongues, and artistic values of the world itself, nestled deep inside the graying streets and sounds of the modern metropolis.   One might say…New York has it all…and has seen it all.   However, nothing on this planet could ever prepare the Big Apple for what was going to enter its doors, and shake the very foundation of its existence.

While thundering above the towering buildings that graced the streets, many people watched as a show of lightning danced across the city's salty sea air.   The sky held an angry, and terrorizing vibe that loomed over the skyscrapers, blocking out the sun's rays for miles around. The large super cell created winds of wrath, making the waves in the surrounding ocean currents to crash against the shoreline harshly.

Standing on the head of one of the decorative eagles, perched along the edge of the

61rst floor, Sabrina stood on the corner of the Chrysler Building.   Her gaze fixed upon the world below her as she struck the top of the spire with several powerful lightning bolts.   The piercing light shimmered over the crown of the building behind her.   The electricity surging through the building as the lights flickered with each hit. Letting its occupants know the impending storm was serious.   She watched the busy streets below her, feeling the pulsing energy flow throughout her body as the lightning crashed above her.   Her eyes flashed a glow while staring at the loud metropolis, announcing the arrival of her powerful mind.   She whispered a threatening murmur into the air with her lips…slow and faint, holding Clementine close to her chest.

"I'm here now, Clair….*I feel you*…."

Author's Notes

In regards to the publication of my book, this is actually the second time I've published this story. The first publication was back in 2010, and was titled "Power of the Gods: Sabrina's Beginning". However, that title is no longer published since I've re-edited my book considering the developing storyline over the recent years in my writing. This book shall now be the opening of my Power of the Gods series.

Several sources inspired me when writing this book, and music was one of them. I've always told people, that music is an excellent source of inspiration. It's beautiful, powerful, emotional, and unlike anything else in this world. It truly is something special on how it influences us, and our personal thoughts. All songs mentioned in the book served as inspiration for me when I wrote the events they were referenced in, and because of my personal liking. The songs "Frozen" and also "A Dangerous Mind" by Within Temptation, were another source of inspiration, even though I hadn't mentioned them. The short poem "Black Umbrellas" in the opening of chapter twenty-three, was written specifically for that part of the story.

As for Sabrina's future, my "Power of the Gods" series will continue very soon. The second book will be titled "Power of the Gods: Sabrina's Reprisal". Sabrina has much to see, and many people to meet. There are powerful minds at work, and she will soon learn that she's not the only person in the world...who is "unique".

Printed in Poland
by Amazon Fulfillment
Poland Sp. z o.o., Wrocław